C000213536

DEAD WRONG

THE KERI CHRONICLES, BOOK ONE

A.C. ARQUIN

WORDS ON THE WIND, LLC

Copyright © 2022 by J.S. Arquin

All rights reserved.

No part of this book may be reproduced in any form or by any electronic or mechanical means, including information storage and retrieval systems, without written permission from the author, except for the use of brief quotations in a book review.

1

Red light dripped down the walls, bass thumping through the Alley Cat like a living thing. Curves of flesh strained against thin strips of fabric, or, in the case of the girls onstage, burst free of their restraints. The humid air was thick with alcohol and sex.

Valora Keri squared her shoulders and breathed it all in, the knife in her hand going snick, snick, snick as she sliced a lime into wedges. She'd been tending bar in the Alley Cat for a little over a year now. The strip club was grimy and loud and full of sleazeballs, but the money was good and there was never a dull moment.

"Get your sweet ass over here and give me a vodka tonic."

Case in point.

Val gave the man leaning on the bar the side-eye. He was middle-aged and balding, with an expensive suit and a sheen of sweat across his scalp. A shiny comm implant had replaced his left ear. He leered at her, teeth grinding behind his smile, pupils huge, holding up a credit chip between two fingers. A tattoo adorned the back of his hand, a stylized cross inside a circle, the symbol of the Black Knights, the religious cult who controlled the drug trade in Polk Gulch.

"*Hurt him*," Mister E whispered in her mind. "*Make him bleed.*" His

Cheshire Cat grin appeared, floating above her shoulder. His golden
eyes glowed.

Her pulse jumped at the suggestion, but Val ignored both her inner
demon and the gangster. Mister E was invisible to everyone but her,
and as for the guy in the suit, she didn't care who he was, or what
organization he was part of. At this bar she was in control, and nobody
got to speak to her like that.

Val angled the knife toward him, letting the red light gleam along
the edge.

"You might want to choose your words more carefully when you
address a girl with a knife in her hand." She whirled and tossed it in
one smooth motion, spinning the blade end over end. It sank into the
dart board at the end of the bar with a satisfying *thunk*.

"*It would have made an even better sound sinking into his skull,*" Mister
E complained.

"But then I'd have to clean his blood off the bar," Val shot back
under her breath. "And I've got enough work to do."

She left the suit with his mouth hanging open and went to help a
customer at the other end of the bar. Bottom line, the guy was an
asshole, and she dealt with assholes all day, every day.

She put him out of her mind and nodded as Gina the cocktail waitress shouted her order. Val was lucky to even have a job, and she
knew it. San Francisco was one of the handful of cities in the US that
hadn't completely fallen apart when the rest of the country collapsed,
fracturing into tribes, corporate compounds, and small-town fiefdoms. As the former capital of Silicon Valley, SF still had a semblance
of civilization, but it was a far cry from its tech-billionaire heyday.
You'd be an idiot to enter certain areas of the city without body armor,
and organizations like the Black Knights ruled entire neighborhoods.
Even a place as rough as the Alley Cat counted as comparatively
civilized.

"Hey, Val. Are you going to let me make all your dreams come true
yet?" Jack sauntered up to the bar, turning his thousand-watt smile
on her.

"All my dreams, huh? Have you got a slice of butterscotch cheese-
cake tucked into those jeans?" Butterscotch was Val's absolute favorite.

Butterscotch candy, butterscotch syrup. Throw butterscotch on it and she'd eat just about anything.

She scooped up a clean glass and started mixing Jack another White Russian.

Jack was a regular, and he was prettier than most of the girls who worked here. Long eyelashes, ice-blue eyes, sculpted cheekbones, perfectly waved blond hair, and a tight t-shirt showing off his pecs beneath an open jacket. He liked to flirt, and Val had always figured that was all it was. But lately his eyes had been lingering on her with an intensity that hadn't been there before. She wasn't sure how to handle it, so she'd been doing her best to ignore it.

Jack's smile got brighter.

"Maybe I do. Let me take you out to dinner and you can find out."

Val stiffened, heat rising to her cheeks. That wasn't only flirting. He'd asked her out directly, which put her in a tough spot.

When you worked in a strip club you got hit on. A lot. It came with the territory. Because of that, Rule #1 was No Dating Customers. It was a hard line and she'd never crossed it.

"I wouldn't mind giving him a tongue bath," Mister E purred.

Val's blush deepened. "You are not helping."

"Meow."

She bent down and pretended to search for something in the mini-fridge, stalling for time. Turning Jack down and keeping things professional would be the safest play. Rule #1 was there for a reason. Guys could get weird if things didn't work out, and she didn't need that kind of energy in her workplace. Also, a club like the Alley Cat attracted a lot of trophy hunters -- guys who thought of girls as notches on their belt. And even though Val wasn't as pretty as most of the dancers, it was well known she was unattainable. That in itself could be a powerful attractor for that type of man.

Still, Jack might be worth making an exception for. It had been a long time since Val had scratched that particular itch, and Jack definitely made her feel itchy.

But there was no way she was saying yes the first time he asked. He'd have to work a lot harder than that if he wanted her to break Rule #1.

She delivered his drink with a smile.

"Sorry, Jack, I'm all booked up this week."

He didn't blink. "Next week?"

"Booked then, too."

A flicker of annoyance crossed his face, there and gone so quickly she might have imagined it. Jack wasn't used to getting turned down. Then the smile was back, even brighter than before.

"At least give me your number."

"Perhaps." She sang lightly as she walked away, *"Perhaps, perhaps, perhaps..."*

Gina stepped up to the bar, but Jessie was dancing onstage now, and she liked the music for her set extra loud, so Val had to lean towards the waitress's pink buzz cut to hear her order. As she mixed the drinks, she didn't glance at Jack or the asshole at the far end of the bar. Let them stew. It was good for men to not get what they wanted once in a while. It built character.

Gina and the rest of the girls were sweet and hard working. And if they drank too much, did too many drugs, and had personal lives that were often train wrecks, that was simply par for the course when you made a living shaking your naked ass onstage. Had Val been a dancer, she'd have been blind drunk at work most of the time too.

Not that she would ever get up onstage, no matter how many times her customers begged her to take a twirl around the pole. Behind the bar, she held the power. She was an unattainable goddess, beyond their sweaty grasp. If she ever crossed that line, she'd become just another girl in their minds.

Which made no sense to Val. She couldn't imagine the courage it took to dance naked in front of strangers night after night. The thought of getting up on that stage terrified her. She might look tough behind the bar, but as far as she was concerned the dancers had more guts than she ever would.

Sadly, most of them had no idea how powerful they were. Case in point: Ruby, who was now leaning into the Black Knight at the end of the bar, straddling the barstool next to him in her green sequined dress. The dress was getting frayed around the edges -- it was Ruby's favorite, and she wore it almost every night, like a suit of well-loved armor.

Ruby had a big heart and she often brought in plates of homemade cookies for the girls. When Val had first arrived in the city, knowing no one, and with nothing more than a letter of recommendation from a club in Kansas City, Ruby had cheerfully helped Val find a place to stay and shown her around the city. The dancer had an adorable toddler too, a little girl with blond curls and eyes as big as the moon. Just like her momma.

Unfortunately, Ruby was better at taking care of other people than she was at taking care of herself. Beneath her sequined dress, Ruby was desperately insecure. She was the kind of girl who'd let some ogre hit her and then go crawling back for more, apologizing for making him lose his temper. As if his violence were somehow her fault.

Val worked her way back down the bar and finally returned to the Black Knight after serving every other patron first. He was pawing at Ruby now, one hand on her thigh, thick fingers sliding up under the hem of her dress. Ruby was smiling and batting her eyes, pretending to like it while she tried to sell the guy a private dance.

Val caught Ruby's eye.

"You need anything, honey?" Meaning: Are you all right? Do I need to call the bouncer?

Ruby giggled in that fake little-girl way she did when she was working.

"No, I'm just perfect, sugar." She winked at the Black Knight, big and slow.

Val fought back a scowl as she watched the gangster puff up. Ruby definitely had him on the line. Of course, hooking them wasn't the hard part. It was controlling them once you had them hooked.

The guy sneered at Val as she finally slid his vodka tonic across the bar. "You're a real piece of work, you know that?"

Val's smile was all teeth. "Thanks for noticing. Can I get you anything else?"

The Black Knight slid a hundred credit chip across the bar and leered. "Just your number."

Val's eyebrows climbed her forehead. This guy really thought the sun shone out of his asshole. She could see Ruby fighting to keep her smile glued on. The prick had one hand up her skirt and he was asking for Val's number. That took nerve.

Val plucked the hundred off the bar and considered it, then slipped it into her apron pocket.

"Thanks for the tip," she said, turning away.

"Hey, what about my number?"

She ignored him, leaving Ruby to soothe his ego while she went to the kitchen to grab clean glasses. Just a typical night in the Alley Cat.

Junior was in the kitchen munching on a plate of cheese fries. The big bouncer froze like a kid with his hand in the cookie jar, watching Val out of the corner of his eye. His wispy mustache had cheese on it.

"Don't worry, Junior. I don't see a thing."

He grinned and scooped up some more fries.

"*Gracias*, Val."

"*De nada.*" Val pulled a rack of clean glasses out of the dishwasher and shoved another one in. "Who's watching the door while you're in here stuffing your face?"

"Carla's covering for me."

"Carla's doing you favors, huh?" Val smirked at him, and Junior couldn't meet her eyes.

"It's nothing, Val," he said, a blush rising to his cheeks.

Junior was a big teddy bear. Soft-spoken and solid. Loyal. He treated the girls like his little sisters back in Mexico. All except Carla. Carla he treated like a tiara sculpted from ice. Like she was the most delicate and beautiful thing he'd ever seen. Carla mostly ignored him, but if she was doing him favors now maybe she was starting to come around.

Val hoped that was the case. She liked Junior, and she thought he deserved to be happy. She didn't think much of Carla, but Junior's opinion was the only one that mattered. If having Carla would make Junior happy, then Val was in favor of the match.

She carried the glasses back out and slid them onto the shelf behind the bar. Two more customers were waiting, so she took care of them before she locked the register and headed around the corner to the restroom.

The hallway was painted black: walls, floor, and ceiling. Just like the rest of the club. A single red bulb hung over a mirror in a heavy gilt frame halfway down, making it seem like you were in some kind of gothic nightmare. Val thought it was a little overdone, but not entirely inappropriate. The Alley Cat was a den of sin, after all.

She did her business, carefully hovering over the toilet seat as she peed. The Alley Cat was not the type of place where you wanted to use the seat. She washed her hands and checked herself in the mirror. Val was just below average height, with curly hair that changed color frequently and an olive complexion. She had a tough shell, and every inch of her shouted it, from her high black boots, sleeveless black shirt and battered leather jacket to arms that were a little too well-defined to be considered soft and feminine. She wore minimal makeup, just a hint of blush to accentuate her cheekbones and a ring of eyeliner around her most prominent feature: her golden eyes.

She had irises like Spanish doubloons, flashing in the light and glowing softly in the shadows. They shone like the sun when she flexed her magic.

Right now, though, her eyes were sunken and tired. Work was always exhausting, keeping her up until four or five in the morning most nights, and lately she'd been having drama at home with one of her roommates as well, which was robbing her of rest even in her off hours. She couldn't remember the last time she'd gotten a full eight hours' sleep. It was impossible to tell where the bags under her eyes ended and the eyeliner began.

A noise caught her attention as she pushed back out into the hall-way. Turning her head, she noticed the door to the storage room was cracked open. She tensed as she heard the noise again. Voices inside the room.

Mister E perked up, and her fingertips tingled as her power rose with him. She tasted honey and smelled sage, just like she had that day in the mountains when she was just a girl. The day the power first crawled inside her. The day she killed her mother.

Val didn't know what Mister E was, exactly. She thought of him as a cat-demon, but he could just as easily be a ghost. Or a god. Whatever he was, she had accidentally released him, and in return he gave her power.

But Mister E was capricious and bloodthirsty. Old-Testament savage. He had lain dormant for millennia before young Val stumbled upon him, and his ideas of power and violence did not fit in the modern world.

She tried to push the power down. She didn't want to hurt anyone. Not again.

But her body gave the lie to her thoughts. Her hands bunched into fists. Her jaw set. Her weight balanced on the balls of her feet.

The music was too loud for her to hear words, but as she slid up outside the door, she recognized one of the voices. Ruby, screeching in pain.

Val shouldered the door open and flipped the light switch. The Black Knight had Ruby pinned against the metal shelves, his fist in her hair, yanking her head down and back. His other hand was under her dress again, except now he had the green sequins pushed up to her hips. He turned his face toward the door, surprised by the sudden light.

"Get away from her," Val snarled.

The gangster glared at Val, jaw muscles working as he ground his teeth. "Shut the door. This is none of your fucking business."

The power swelled, filling Val with heat. She made a fist around the register keys, two of them thrust forward between her knuckles.

"I'm making it my business. Get the fuck away from her. Now."

2

The Black Knight sneered. "You are making a very big mistake. Do you know who I am? Believe me, you want to give us some privacy. Turn the light off on your way out."

She tightened her fist around the keys. "I'm not saying it again. Last chance. Let her go."

"*Yes,*" Mister E hissed. "*Cut him. Make him bleed.*"

The gangster's expression turned ugly. He shoved Ruby to the floor and squared up to Val.

"You want a piece of me, bitch? Come on. I got what you want right--"

He never had a chance to finish his sentence. Val lashed out with her fist, keys tearing a jagged hole in his cheek. He cried out, pressing his hands to the wound, bright red seeping between his fingers. The scent of the blood filled the small space, sharp and metallic in her nostrils, and the power inside her surged. She saw a vision of a battlefield, foes falling before her like wheat.

Val grabbed him by the front of his shirt and hurled him out into the hallway. Her power gave the throw a little extra force, and he slammed face-first into the opposite wall.

Her blood sang with the release, and Mister E was there again, floating over her shoulder. His golden eyes gleamed as he flashed his maddening Cheshire Cat smile.

"Don't finish him too quickly. I want to enjoy this," he purred.

She brought her fist down. Bright blood spattered the wall. She hit the asshole again and again. It felt good to let go, to let the power sing within her. This was what she was made for. It would be so easy to bash his skull in. Snap his neck like a twig...

"Val?" A hand touched her shoulder.

She lashed out, snarling, her face speckled with blood as she flung this new opponent away from her, the body hitting the opposite wall with a thud. She stepped forward, fist cocked, ready to pound whoever it was into pulp.

Ruby cringed at the base of the wall. She cried out, her eyes wide, face white. Terrified. Not of the gangster, but of Val. She was terrified of Val.

The realization hit Val like a cold shower. Mid-punch, she diverted her fist away from Ruby's face, smashing through the drywall beside the dancer's head instead. Inches from disaster. She ground her teeth, fighting against her violent urges, against Mister E egging her on, shuddering with the effort. Pushing the power back down into the dark where it lived. Locking it away inside her.

"Sorry," she ground out between clenched teeth.

She left Ruby cowering and put the asshole in an armlock, wrenching his wrist up behind his back. She might have torqued his arm a little harder than necessary, but at least she wasn't caving his skull in. That was a victory in itself.

He spluttered and cursed, but Val had all the leverage now. There was nothing he could do as she frog-marched him across the bar. The regulars laughed and jeered.

"Atta girl, Val!"

"You show him who's boss!"

Val didn't take any pleasure in their cheers. She knew how close she'd come to hurting Ruby. To doing the very thing she was trying to prevent.

Junior poked his head out of the kitchen, blanching when he saw what the ruckus was. He hustled over to her.

"You want me to take this guy, Val?"

"No, I've got him. You could open the front door for me, though."

"Sure, no problem." He ducked his head and scuttled ahead of her.

Mist ghosted the street outside, cool and damp against her skin, softening the pale moon that shone above the neon sign of the Alley Cat. The faint breeze smelled of sea and salt. Garbage trucks ground and clanged down the block, interrupting the hustle of the working girls on the corner. A typical Friday night in San Francisco.

Val tossed the bleeding man onto the sidewalk. Her power tried to flare up inside her again, but she held it in check. Throwing the guy ten feet through the air was not something she wanted to do in front of witnesses.

"This guy's eighty-sixed," she told Junior. "I don't want to see his face inside again."

The Black Knight snarled up at her, dark blood smeared down his cheek and neck.

"You're going to pay for this. You don't know who you're messing with."

"Oh? Hold on, I've got something for you." Val made a show of rummaging in her pockets, then held up her empty hands and shrugged. "Nope, sorry. I'm all out of fucks."

As if to punctuate her words, the sky opened up. Rain bucketed down so hard it seemed like a giant was dumping an enormous water tank out of the fog. In seconds, the asshole was soaked.

There was something else too. Little slices of silver that caught the light. A couple of them wriggled in the gangster's hair.

"What the hell?" Junior said.

Val squatted down to get a closer look. They were fish, little ones, no bigger than guppies. Flopping around on the sidewalk. Bouncing off the cars parked on the street. Thousands of tiny fish falling from the sky. Mister E scampered around the sidewalk pouncing on them, looking almost like a normal cat.

She looked up to find the moon still visible through the fog overhead. It didn't even look overcast. She shivered. It was a Wild Storm.

The Wild Storms had started when she was a child, right around the time she'd first met Mister E. No one knew what caused them, though a popular theory insisted the storms had something to do with the sudden reversal of the Earth's magnetic poles. No one was sure which event was the chicken and which was the egg.

The Wild Storms sprang up without warning, bringing magic with them, changing everything they touched. Sometimes those changes were harmless, like a storm of tiny fish on a clear night. Other times the storms created monsters.

Monsters like Val.

As quickly as it started, the downpour petered out. The whole thing had lasted less than a minute, but it had come down with such fury that it left the entire block glistening, the gutters streaming. And full of tiny, flopping fish.

Val turned to go back inside, muttering to herself, "Curiouser and curiouser."

Mister E leapt back up onto her shoulder, his golden eyes shining, grey tail wrapped around the back of her neck.

"Well, that was exciting." He licked his paw, and Val saw it had been dipped in blood. She shuddered.

"You're disgusting."

"Says the woman who spilled the blood in the first place." Mister E was unperturbed.

She found Ruby huddled on a barstool, the broken strap of her green sequined dress hanging down her back.

"Are you all right?" Val poured Ruby a shot and slid it across the bar.

"Yeah." Ruby downed the shot in one smooth motion and tried to smile. The smile came out lopsided and thin. Her hands toyed with something gold.

"What's that?" Val asked.

Ruby looked startled, as if she hadn't realized she was holding the thing. It was long and slender, a finger-length piece of gold tube. "Oh, nothing. Just something I found. It's my good-luck charm." She tucked it back into her purse.

Val poured the dancer another shot.

"Thanks, Val. Keep 'em coming. I think I'm done working tonight."

Ruby seemed stretched thin, her skin gone grey. Had she always looked this tired?

Val thought back to her first month in the city, when Ruby had taken Val under her wing and shown the new arrival around. In her memories, Ruby was always smiling and laughing, pointing out birds perched on wires and little flowers growing in the cracks of the sidewalk. No, back then she'd been full of energy and life. Something had changed.

Val reached out and put her hand on Ruby's.

"Hang in there, yeah? There'll be better days."

Ruby studied the bar, not meeting her eyes.

Val sighed and went to get another rack of clean glasses.

In the privacy of the kitchen, finally away from public scrutiny, she started to tremble. She leaned against the wall, face pressed into her hands, shoulders shaking. She'd done it again. Lost control and hurt someone. Maybe he'd deserved it, but she'd almost hurt Ruby too. The blood lust had taken control, and in that moment Val had wanted blood every bit as much as Mister E did. If Ruby hadn't interrupted her, she might have killed the guy.

Tears slipped through her fingers. She cursed and wiped them away.

"Why can't I just do something good for once?"

Mister E hopped up on the counter, cocking his head at her. "*Would it have been better to leave him alone? Let the man have his way with the girl?*"

"That's not what I meant. I could have stopped him without punching him in the face with keys. Good people don't do that sort of thing."

"*People do what needs to be done. The end result is all that matters.*"

She barked a bitter laugh. "That's easy for you to say."

Someone called out from the bar, "Hey! Can I get some service out here?"

"Shit." Val took a deep breath and pushed herself away from the wall. Blinked away the last of the tears. Slipped her public mask back into place. She checked her face in the mirror over the handwashing sink. "Goddamnit. Now I have to go fix my eyeliner."

Five hours later, the glow of victory was long gone. Val felt as worn out and trampled as the sticky floorboards. Everything hurt, especially her feet and legs. Knee-high black leather boots were great for attracting tips, but less great for standing in over eight hours. All she wanted to do was go home and sink into a hot bath.

The Alley Cat was finally closed, and both Ruby and the customers had been sent home. A few of the girls were unwinding with after-shift drinks in the big red upholstered corner booth. Stacks of crumpled dollar bills covered the table as they counted their tips and traded stories with Junior while Val closed up the bar.

Shrieks of protest rose when Val killed the music and turned on the harsh overhead work lights.

"Come on, Val! It isn't even five yet."

"I'm done cleaning up and I'm tired," Val said. "You don't have to go home, but you can't stay here. Go to Roxie's if you want to socialize. Have some breakfast. God knows you all need to eat more."

They booed and blew her raspberries, but gathered up their things and left. The girls knew better than to argue with Val at the end of a long night.

"You want me to stay and walk you out to your bike?"

"No, I'm fine, Junior. Thanks, though."

"OK." Junior didn't move. He just stood there with his hands in the pockets of his big hoodie, watching her with his soft brown eyes.

Val smiled and grabbed her leather jacket, bag, and keys, then turned off the lights and set the alarm system before clicking the bolt shut on the front door. Mister E strutted along in front of her, his dainty paws not quite touching the ground. Junior stayed beside her as they circled the building, heading for the tiny parking lot by the alley in the back.

The street was quiet now, the working girls all gone from the corner. The cold breeze pimpled her skin. The city slept, frozen in the brief lull between the nightwalkers and the early risers.

There was no trace of the downpour from earlier, and the tiny fish had vanished along with the puddles. Val pressed her lips together and scowled. Add it to the list of weird things that had been happening. Individually, they might be bizarre anomalies. But put them together and she suspected they added up to something. And that something smelled like magic.

She didn't know what it all meant, but she was sure it was nothing good. In her experience, magic never was.

They approached the back of Junior's beat up little Honda. A peeling sticker on the bumper read, "La Familia".

"How many sisters have you got Junior?"

"Seven." He smiled shyly.

"Older or younger?"

"Two older, five younger. I'm the only boy. The man of the family."

"You give them money?"

"Of course. All the money. Why you think I work in a place full of *loca* women? I need lots of money."

Val laughed. "You and me both, Junior."

Val pulled on her helmet and threw her leg over her motorcycle while Junior crammed himself into his beat up little Honda. Mister E perched in the sidecar of the Ural. The Russian motorcycle was an ancient thing, the engine coughing and growling as she kicked it to life. It was a beast with no electronic parts. Which suited Val just fine. Her power didn't always play nice with electronics.

Junior waved to her through the window as he pulled out onto the street. She was nosing the Ural out after him when Mister E whipped his head to the side like a pointer, making her pause.

Something was in the alley at the far end of the parking lot. Off in the shadows, where the streetlights didn't reach. She couldn't see it so much as sense it, her blood tugging in that direction like metal filings to a magnet. Something over there felt wrong.

She backed up the bike and turned it until the headlight shone into the dark corner. What the light revealed made her stumble away, hot bile rising in her mouth.

A woman lay in a dark pool upon the asphalt. Her limbs were bent at unnatural angles, with bits of bone visible. Her belly was sliced open, spilling loops of thick grey intestines. Val couldn't see the woman's face, but she didn't have to. She would know that green sequined dress anywhere.

3

SFPD's Tenderloin Station was not a nice place. The tile floors were scuffed and cracked, the brick walls crumbling. Charged with policing one of the poorest and most crime-ridden sections of the city, the cops who inhabited it were overworked and underpaid.

Val sat on a metal chair in a small "interview room." She sipped terrible police-station coffee from a paper cup, the overcooked brew buried beneath enough white sugar and chemical creamer to make it almost palatable. It was her third cup. They'd kept her there for hours, waiting for a Detective Chen to arrive, and Val was jittery and exhausted, physically and emotionally. The coffee was the only thing keeping her upright.

Detective Chen now sat across the table from her, tapping a pen against an old-fashioned notebook flipped open in front of him. His face was unlined except for the faint crow's feet at the corners of his narrow eyes. His close-cropped black hair had a touch of silver at the temples.

Chen was as unreadable as the bay and twice as salty. He'd seen it all and then some: junkies, dealers, pimps, whores, pickpockets, and muggers were as unremarkable as the oil stains on the streets. It took a lot to make him sit up and take notice.

Ruby's death had caught his attention.

He flipped through the pictures in front of him and shifted in his chair, clicking the pen with his thumb. He looked almost as tired as Val felt. He cleared his throat.

"Sorry to keep you waiting so long, Miss Keri. Hell of a way to start the day."

"Hell of a way to end one too," Val mumbled. "Especially for Ruby."

The detective looked uncomfortable.

"Yeah. Well. I know you've already given a statement, but I'd like you to go over it again with me. Please start at the beginning. You say there was an altercation with a patron earlier in the night?"

Val scrubbed her hands over her face and told the story again. The Black Knight at the bar getting handsy with Ruby, and how she'd caught him trying to force himself on her in the supply room. Throwing the creep out onto the sidewalk and the fish rain shower. Finding Ruby's body as she was leaving the parking lot.

Chen scribbled in his notebook.

"When you discovered the man and the victim in the supply closet, what did you do, exactly? Walk me through it step by step."

"I pulled him off her and frog-marched his ass out the door."

"He didn't resist?"

"Of course he resisted," Val snorted.

"How did he resist?"

"He called me a bitch and told me I'd close the door if I knew what was good for me. He asked if I knew who he was."

"And did you know who he was?"

"No, I never saw him before."

Chen looked skeptical. "So you overpowered a grown man and escorted him out of the establishment all by yourself. That's your story? What are you, five-two? One-fifteen?"

"Five-four, one-twenty," Val said. "And yes, that's my story because that's what happened."

Chen hummed.

"This isn't the first physical altercation you've been in, is it?"

"I don't know what you mean."

"You assaulted a man at Division and Van Ness on September twelfth of last year, is that correct?"

"He was a stim-junkie who wouldn't leave me alone."

"You broke three of his fingers and cracked two ribs."

Val glowered at the detective.

"I was protecting myself. Is that a crime?"

"You were in another physical altercation on December eleventh, this time with a woman. You knocked out several of her teeth."

"She thought I was looking at her boyfriend. She called me a cunt."

"And were you?"

"Was I what?"

"Looking at her boyfriend."

"I don't see what that has to do with--"

"Answer the question."

"No, I wasn't looking at her boyfriend. He was some beefy construction guy. Not my type at all."

"So you remember what he looked like. That suggests you were looking at him."

Val felt her power stirring. Where did this detective get off questioning her like this? She was not the suspect here.

"I looked at him after she said I was looking at him. Just to see what the hell she was talking about," Val ground the words between her teeth.

"I see." Chen made a note on his pad. "And then on February fourteenth--"

"What the fuck does this have to do with anything?" Val snapped. "My friend was killed last night. You need to be focusing on her, not me."

"Do we? And why is that?"

"Because she's dead! She's dead and the psycho that killed her is still out there walking around!"

"In my experience, a number of violent incidents centered around one individual constitutes a trend. When that individual is a member of your particular... shall we say sub-culture? ... that often compounds the problem."

"My sub-culture? What the hell does that mean?"

"I think you know what it means, Miss Keri."

"You mean the magical community," she growled.

"And is it?"

"Is it what?"

"A community. Do you all drink blood together under the full moon, or whatever it is you do? Do you kill people in alleys for fun?"

"Fuck you. I'm done with this interview." Val pushed back from the table and stood up.

"Sit down, Miss Keri," Chen barked.

Val glared at the detective and remained defiantly on her feet.

Chen returned her stare, his eyes hard. His voice was cold as slate. "If you do not sit down, I'll throw you in a cell so fast it'll make your head spin. Sit. Down."

Val crossed her arms over her chest, breathing hard through her nose. He'd pushed her buttons and made her lose control. Fine. Round one to him. She remained standing for a few more seconds just to make a point, then sat stiffly on the edge of her chair.

"If you answer my questions, this will go a lot smoother for everyone involved. I've got a file on you, and on a lot of freaks like you. There have been an awful lot of murders in this town since your kind started showing up." Chen paused.

"Was there a question in there?"

The detective leaned forward, elbows upon the table. "In my experience, you people like to cover for each other. You think you're in some kind of special club that puts you above the law. Let me assure you, Miss Keri, you are not above the law. I think you know more than you're telling me. What are you hiding?"

"I've told you what happened. I don't have anything else to say to you."

Chen stared at her, silent and waiting. Val stared right back, glowering and grinding her teeth.

Finally, the detective gave a little hmmm, and made a note on his pad.

That hmmm infuriated Val, and she almost lost her temper again. But that would be giving him what he wanted. And she'd be damned if she'd give him the satisfaction.

.   .   .

It was well after noon by the time Chen finally let her go with an order that she not leave town in case he wanted to talk to her again. Right. Like she had anywhere to go.

Her eyes were gritty, her bones ached from fatigue, and on the whole she felt like dried dog shit smeared across the sidewalk. She was exhausted, but too wired and shocked to sleep. She thought about getting some food, but her stomach felt queasy from all the cheap coffee and chemical creamer. Her thoughts churned as she maneuvered the Ural down the city streets. Without conscious planning, her path led her back to the narrow lot behind the Alley Cat. The alley in the far corner was blocked off by bright yellow police tape, but the cops had come and gone. The lot was deserted.

She stared past the tape at the dark bloodstain soaked into the asphalt. Who could have done such a thing? And why?

The Black Knight was the obvious suspect. He was an entitled asshole, and he'd threatened her to boot. But it was a big step from hostile asshole to murderer. An image of Ruby's mutilated body flashed through her mind and she shuddered. Only a monster would do something like that.

Like most nightclubs, the Alley Cat was sad and dirty in the harsh light of day. Painted-over windows covered in a layer of grime. Neon signs dark. Every stain and crack in the pavement felt like a record of hopelessness and desperation. The stench of exhaust clouded the air as an ancient delivery vehicle rumbled by. Construction sounds rose from the collapsed underground line they were digging out somewhere beneath the surface.

The girls all claimed that working at the Alley Cat was temporary. Some of them wanted to save up enough money to move on to a better life. Some were paying for an education. Some were just trying to survive.

For Ruby, that struggle had come to an end.

Val wondered what would happen to Ruby's daughter. The sweet little girl with the big eyes and the curls. Guilt twinged as she realized she couldn't remember the girl's name.

She glanced around to make sure no one was watching before ducking under the police tape to kneel beside the stained asphalt. An entire life -- friends, family, loves and losses, childhood and parenthood -- and this was all that was left. A dark spot on the ground. Val took a deep breath and laid the tips of her fingers on the stain.

The blood woke Mister E immediately. The cat leapt to the ground and prowled around it, sniffing and purring. He rubbed his cheek against the stain.

Emotions assaulted Val -- hunger and rage, fear and despair, desperation and pain. She fought the urge to snatch her hand away and forced herself to focus, sorting through the storm of impressions. First she had to separate Mister E's reactions from the echoes of Ruby left behind in her blood. That part was easy; Mister E's urges weren't even remotely human.

With every hour that passed, the echo of Ruby's soul would fade. In a week, her blood would be just another stain. But now, less than twelve hours after her death, the dancer's presence was still fresh and strong. Ruby's wild fear surged through Val, along with rapid-fire impressions of the doomed woman's final moments. Darkness and something charging toward her. There was panic and terrible pain, and something else, a taste of magic, old and powerful... Then there was more pain, and Mister E hissed as Val jerked away from the stain and landed on her ass, gasping in the grey light.

She sat hugging her knees for a few minutes, trembling, fighting to get herself under control. It took a tremendous effort. The echo of Ruby's death whipped her emotions into a frenzy, and she wanted to hit something, to hurt something. To make the responsible party pay.

She forced herself to take a deep breath. Unclench her fists.

The killer was gone. There was nothing she could do right now. She had to be patient. She swallowed Mister E's bloodlust, forcing it down breath by painstaking breath. She finally shoved the cat-demon back inside his mental cage and locked the door.

Val opened her eyes and blinked. Her ass was asleep. Her comm told her she'd been sitting in the parking lot for an hour and a half. Flaming toads. She was lucky someone didn't notice her and call the cops.

She pulled the Ural out into traffic, then turned south on Van Ness. Her wheels hummed up onto the metal grating of the Van Ness bridge, the Market Street chasm yawning beneath her. The south side of the city had been cut off by the earthquakes that had flattened much of California. Where Market Street used to be was now a massive rubble-filled canyon. Water from the bay filled the east end of the canyon. The west end was unstable, periodically swallowing chunks of the Castro District in massive rockslides.

The canyon was crossed by a single bridge at Van Ness. It was a hell of a traffic bottleneck and would have been worse if a significant percentage of the personal transports in the city weren't bicycles and aircars. Ground-bound gas-guzzlers like Val's Ural were dinosaurs, slowly going extinct.

As Val rode, she tried to sort through the impressions she'd gotten from Ruby's blood. Ruby's panic and fear had been too strong to allow Val many clear images, but a couple of things came through.

First, the attacker was male. Not exactly news, but at least it confirmed her suspicions.

Second was that taste of magic. Something old and powerful. This wasn't a mundane murder. Something more was going on.

But the third thing was the one that made her grip tighten on the handlebars. In Ruby's memories, she'd felt no trace of a murder weapon. No knife, no machete, no sword. The guy had disemboweled her with his bare hands. With his claws.

Which meant Chen had been right about one thing. The murderer wasn't a guy at all, but a nightmare. A nightmare that had killed her friend.

Val's face twisted into a snarl.

"Not in my town, you fucker."

4

Twenty Years Ago

Valora Keri was running, her six-year-old arms pumping, black hair flying behind her, bare feet slapping the dusty ground of the tiny village. Dark clouds boiled overhead, swallowing the sun, the rising storm carrying the scents of sage and ice across the rocky mountainside.

Valora didn't notice any of that. Her attention was fixed on the taunts of the children chasing her over the hills.

She pounded past the abandoned factory, dodging craters left by the war. The world was in shambles, decimated by climate change and collapsing economies. Humanity was hanging on by its fingernails. But Valora didn't know any of that either. She only knew the other children were mean to her.

She didn't know why they tormented her. She tried to fit in, tried to play their games, tried to be who she thought they wanted her to be. But everything she did went wrong. No matter what she said, they twisted the words that came out of her mouth, made her out to be

stupid and ugly and wrong. She didn't want to be wrong. She just
wanted to play with the other children. But they wouldn't let her.

Lightning flashed overhead, causing the hair on the back of her
neck to rise.

The voices were getting closer. Fear, anger and despair filled her
heart. Every day was a struggle. A gauntlet of taunts and scorn. Tears
carved tracks down her grimy cheeks, dripping from the point of her
chin. Thunder rolled over her, echoing off the surrounding peaks.

She rounded a standing stone and redoubled her speed. The ruins
of the ancient temple were just ahead, full of nooks and crannies and
hiding places beneath the crumbling stone. If she could make it to the
temple, she'd be safe.

Her tormentors got there first.

Andrei caught her ankle with his toe and she tumbled, the rocky
ground tearing the skin off her palms and elbows. The other children
surrounded her, squawking like crows. A little murder waiting to
happen.

They chanted, calling her all the names they knew, laughing and
spitting at her, egging each other on. Even sweet, blonde Katrina --
who was nice to Valora when they were alone, who liked to chase
bumblebees and laugh at the way their fuzzy butts stuck out of the
flowers -- even Katrina took part, driven by the crushing weight of
peer pressure, the inexorable urge to fit in.

Valora sobbed and tried to get away, but they caught her and
pushed her back down in the dust. Her fear turned to desperation and
rage, rising like the storm. In that moment she hated them. Hated
every one of them.

Her eyes locked on Katrina. She hated Katrina most of all. Hated
her two faces. Hated the way she pretended to like Valora, when in her
heart she really despised Valora the same as the other children.

Fear and rage filled her like the black clouds, hazing her vision,
turning everything red. Lighting flickered, striking the ruins off to her
left, cracking stone that had been standing for centuries. The roar was
louder than anything in the world.

Valora didn't hear it. Her senses were all wrapped up in her rage.
Beneath her feet, the lightning crackled down through the mountain,

flickering through glacial ice until it touched something. A frozen thing that thawed. A prison that softened.

Something powerful awoke. Escaped into the dark. Something that had been locked away for thousands of years.

That something found Valora. It whispered in her ear.

I can give you the power you seek. The power to avenge these wrongs. Smite your enemies. All you have to do is say yes.

Valora didn't think about where the voice in her head came from. What it might be, or what it was asking. She was six. She wanted to fight back. She wanted to hurt the bullies. Wanted to stomp on them like ants. Poke sharp sticks through their bodies. Rip their wings off and pour honey over them.

She'd have agreed to anything in that moment.

She whispered the word, "Yes."

Power filled her. It swelled her body, pressure against the back of her ribs, behind her eyeballs. It felt like she'd swallowed the storm. She couldn't move. One more breath and she would explode.

Then she did explode.

The power entwined with her fear and despair, her hatred and rage. Through her eyes, it found a target.

A whirlwind sprang up around her. Her own private storm. The wind howled, gathering dust and pebbles and rocks and hurling them away from her with hurricane force, shredding her tormentors' clothing. The taunts of the children changed to something else as small sticks and twigs drove into their flesh like spears, impaling their arms and legs. A rock went through Andrei's leg like a bullet, shattering bone, missing an artery by millimeters.

But the storm aimed the biggest blow at Katrina.

A branch as thick as a man's arm punched straight through the girl's chest, leaving a hole wide as a saucer. Valora could see the ruins of the girl's ribcage right through the hole. Katrina's wide blue eyes caught hers, blinking in shock. Her mouth opened and closed, a trickle of blood dribbling over her bottom lip.

The thing inside Valora crowed in triumph, exulting in the blood. It wanted more.

Suddenly Valora's mother was there, clutching at her arm,

screaming at her over the roar of the wind. Valora pushed her away without a thought, the wind hurling her mother through the air. Her skull smashed into an ancient stone pillar with sickening force. She collapsed to the ground, leaving behind a bright red smear.

Valora recoiled in shock. The wind died as quickly as it had sprung up. For a moment, the hillside was deathly silent. Valora smelled sage. She tasted cold honey.

For the rest of her life, Valora would see this moment in her nightmares, in horrible photographic clarity. Would feel the spit drying on her face, hear her tormentors' banshee wails carried on the wind, taste the incongruous sweetness in her mouth. See her mother lying in a puddle of blood.

And in her dream, she would always smile.

Then she would wake up screaming. Wondering what kind of monster she'd become.

5

The flip side of magic returning to the world was that the monsters had come back as well. Or maybe they'd never left. Val hadn't had time to ask the ones she'd met personally. She'd been too busy trying not to get killed.

She wrapped her arms around herself and leaned her face against the cool glass of the bay window, watching a rusty garbage truck block traffic as it scooped up cans on the street below. A line of annoyed bikes stretched behind it, contrasting with the glint of a hovercar flashing across the sky above. Hovercars had been a luxury product when everything went to shit, and they'd never come down to a price point that was attainable by the average person. So the fat cats breezed across the sky, while the rest of humanity was stuck behind garbage trucks. Some things never changed.

The flat at Sixteenth and Valencia had seen better days. The white paint on the windowsill was grey and peeling. The walls were warped and the stained hardwood floors should have been replaced decades ago. It was old and overpriced and falling apart, like a lot of historic Victorian houses in the city. On the other hand, the Mission District location was great: easy walking distance to dozens of bars, restaurants and shops, and just a couple of blocks away from the sunshine of

Dolores Park. The park had become a shantytown of homeless people and stim-junkies, but still, it was open space. That had value in a city.

In San Francisco properties could generally be described as affordable, well-located, or new. If you were lucky, you got one out of three. If you were extremely lucky, you got two.

Val figured she'd gotten one and a half. Well-located, check. New, definitely not. Affordable could go either way, depending on your perspective. A biotech worker would consider her flat a steal, though they'd be less than thrilled with the leaky faucets and roaches. For Val, the flat was at the upper reaches of what she could afford. And that was with a pair of housemates, of course. Only the ludicrously wealthy could afford a flat in the city without housemates.

As was often the case with young people in a bustling city, she rarely saw her housemates. They all had busy lives, and her nocturnal schedule meant she was generally sleeping while they were awake and vice-versa.

Thanks to her unusual morning, today did not fit the normal pattern. She could hear Malcolm banging around in the kitchen, singing along to "I Will Survive."

Her stomach growled like a wolverine. Food sounded good. Really, really good.

She leaned into the kitchen doorway and watched Malcolm's back as he shook his ass and used a whisk as a microphone. The kitchen was small, with a black and white checkerboard tile floor and a tiny table with two chairs wedged up against the side of the refrigerator. Malcom was wearing green velvet pajama pants and a t-shirt that featured a kitten flying across the milky way, shooting rainbow lasers out of its eyes. Fortunately, he was mostly lip synching. Malcom could dance with the grace of a woodland nymph. Sing, not so much.

Malcolm spun around and screamed. The whisk clattered to the floor. He fell back against the stove, gasping.

"Girl, you almost gave me a heart attack!" He glared at Val, fanning himself with his fingers. "Trust me, you do not want dead black queen all over your floor. We stain. You'd be scrubbing that shit up for weeks."

The corner of Val's mouth quirked.

"Sorry, I wasn't trying to be sneaky. What are you doing home? Don't you have work today?"

Malcolm raised an eyebrow at her. "It's Saturday. You know, the weekend?"

"Oh, right. I forgot."

"You forgot what day it is? You must have had a much more interesting Friday than I did." He studied her critically. "And maybe not in a good way. You look like warm death on a sesame seed bun."

"I had a long night."

"Are your panties in your pocket? No? So not a sticky walk-of-shame kind of long night. Too bad. Sit down and I'll make you some of Malcolm's patented banana-chip pancakes. Sure cure for hangovers, broken hearts, and parking tickets. You want some coffee?"

"God, no. I'm already vibrating at a subatomic level. Any more coffee and I might accidentally time travel." Val shuddered and lowered herself into one of the creaky wooden chairs.

"Tranquil tea?"

She managed a small smile.

"That sounds perfect."

"You've got mail," Malcolm said over his shoulder. "Another letter from New York."

Val pulled the envelope from behind the salt shaker and ran her fingers over the familiar handwriting. New York. Memories came flooding back, not all of them good. She put the envelope back. She was not ready to deal with New York right now.

Malcolm delivered the steaming coffee mug and said, "You look like you've got quite a story. Tell me all about it while I whip up the batter."

So she did, starting with the Black Knight assaulting Ruby at the club, the rain of fish, Ruby's body in the parking lot, and ending with her hours of questioning at the SFPD station.

Malcom slid two plates of steaming pancakes onto the table and settled into the chair across from her. Her stomach rumbled like the San Andreas fault as the smell of warm chocolate and banana hit her.

"Fish rain? Really? Climate change has fucked this city up good. I remember when it was always sunny here. Nobody told me in five years it'd rain more here than it does in Seattle."

"That's what you're focusing on from all that? The fish?"

"Fish rain is all I can handle on an empty stomach. Let me get some pancakes in me and we can talk about the rest." He pointed a fork at her plate. "You better eat those while they're still hot. You want to get the chocolate chips while they're all melty. Also, I got you some butterscotch syrup."

"Oh my god, Malcolm. You are a god made flesh."

Val drenched the pancakes in butterscotch and shoved a bite into her mouth. Malcolm was right, the pancakes were amazing. For a while she allowed herself to get lost in a wonderland of melted chocolate chips, warm banana, butterscotch and butter.

She resurfaced sometime later, stuffed like a teddy bear. On the other side of the table, Malcom was polishing up his plate.

Val cradled her tea and leaned back in her chair. "Thank you. That was heavenly."

"I told you. Banana-chip pancakes make everything better." He took a sip of coffee and crossed his legs. "So. Your friend was murdered. That's some crazy shit."

"Yeah. Crazy shit."

"You think the Black Knight did it?"

"I don't know. I mean, he was an asshole, but the way Ruby's body was mutilated..." She shuddered. "I just can't imagine someone doing that."

"Well, clearly someone did."

"Maybe."

"Maybe? What, you think she did it to herself? Or was she mauled by a bear in downtown San Francisco?"

"I don't know what I think. But there was something wrong about that corner of the parking lot. Bad energy. It's why I noticed the body in the first place."

Malcolm rolled his eyes.

"You talking about magic again?"

"Maybe."

"Honey, you know I love you, but you've got to stop talking about that magic shit. It makes you sound cracked like an old teapot."

Val rolled her eyes right back at him.

"Just because you don't believe it, doesn't mean it's not real."

"Mmmmhmm." Malcolm gathered up the plates and took them to the sink. "I think you should go get some sleep while you can. They're going to be shoring up the old BART tunnels under Sixteenth tomorrow, and none of us will be getting much sleep for who knows how long."

"Here too? Wonderful." Val frowned over her mug. "They've been digging underneath the Alley Cat for weeks. Fucking jackhammers and dynamite are following me wherever I go."

"Like I said, you'd best sleep while you can. Today's going to be the last quiet day for the foreseeable future."

As if to underline the point, a door slammed at the end of the hall. Julie came stomping into the kitchen, chunky headphones covering her ears. She ignored them both and went straight to the refrigerator. She grabbed a bottle of orange juice, slammed the refrigerator door, and stomped out.

Just before she passed through the doorway, she growled, "Fuck this freakshow. I'm moving out at the end of the month."

Val stared at Malcolm. "Wait, what? On two weeks' notice? Seriously?"

Malcolm spread his hands in a helpless gesture. "I mean, you did cost her a boyfriend."

"I didn't cost her shit! He came into the Alley Cat while I was working! If he and Jessie got a little too friendly that has nothing to do with me!"

"Hey, don't shoot the messenger. I'm just telling you what she told me."

"Flaming toads. I don't have time for this shit."

She sighed and pushed to her feet. Her name was on the lease. If they couldn't find someone to fill Julie's room by the first, Val would be the one on the hook for the extra rent.

"See you later, Malcolm."

He waggled soapy fingers at her. "TTFN."

"TTFN?"

"Ta-Ta For Now."

"Is that what the cool kids are saying these days?"

"Nope, just me and Winnie the Pooh."

"Winnie the Pooh? You never struck me as the type."

"What type? Everybody loves Winnie the Pooh. Though, I prefer Tigger myself. T-I-double-Guh-RRRRRR," he said, making finger claws at her.

Val laughed and stumbled down the hall. The warm tea and pancakes had done their job. Fatigue was crashing down on her like a mountain. She barely managed to remove her clothes before collapsing into bed.

As she drifted off, her mind replayed the events of the long night. The last thing she saw was Ruby sitting at the bar, downing shot after shot, her smile brave and trusting. Alive with the belief that Val was going to protect her.

6

Valora's father sent her away.

It was all he could do to keep the other villagers from stoning her to death. Two children were dead, along with Valora's own mother. No one could prove it was Valora's fault, but the fact that she was the only child to come out without a scratch made them suspicious. And her eyes had changed. Her irises were now an intense gold, like the morning sun breaking the horizon.

The villagers muttered about witchcraft and demons, and made the sign against evil when they walked by Valora's house. But no one had actually seen what happened, and Valora's own memories were blank. Like someone had wiped the chalkboard in her mind clean with a single swipe. The police weren't sure what to do, but they were investigating.

Her father locked her inside their home and forbade her to set foot outside, lest someone see her and fly into a rage. Valora withdrew into herself, rarely responding when anyone asked her a question.

"She's lost her mind," her father said. "Her mother is dead. She needs to be sent to a madhouse."

"No!" her grandmother disagreed. "We don't know what happened up there, but it's clear she's been through a great shock. She needs her family."

In the end, when it became obvious the authorities were going to take the girl away regardless of their wishes, her father found another solution. They sent her to live with his sister in America.

At the airport, Valora's grandmother sobbed and hugged her tightly. Her father stood apart, smoking, his face grim. The girl stayed silent, her gaze far away, hardly aware of what was happening.

Valora never saw them again.

Her Aunt Marya turned out to be a short-tempered woman with a pinched face and three children of her own. She was not happy to see Valora, and put her in a room with the youngest child, Niko, who was not yet two years old. She gave Valora a foam mat in the corner to sleep on and a single drawer to put her few clothes in.

The other children were excited to have a new playmate. The girls, Sasha and Anna, were close to Valora's age, and they tried to get her to join in their games, but Valora remained silent and withdrawn. She couldn't have talked to them even if she'd wanted to; their rapid American English flowed past her like a river, all noise and melody, but with few understandable words for her to hold on to.

Everything was different in America, bigger and louder and shinier. Valora didn't understand why her father had sent her there. She missed her village. She missed her friends and home. She missed her mother.

She didn't know what had happened that day in the ruins, in the blank spot in her mind, but she knew it was something terrible. She spent most of her time sitting on the floor in the baby's room, rocking and whispering to herself, trying and failing to remember. Her cousins were nonplussed, to say the least.

About a week after Valora arrived, Sasha and Anna walked into the baby's room and stopped dead. Their eyes stretched as wide as the ocean.

Valora sat on the scrap rug on the floor, muttering to herself. This was not unusual. Unusual was the fact that a tiny whirlwind puffed around her, lifting the baby's blocks into the air, spinning in a slow constellation. To their credit, the girls did not scream or run away or call for their mother. They stood and watched in wonder as little Niko giggled and jumped and tried to catch the floating blocks, his baby hair tufting in the wind.

When Aunt Marya found out, she had a very different reaction.

Valora was banished to the attic, her foam bed shoved between boxes of old books, clothes, and furniture. Aunt Marya forbade her to come down from the attic unsupervised.

The air was hot and thick in the attic, with cobwebs drooping in the spaces between the rafters. Moths danced in the soft light filtering through the dusty windows. At night, the room creaked and groaned around her.

Despite all this, Valora found she liked it up there. It was quiet, and people weren't constantly staring at her or talking American at her. They just left her alone.

She spent her days reading books and exploring, poking around in the dusty boxes. She unearthed old clothes and photographs, ice skates and baseball gloves stiff with age. An abandoned wasps' nest lurked beneath one of the rafters, a grey honeycomb as big as her palm. Inside an old wooden chest she saw small black turds she was sure were mouse droppings, although she never saw any mice.

The cat might have had something to do with that.

It came sauntering out from behind a rusty old sled one day while she was reading a yellowed copy of *Alice in Wonderland*. Its grey-striped fur was so dark it looked purple, and it wore a black hat, which leaned at a jaunty angle as it leapt up onto a box and sat, regarding Valora with eyes as golden as her own. It puffed on a candy cigarette and blew a smoke ring.

"Would you like to play a game?" it asked.

Valora nodded, excitement coursing through her. Even though she'd never seen the cat before, something about it resonated inside her. It felt right. They belonged together.

The cat yawned, exposing needle-sharp teeth as it stood and stretched.

"I'll hide. You seek. Start counting." It leaped from the box and disappeared into the jumble.

After a few games, she asked it, "Do you have a name?"

The cat shrugged. *"Many. There are names and then there are names, if you know what I mean."*

Valora wrinkled her nose. "I don't know what you mean."

The cat twitched its tail and blew another smoke ring.

"There are names others call you, and names you call yourself. Then there's your true name, which is only spoken by your heart to itself. The heart has no tongue, and so none but another heart may hear it."

This was all a little deep for a six-year-old. Valora tried another tactic.

"What should I call you?"

"Call me what you will. Names are written in sand. The name you call me now may not be the name you call me later, regardless."

"Later? Like tonight?"

The cat chuckled. *"No, later in your life. When you are all grown up."*

Valora thought long and hard. Then she smiled.

"I will call you Mister E."

Mister E arched an eyebrow. *"Mister E? That seems very formal. Are we not going to be friends?"*

"We are, but we've only just met. I will call you Mister E until I get to know you better."

"That seems fair." Mister E cocked his head at her, his golden eyes shining. *"Now, is it your turn to hide, or mine?"*

Mister E became Valora's constant companion. They played games together, or chased moths, or lazed in the dusty sunbeams that shone through the attic windows.

"Why do you smoke candy cigarettes?" she asked him. "Why not real ones?"

Mister E shuddered. *"No, thank you. Those things will kill you. And these taste much better."* He blew her a smoke ring to emphasize his point. It shimmered in the sun.

Months passed. Valora unearthed a box of old books and Mister E would read to her, doing the most excellent voices for all the characters. As her English got better, she would sometimes read to him too.

Reading was hard, though, and living in America was even harder.

Valora missed her mother and father and grandmother. She missed the mountains and rocks and trees of her village. She missed the other children, even if they had been mean to her.

She was often sad or frustrated or angry. And despite Mister E's company, she was lonely. Her feelings built up inside her, filling her like a dense fog. They would expand within her ribcage, pushing outward at her skin until she felt like a fat, swollen sausage, or a balloon. The pressure would grow and churn until she couldn't contain it. On those days she was surprised her feelings didn't leak out of her mouth, like frozen breath on a winter's morning, or smoke from a dragon.

"You can't keep your feelings bottled up inside like that," Mister E told her. *"You have to let them out."*

He taught her to release the pressure by lashing out at something, directing her emotions at a target. This often had spectacular results. The wind would howl and swirl around her, blowing faster and faster, then rush forward in a great gust, hurling boxes and baseball gloves and clouds of dust across the attic, producing very satisfying bangs and crashes.

Mister E was right. She always felt better afterward.

Her experience in the nursery had taught her to never let her emotions out around other people. If she was outside the dusty little room when she felt them building, she would immediately dash up the stairs and slam the door behind her. If Aunt Marya and Uncle Victor heard the sounds of things smashing that followed, they wisely never said a word about it.

One day, about six months after Valora arrived, Aunt Marya woke in an exceptionally good mood. It was a beautiful spring day outside, with fluffy clouds skipping across the blue sky and bees buzzing around the flowers in her garden. She decided to pack a picnic basket and take the children out for a day in the park.

Greenway Park was massive and sprawling, with green lawns alongside acres of rolling hills and forest. Aunt Marya chose a shady spot beneath a wide maple tree, between a playground and a stretch of dark forest. Sasha and Anna squealed and ran for the swings, while little Niko toddled around picking daisies.

Valora stood frozen, overwhelmed by the open space and light, like a house cat plopped into the wide world. It was all too big and bright, with no walls to protect her. She felt exposed and vulnerable. As her anxiety rose, the fog within her rose as well, making her skin feel too tight, stuffed full of feelings with no outlet.

"There are some trees over there," Mister E told her. *"No one will see you in there."*

She slunk away from the noise of the playground, away from the sun and the shrieks of the other children, until she found herself beneath the cool canopy of the forest.

Valora crouched at the base of a massive oak tree, nestled in a crook between the roots. It was cool and protected here, and she tried to calm down, to breathe in the pine-scented air and feel the bark beneath her fingers. But it was no use. The noise from the playground intruded: squeals, laughter and sobs. Shrieks of indignation and cries of pain.

The ruins of the old temple flashed through her mind. Children taunting her. Chasing her. Calling her names. Her fear and anger rose, growing stronger and stronger, pushing out against her ribs until she thought she would burst.

It was no use, she couldn't contain it. She had to let it out.

She tried to control it, to let the power trickle out of her slowly, like a hose with a kink in it. But the pressure was too great. As soon as she allowed a tiny bit to escape, the wind spun out of her control, roaring into a cyclone, flinging dirt and stones, flattening bushes and plants. It chewed up the ancient trunk behind her, leaving a deep scar in the thick bark.

She couldn't say how long it went on for, but when the power had finally drained away, she slumped against the massive roots, feeling empty and exhausted. A circle of bare dirt surrounded her, a thirty-foot swath of uprooted plants and broken bushes. She had been facing the park, and the cyclone had cleared away all the underbrush separating her from the wide green lawn. The lawn was strewn with branches and leaves, dirt and rocks from her explosion, the playground clearly visible.

Aunt Marya stood staring at Valora, mouth open, her eyes filled with terror.

7

As everybody knows from every cop show ever, the main thing about stakeouts is that they're about as exciting as a committee meeting on infrastructure. Val was learning the painful truth of that as she sat sipping coffee in the Ural's sidecar, leaning back and squinting in the afternoon sun, watching the entrance to the Temple of the Black Knights down the block. She'd only gotten a few hours of sleep, and her eyes were dry and grainy. She felt cranky and stretched thin from too much caffeine and not enough sleep. But she had to work that evening, so she had to use the time she had.

The good thing about the Black Knights was they were a religious organization as well as a criminal one. So their headquarters-slash-temple was big and obvious and out in the open.

The bad thing was, she couldn't just walk in there without an invitation. It wasn't that kind of religion.

So Val was reduced to lurking. Waiting and watching. A good old-fashioned stakeout.

Unfortunately, foot traffic in and out of the temple was light, and she hadn't seen the asshole she was looking for. Which wasn't exactly shocking. If the guy she'd kicked out of the Alley Cat murdered Ruby, he was probably laying low.

But the only thing Val knew about him was that he was a Black Knight. Which meant she had exactly one lead. And that lead brought her to the Black Knights' temple. So here she was, sitting around like a dumb ass, wasting an afternoon on the street and feeling like she was doing nothing.

"Religion was a lot more exciting in the old days." Mister E lay stretched across the seat, half-dozing in the sun. *"Fertility rites, human sacrifices, orgies. That's why so many people have stopped believing these days. Modern religions are no fun."*

"I don't think the person being sacrificed would agree with you."

"You're always so negative," he pouted. *"Sacrifice days were the culmination of a week-long festival, full of music and art and wine and sex and food and competitions and games. A whole street market would spring up around the site, with vendors traveling for days to be there."*

"Did they take selfies with the condemned?"

Mister E gave her the side-eye. *"Being chosen as sacrifice was a great honor, I'll have you know. The family of the chosen would receive a fabulous bounty from the village. Giving a child to the gods could literally set the rest of the family up for life."*

"Wait. A child? You sacrificed children?" Val was appalled.

"Well, I didn't sacrifice them. Their parents did, of course."

"How could someone sacrifice their own child?"

Mister E yawned and turned over so the sun could warm his belly.

"First of all, the world was more dangerous back then, and children weren't nearly as precious as they are now. Families had a lot of children, and half of them never made it to adulthood anyway. So sacrificing a child wasn't a big deal."

"Sacrificing children is sick."

"Spoken like someone who has never spent a day with a screaming toddler."

Val sighed and ground a knuckle into her eye socket. "I don't know why I bother talking to you."

She fidgeted with the buttons on her leather jacket. Her hands itched to be doing something. She wasn't good at sitting still, especially not when she had a friend to avenge.

She kept seeing flashes of Ruby. The sun dancing in her hair as she showed Val around the waterfront. The smile in her eyes when she arrived at the Alley Cat with cookies. Her fraying green sequined dress. Her broken body in the parking lot. Her intestines pulled out onto the asphalt.

Ruby didn't deserve to die like that. No one deserved to die like that.

She thought of Ruby's daughter again, the little girl with the curls and the big eyes. She should go check on her. Make sure someone was taking care of her.

She added it to the list. One more thing for her to cross off. But first, she needed to find Ruby's murderer.

She perked up as a Black Knight descended the steps of the temple and turned in her direction. He was a tall skinny guy, with sallow skin and sunken cheeks. He walked with his hands buried deep in the pockets of his denim jacket.

As he got near, Val levered herself off the Ural.

"Hey," she called. "Can I ask you a question?"

The guy scowled at her suspiciously. "No."

She stepped towards him. "Please, it'll only take a minute."

"Fuck off."

Val smiled. "Sorry, not the answer I'm looking for."

She closed the distance between them with two quick steps and shoved the guy hard. She'd chosen her location carefully, parking the Ural directly across from a narrow alley between two old brick buildings. The shove sent the Black Knight stumbling into the mouth of the alley. Val followed, pinning him against the bricks with a forearm against his throat.

He snarled and took a clumsy swipe at her. Val ducked and hit him with two quick blows to the stomach. The wind huffed out of him.

She snarled into his face. "Naughty-naughty. None of that now." She swiveled and threw him face-first into the opposite wall. He bounced off the brick and went down on all fours, the knees of his jeans landing in a dirty puddle. Val came down behind him and clamped an arm-lock around his throat. She bent low, whispering in his ear.

"Now. I've got a few questions for you. Answer them and we can both go about our day, no harm done. Understand?"

Sputtering and cursing, he clawed at her arm. Val squeezed harder.

"I said, understand?"

The man's face grew purple, his movements weaker. Finally he sagged, and Val loosened her hold just enough to let him wheeze and suck air.

"You don't know who you're messing with. You're going to regret this."

"That's funny. I met one of your guys last night and he said the same thing." She leaned in close, tightening her forearm around his neck to show she meant business. "That's what I'm here to talk to you about. One of your brothers was in the Alley Cat last night. Middle-aged, balding guy. Sharp suit. A silver comm where his left ear should be. I want to know who he is and where I can find him."

"I don't know what you're talking about," the guy snarled.

Val could tell by the way he tensed at the description that he was lying. He knew who the guy was, all right.

"Wrong answer," Val cranked down on his neck again, choking him out until he went limp in her arms. When she finally let him breathe, he coughed and wheezed for a full minute.

When he finally got himself under control, she asked again. "This is your last chance. Tell me what I want to know, or this alley will be the last thing you ever see. If I have to choke you again, I'm not going to stop. It all comes down to one simple question, really. Is protecting this asshole worth your life? Think about your answer carefully. Now. Last chance. Who is he, and where can I find him?"

The guy stiffened, and she could practically hear the wheels turning as his self-preservation instinct battled itself. On the one hand, if he ratted out his brother Knight and the organization found out he'd done it, his long-term survival prospects weren't very good. On the other hand, if he didn't tell her what she wanted to know, he wouldn't live long enough to have any long-term survival prospects.

"Don't even think about lying to me. I'll know if you're telling the truth or not."

She could feel his decision teetering. Whichever way he stepped there was danger. She almost felt sorry for the guy. Almost.

"Time's up." She started to squeeze.

"No, wait!" he choked. "His name is Edward Hopkins. He's a lieutenant in the organization. I don't know where to find him."

Val tightened her arm at that, and the guy's voice tightened in panic. "I'm telling the truth. I don't know where he lives. Please. I've given you his name. That's all I know."

Val considered. He seemed to be telling the truth. His information wasn't as useful as she would have liked, but it was something. Now she at least had a name to go on.

"Thanks," she said. "Go to sleep now, and dream of a better world."

She clamped her forearm around his windpipe once more, and kept it clamped until his struggles ceased. She left him lying facedown in the alley, his pant leg soaking up the dirty water from the puddle. He might wake up with a headache, but he would wake up.

As she kicked the Ural back to life, she turned the name over in her mind, bright and shiny like a new penny. Edward Hopkins.

8

———

Halfway through her shift that evening, Val's boss called her into his office. Tommy Walker's domain was up a metal flight of stairs next to the DJ booth, up above the seating area. Big one-way windows covered an entire wall so he could monitor the club. Tommy liked to sit up there in his leather chair and watch over the floor like a medieval lord, master of all he surveyed.

He was sitting there when Val walked in, his walnut hair slightly mussed. He wore a white silk shirt with a black octopus silhouette, the tentacles going down his arms, making him look like a Hollywood producer or some kind of manga villain. His eyes were red and Val wasn't surprised to see traces of white powder dusting the rim of his left nostril. He was studying a picture of a long golden object on the desk in front of him, but he quickly tucked it away when Val approached.

"What's this I hear about you wanting to close my club?" he said before she'd made it two steps inside the door.

Val rolled her eyes.

"Ruby was killed in the alley, Tommy. Show some respect."

"You need to show some respect when you speak to me," Tommy

jabbed a finger at her. "This is my club and I call the shots. Don't go behind my back and talk to the girls before you talk to me."

"I wasn't going behind your back, I was just talking. I thought it might be a nice gesture if we closed for Ruby's funeral so the girls could pay their respects."

"You're not paid to think. Your job is to pour drinks and look sexy. That's it."

Val clenched her teeth and fought down an image of her fist and Tommy's face coming together. She took a deep breath.

"Look, Tommy. The girls are shook up, OK? They're scared. Ruby was killed in the alley right next to the club. The same alley a lot of them walk through every night to get home. Going to Ruby's funeral would help them grieve. Give them some closure. It would also be a nice gesture on your part, make it look like you actually cared about them. It might make them feel a little safer."

"I'm going to have Junior check the alley every hour. And he'll personally escort the girls to the taxi stand. That should make them feel safe enough."

"Thank you. That's a good idea." And the least he could do. "Look, the funeral is going to be during the afternoon. The club's not busy then anyway. Just consider closing for a few hours so the girls can show their respects. Maybe you could come too. I know it would mean a lot to them."

Tommy scowled. He was opposed to anything that cost him money. He had expensive habits to support, after all.

"I'll think about it," he said. "But next time you come to me first before you go talking to the girls about things."

Val forced a tight smile.

"You got it, boss. Anything else?"

"Yeah, I don't want to see you roughing up my customers like that ever again. Now the Black Knights are up my ass. Show some self-control, for Christ's sake. That man was a paying customer."

"A paying customer who was getting handsy with Ruby in the storage closet."

Tommy held up a placating hand. "And you did the right thing in stopping him. Nobody rides for free. But the way you handled it was unacceptable. You can't go around beating the shit out of customers. Do it again and you're fired. Is that understood?"

Val ground her teeth behind her smile.

"Sure, Tommy. Whatever you say. Can I go now?"

"Yeah. Oh, one more thing. Your till was ten credits short last night. I'm taking it out of your pay. Now get back to work." He shooed her away like a fly.

Val stomped back down the stairs past the DJ booth. Malina was in there, curly hair bobbing to the music, one brown hand holding her headphones against her ear as she cued up the next song. Val barely saw her. She was seeing red.

Mister E perched on her shoulder, growling, his tail twitching. He fed on her anger, stoking it higher. Tommy was a dust-brained prick. She should quit. Kick him in the balls and storm out in front of everyone. Ride off into the sunset like a conquering hero.

Yeah, right. An unemployed hero with an empty bank account who would have to pay double rent if she couldn't find a new roommate in the next two weeks. While trying to find a new job in a city where bartending gigs were worth their weight in gold. Fat chance.

Jack had the misfortune of trying to flirt with her the second she stepped behind the bar.

"Hey, gorgeous. You're extra sexy tonight."

"You're not as charming as you think you are, Jack," she snapped.

A mystified expression replaced his smile.

"What did I do?"

Val delivered his White Russian and stomped away.

She spent the rest of her shift in a thundercloud, glowering at everyone who approached the bar.

After a couple of hours, the barback cornered her in the kitchen. Lisa was tall and willowy, with straight blond hair pulled up in pigtails. She liked to wear tight vintage athletic jerseys and black jeans that made her look like a twig. Her nails were always immaculate, and today each one was painted a different color. Val knew Lisa made art, some kind of sculptures. The barback didn't talk much; usually the girl was lost in her own world.

So it was a surprise when Lisa interrupted her while she was grabbing a rack of clean glasses.

"Are you all right, Val?"

"I'm fine."

"It's OK to be sad, you know." Lisa laid a hand on Val's shoulder.

"Don't touch me." Val jerked her shoulder away. "I said I'm fine."

Lisa bobbed her head and studied her toes, but she didn't walk away. She leaned in and lowered her voice.

"I heard Ruby was in debt to the Russians."

Val stared at her. "Vasilevski's Russians?"

Lisa's eyes darted around, as if just saying their name would summon them. "Yeah, that's what I heard."

"Where did you hear that?"

"Some of the girls were talking."

Val scowled and pushed past Lisa.

The barback called after her, "If you ever want to talk, I'm here..."

Val ignored Lisa's compassion. She didn't need to be sad; she had plenty of anger to keep her moving. And she didn't need to talk. What she needed was answers.

The night slid by in a neon haze of cold drinks, loud music, naked girls, and assholes who thought they were Jesus reincarnated. Val did her job mechanically, an automaton running on pure rage. She kept a lid on her power, but just barely. Mister E paced the liquor shelves and growled, his fur fluffed to twice his normal size.

The names Edward Hopkins and Vasilevski turned over and over in her mind. Now she had two men with a motive. They were both violent and powerful enough to have murdered Ruby, but was one of them a monster? That was the question she needed to answer.

Some time after midnight, Val glanced up and froze. Vasilevski himself had just walked in, along with two of his square-jawed bodyguards. The trio slid into one of the dark booths against the far wall.

Andrei Vasilevski was a short, intense man with dark eyes that bored right through you. He was the head of the Russian mafia in this part of the city -- hell, maybe the whole city as far as Val knew. He came by the Alley Cat at least once a week: Val figured he was Tommy's source for dust. Sure enough, Tommy descended from his office almost immediately, making a beeline for the Russians' table. He caught Val's eye and circled his index finger in the air, which meant he wanted a round brought to the table on the house. There was no need to ask what kind of round to bring. The Russians only drank one thing. Vodka. Always vodka.

Val poured the shots on a tray and carried them over to the table. Her heart was in her throat. Did these guys kill Ruby? An image of the dancer's mutilated body flashed through Val's mind. Had one of them done that? Was one of them her monster?

She plastered on a professional smile as she delivered the shots.

The men raised their glasses and toasted, then downed the shots in one smooth motion, as Val had known they would. She scooped up the empties and delivered the second round, which she already had waiting on the tray.

The men ignored her. Not a single "thank you" in the bunch. Assholes.

Back behind the bar, she kept one eye on their table. How could she find out if they'd killed Ruby? She chewed over different angles of attack, but none of them seemed promising. For the first time, she wished she was a dancer. Then she could get one of the Russians alone and get him talking. The girls were good at that.

Val eyed the girls on the floor. Would any of them be discreet enough to do the job? She considered Jewel, Candy, Tiger, and Domino in turn. No, she couldn't ask any of them to get involved. It was too dangerous. If the Russians killed Ruby, what was to stop them from killing again?

She was the only one who could defend herself if it came to that. She had to do this alone.

Her chance came when Vasilevski left the table to go to the little boy's room. Val waited in the hallway outside with a pair of drinks on a tray, and when Vasilevski emerged, she ran right into him, spilling the drinks everywhere.

"Oh! Mr. Vasilevski, I'm so sorry. Step over here, I'll get a towel and get you cleaned up." She gestured toward the kitchen.

Vasilevski glowered at her, eyeing the liquid on his lapel. This was the risky part. He could accept that it was an accident and allow her to wipe off his suit. Or he could fly into a rage, slap her around, and get her fired. She could see violence building in the gangster's dark eyes. The moment balanced on a knife's edge.

She was saved when Lisa stepped out of the kitchen door.

"Oh shit," the girl said, taking in the scene at a glance. She grabbed a clean towel from the shelf above the dishwasher and held it out in one smooth motion. "Here."

"Thanks, Lisa. I've got this." Val glanced meaningfully at the door. Lisa took the hint and retreated into the kitchen.

Val wiped down the front of Vasilevski's jacket with the towel. She'd tried not to spill too much on it -- she wasn't suicidal after all -- and she was relieved to see the damage wasn't too bad. As she wiped up the liquid, a pendant on a gold chain fell free of his collar. The pendant was long and thin, like a tiny tower. It looked familiar, but she was too focused on Vasilevski to remember where she'd seen it before.

"I'm really sorry, Mr. Vasilevski. I've been frazzled ever since Ruby died." She watched him carefully as she said this. His hard expression didn't change. "Or maybe you haven't heard about Ruby?"

Wary interest flashed behind his eyes. And something else. As he inclined his head to one side, his fingers plucked at his pendant, tucking it back inside his shirt. She wasn't sure what that meant, but at least it showed that he was listening. She pressed on, speaking quickly.

"Ruby was killed in the alley behind the bar last night. It was really brutal. I saw her body with my own eyes..." She felt tears rising and didn't bother to hold them back. "You liked her, didn't you? I know she hung out at your table a lot."

"She owed me money."

Val's heart skipped. The gangster had just confirmed his motive.

"Not a lot, I hope?"

He did the head-tilt thing again. "Enough."

Val reached deep and pulled up a smile.

"Well, I'm sorry to hear that. I guess everyone loses with her dead."

The Russian stared at her for a long moment, weighing her with his eyes. Trying to figure out how much she knew? Deciding if she was a threat?

"*Da*," he finally said. "Everyone loses." Vasilevski shouldered past her and made his way back out into the club.

Val sagged against the wall as the Russian left the hallway. Her legs shook with adrenaline. That had been a risky play. And for what? Vasilevski had confirmed his motive but given nothing away. If he'd had Ruby killed, his poker face was seamless. Val was no closer to the truth than she'd been before.

9

After the incident in the park, Aunt Marya handed Valora over to state custody. She spent a decade bouncing between group homes and foster homes, never living anywhere more than a year. She discovered social rules were twisty, slippery things, different everywhere she went. After many failed attempts at making friends, she stopped trying. She became withdrawn and guarded. Prickly.

Valora was terrified of the power within her and she fought to suppress it, often with disastrous results. It would build up inside her, swelling until she couldn't control it any longer, then explode out of her the way it had that afternoon in Greenway Park. Two of her foster home experiences ended with suspicious explosions in the house, and Valora was labeled as violent and destructive.

Mister E was her one constant companion, though no one was able to see him but her. People thought she was talking to herself when he was around, which didn't help her reputation. They put her on various medications and antidepressants, which made the world flat and distant, pressed beneath a sheet of glass. The meds helped tamp down her anger, but they kept every other emotion buried as well. Her world became a dull, grey place.

Meanwhile, the outside world was moving in two directions.

On the one hand, the future had indisputably arrived. Exponential scientific and technological advances, like ubiquitous 3-D printing and home CRISPR kits, meant that flying cars, gene-modding, and DIY cyborgs had become as common as blue jeans once were. Cities like New York, Chicago, Atlanta and San Francisco looked like the Los Angeles of 2019 envisioned in the *Blade Runner* films. Humanity was changing by leaps and bounds, becoming almost unrecognizable.

At the same time, the planet was collapsing. Natural disasters piled up year after year. Small towns were destroyed by hurricanes, tornadoes, floods and fires. People spent months rebuilding, only to be flattened again. Entire counties were abandoned, wide stretches of the country becoming uninhabited wasteland. Emergency services were strained past the breaking point. Homelessness and poverty became rampant, desperate people turning to crime and savagery. Affluent neighborhoods became walled compounds. It strained the federal government past the breaking point, and states were left to fend for themselves. Eventually, many of them decided that was the way they preferred it. The United States collapsed into a loose federation of independent states, then crumbled further into collectives, fiefdoms, and walled corporate compounds. Anarchy ruled the spaces in between.

At sixteen, Valora had been committed to the Woodlawn Teen Facility in upstate New York, unaffectionately called the WTF by the residents. New York still had a functioning state government, but the system had given up on finding her foster homes and was merely marking time until she became an adult and they could release her into the world. The ward was boring and white and run down and full of juvenile delinquents who were violent or self-destructive or stole or did drugs or had a serious problem with authority. Often all of the above.

One cool October afternoon, Valora was slouching in a sagging armchair in the corner of the lounge, glaring dully at the room, when a new girl entered the ward. She had a flat nose and a wild mane of thick, curly red hair. She was the tallest girl Valora had ever seen, over six feet, and she didn't try to hide it with a self-conscious slouch the way a lot of tall girls did. No, this girl stood up straight and glared a challenge at the world. When the girl's eyes found Valora, something within her stirred. The hairs on the back of her neck prickled. Then the girl was gone, as Bill the orderly escorted her down the hall to her new room.

But the feeling of her remained, swirling deep inside Valora.

At lunchtime, Bill bumped Valora's tray with his elbow as she passed, spilling her milk all over and forcing her to go through the line again. Bill did a lot of things like that; he was one of those petty tyrants, tormenting the inmates in a hundred subtle ways, reveling in his control over the ward.

When Val finally got her new tray, she took it to an empty table at the far end of the cafeteria. She was listlessly stirring her mashed potatoes when someone cleared their throat.

"Is anyone sitting here?" The new girl had a New York accent.

Valora shrugged, and the girl sat down on the bench across from her. Her silver-ringed fingers were long and delicate, her nails painted with chipped black polish. Tattoos adorned her knuckles.

The girl gave Bill the side-eye, then poked at the microwaved mystery meat. "This place is something else."

"WTF," Valora mumbled.

The girl laughed, then looked at her hard when Valora didn't respond.

"What's wrong with you?"

Valora could feel the girl's scrutiny burning into her skin. She shrugged again and took a bite of mashed potatoes. They were made from instant flakes and felt grainy and artificial in her mouth.

"What kind of meds they got you on?"

She tried to dredge up words. It felt like she was pulling them from a deep well, hauling the rope up hand over hand. It took a long time for them to get to the surface. Finally, she said, "I don't know."

"What do you mean, you don't know? You put them in your mouth, don't you?"

"I take what they give me. They don't tell me what they are."

"I'm pretty sure that's illegal. They have to tell you what they're giving you."

Valora pushed her potatoes around on her plate.

"Maybe they did. I don't remember."

The girl made a disgusted sound.

"All right, that's step one. We've gotta get you off that shit. You're like a zombie. You're no good to anyone like this."

At last, Valora raised suspicious eyes to the girl's face.

"Why do you care?"

The girl smiled, a big cocky grin. She waggled her bushy eyebrows.

"I care because you're the only interesting person in this dump. I can feel it."

"What do you mean?" But Valora already knew the answer. She could feel it too.

The girl leaned over the table, her voice little more than a whisper. Her eyes were big and green and intense.

"Magic. You're a witch. Just like me."

Valora felt moisture drip onto her hand. It took her a minute to realize she was crying.

10

The long night was finally over. Val yawned as she locked the door of the Alley Cat and rolled her neck, groaning as she and Junior circled the building to the tiny employee parking lot, her muscles knotted with fatigue.

Junior waited for Val to pull out first so she did, circling the block on the Ural before doubling back after the bouncer turned his little car onto Geary. The night was cold and misty as she parked her bike and approached Ruby's bloodstain. She was exhausted, but this couldn't wait. She needed to get some answers.

She got out her chalk and drew a careful circle around the spot where Ruby had been killed. Then she drew a pentagram inside the circle and placed candles on all five points. Once the candles were glowing, she settled herself in the center.

"*Isn't that a bit cliche?*" Mister E asked. He stalked around the outside of the circle, tail twitching, his golden eyes shining like headlights.

"It might be cliche, but it works for me," she snapped. "If I'm going to do anything more complex than bash someone's face in, I need to create conditions that feel magical."

"Conditions that feel magical? Life is magical. The world is magical. Look at the stars and the moon. Breathe the air. There is magic in every breath. I don't see how you can create conditions more magical than that."

"Look, we can't all be centuries-old magical beings. Some of us have to work at this, OK? Now if you don't have anything constructive to add, please stop distracting me. I'm trying to concentrate."

Mister E huffed and stalked away into the shadows.

Val crossed her legs and focused her eyes on the flame of one of the candles. Fortunately, the murder had happened in the alley, so she was hidden from casual eyes. And it was five in the morning, so the odds of anyone walking in on her ritual were slim. Which was good, because if anyone found her sitting in the center of a pentagram on top of the bloodstain of a recent murder she would have a hard time convincing them her purpose was benign.

She let her breath become deep and strong, stoking her energy like a yogi as she dropped into a meditative trance. Her sleep-deprived mind was sluggish and cranky, but she kept at it and slowly found her connection to her power, building it consciously, incrementally, and without anger for a change. When she had her internal furnace burning good and hot, she focused her will through the candle flame and released the summoning.

People overlooked animals in the city, but that didn't mean they weren't there. Sitting on overhead wires, crouching behind dumpsters, squeezing through cracks in old brick. Animals were everywhere. And more importantly, they saw everything. Like people, they were territorial and tended to make their homes in certain blocks, certain neighborhoods. There was a very good chance that any nocturnal animals in the alley tonight had also been around the night Ruby was murdered.

Now, just seeing something doesn't make an animal a reliable witness. It all depends on the animal. Some animals have good memories, some don't. Some pay attention to the humans around them, while some view them only as dangerous things to be avoided.

When a large black rat showed up at the edge of her circle, Val breathed a sigh of relief. Rats were smart. They paid attention to the world around them and they remembered things. You couldn't find many better witnesses in the animal kingdom than rats.

The rat had indeed been in the alley the night Ruby was killed, but whatever killed the woman had terrified the rat, and it hadn't stuck around to watch the show. Val was only able to get quick sensory impressions: the musky scent of an apex predator, a humanoid shape with eyes flashing in the dark. The sound of a snarl and a scream, getting abruptly cut off as the rat fled.

Val thanked the rat and released it, surfacing from her trance. The fog around her glowed in the predawn light and the candles had burned low. Her body was stiff with cold. A huge yawn cracked her jaw as the magic bled away from her body, leaving her eyes drooping. Time to go, before a garbage collector found her passed out in the alley.

She pulled a small hand broom out of the lock box on the Ural and started sweeping away the chalk circle to keep someone from finding it and calling the police. The last thing she needed was to spend another morning in Detective Chen's interview room.

As she swept away the last of the chalk, the hairs on the back of her neck rose. Something was watching her. She turned slowly, heart pounding in her throat. A low growl tickled her eardrums. There. Red eyes watching her from the shadows of the alley.

Val reached for the knife she kept at her belt. Magic was well and good, but it was even better when you paired it with something sharp and stabby.

There was no warning. One second the eyes were twenty feet away, the next they were right on top of her, claws stretching toward her face. Sharp teeth gleaming and snapping. The stench of rotting meat on its breath.

Val pivoted, arms snapping up in a defensive stance, the knife jagged in her fist. Claws tore at her leather jacket and she lashed out, punching a wave of power across the alley. Bricks crumbled, red dust exploding into the air. Something hit the parked Ural with a crash, and the heavy bike rocked on its suspension.

Val ducked and rolled deeper into the alley, coming up on one knee, knife poised, magic ready. She waited for movement, for the glint of eye or tooth. But there was nothing. Just settling dust and the sound of the big motorcycle creaking as it came to rest. Her attacker was gone.

"It must have run out the mouth of the alley," she muttered. "But where did it come from?"

She grabbed a flashlight from the Ural's lock box. Most alleys cut a clear path between streets, but this one was partially blocked by a crumbling brick wall thirty yards down. At the base of the rubble, she found a sinkhole with a large crack at the bottom. It looked wide enough for a person to squeeze through -- and when she climbed down into the hole and shone her flashlight into it, she saw that, yes, there were footprints in the earth. Footprints with claw marks at the toes.

"So, this is where you came from. Now the question is, were you here by coincidence? Or did you have something to do with Ruby's murder?"

"*Oh, please,*" Mister E scoffed. His eyes shone down from atop a pile of crumbling bricks. "*You know there's no such thing as coincidence.*"

Val sighed. Her feet hurt and her back hurt. Her eyes were full of sandpaper. All she really wanted to do was go to sleep.

"Yeah, you're probably right. Suspect number three, come on down."

"*No rest for the wicked.*" Mister E said, as if reading her thoughts.

"You would know." She scrubbed her hands over her face, willing her tired mind to focus.

She thought about going after the thing, but when she glanced back toward the mouth of the alley she saw it was getting light out there, the street coming alive with morning commuters. No, better to let it go for now. Her best shot was to find out where it came from. Figure out what it was and why it was here.

She shone the flashlight back down into the crack. It descended sharply, but there was a clear path through the debris. Beyond that, the darkness swallowed the narrow beam of light after only a few feet. Anything could be lurking there. She might find Edward Hopkins or Vasilevski. Or there could be more of those creatures. Maybe even a whole nest of them.

"*Rats.*" Mister E leapt lightly onto her shoulder. "*I smell rats. And something else. Something bigger.*"

Val tightened her grip on her knife and pressed her lips into a grim line. Her golden eyes flashed, mirroring the eyes of Mister E.

"Only one way to find out."

11

As she descended, Val couldn't decide if the crack was manmade or if it had opened up in an earthquake. The walls were jagged and unfinished, which suggested earthquake. The path she walked on was smooth as stone, however, which indicated either intentional smoothing or a whole lot of foot traffic. Which meant the trail was either manmade or there were enough feet using it regularly to pack it down flat as a board. If that was the case, more of those creatures were around than she wanted to think about.

She still wasn't sure what the thing was. The brief glimpse she'd gotten of it in the dark alley hadn't been clear at all. And even if it had, she still might not have been sure. There were a lot of magical creatures out there, and she only had personal experience with a handful. And she was probably the most experienced monster hunter in the city.

That was the problem with magic having only recently returned to the world: nobody knew much of anything. They were all making it up as they went along. Not for the first time, she wondered why magic had been gone for so long, and why it had suddenly come back.

Because it had definitely come back, that much was certain. In the early days, some people had wondered if maybe magic had never existed before, and this was its first time blossoming in the mundane world. If all the old myths and stories were only that, and they were just now coming to life. Maybe they were true pioneers, the first generation of magicians anywhere, ever.

The monsters put an end to that line of thinking. One by one, all the old stories were proved true. Val had personally encountered werewolves, ghouls, vampires and other nasties, and she'd heard reports of fairies, demons, and even old gods popping up in countries around the world. No, it was clear that the myths and legends she'd grown up with had at least a kernel of truth in them. And now magic was back, blossoming inside people like Val, turning them into magicians, or witches, or wizards, or sorcerers, or whatever you wanted to call them, and bringing all the trickster gods and specters along with it. And no one had the faintest idea why.

The trickster god theory was Val's personal favorite. Loki, or Anansi, or Coyote, or Pan, or one of the other trickster gods had decided to take magic away for centuries, and then suddenly bring it all back as a grand joke. Right now they were sitting back and laughing at the chaos it was causing, busting a gut at the flailing of the foolish mortals who were having all their earnest faith in technology upended. It was as good a theory as any, though Val doubted it was true. It was too simple, and nothing about magic returning to the world felt simple. Still, it was possible. Occam's razor and all that.

Hell, maybe the trickster god in question was Mister E. She frowned at his back as she followed him down into the darkness. Any being that presented itself as a Cheshire Cat was definitely suspicious.

"Do you know what that thing was back there?" she called out to the cat's back. If you're going to have a magical being around, you might as well make use of the resource.

Mister E's slink didn't pause. "*It all happened too quickly for me to be certain, but I think it was a shifter. Possibly a werewolf.*"

"A werewolf. Fucking fantastic." Val tightened her grip on the knife. She'd run into a werewolf once before and did not have fond memories of the experience.

She wished she had more illumination than her tiny flashlight. The dark down here was thick as syrup, sucking up light without a ripple. And it was too quiet. Living in a city, she was used to a constant background hum of noise: traffic and people and animals and the droning of generators. But down here, there was nothing. The crunch of her feet on the path and the rasp of her breath sounded impossibly loud in her ears. It smelled weird too. Musty and stale. Like a crypt that had been sealed for centuries.

"I wonder if I should have a canary with me," she muttered.

She'd read there were pockets of poison air in places like this. Gases trapped underground for millennia, released by unlucky miners. In the old days, the miners had carried canaries with them to detect deadly air pockets. If the canary keeled over dead, the miners knew to clear the area in a hurry. Not the most animal-friendly method, but effective.

"Maybe you are the canary," Mister E purred, *"and the rest of the city is waiting to see if you drop dead."*

Val scowled. That felt more likely.

"Why do you keep putting yourself in these situations, Val?" the cat wondered. *"Have you got a death wish?"*

"Believe me, I'd rather be home in the bathtub. My life would be a lot simpler if people would stop killing my friends."

"Simpler, but a lot less exciting." The cat grinned, his crescent-moon smile gleaming.

"Excitement is overrated."

She knew she should stop talking. If monsters were lurking in the dark, she was helping them out by making noise. But she couldn't help it. The darkness and silence were too much. Too big. The further she descended, the smaller she felt. If she didn't make noise, she'd disappear completely, never be heard from again.

Maybe she did have a bit of a death wish, if she was being completely honest. She'd never be able to atone for all the things she'd done. The people she'd hurt. Killed. Even her own mother.

Hunting monsters was the only thing that felt big enough, important enough, that it might balance the scales in some small measure. Not balance them completely, because that was impossible. But if she didn't do something, guilt would eat her alive. She had to keep moving, keep fighting, keep putting herself in danger. Even if that was borderline suicidal at times.

Also, this time it was personal. Ruby had been her friend. And the monsters had killed her behind the Alley Cat. On Val's turf. There was no way she could ignore that.

So she had to be down here. Searching for a monster's lair in this musty crevice in the earth. Armed with only a knife and a flashlight.

Yeah, she was definitely the canary.

A breath of fresh air swirled against her face. A breeze? And was that light up ahead?

The crevice opened into a vast tunnel before her as she rounded the next bend. Work lights were strung along one wall, the bulbs surprisingly bright. An enormous digging machine sat inactive in the center of the shaft, a quiescent leviathan. A smaller backhoe sat in the shadow of a dump truck beside it. The words "Royal Construction" were painted in purple and gold letters on their sides.

"The old MUNI tunnel," Val whispered. "Of course."

The earthquakes had destabilized many of the old transportation system tunnels, and the city was engaged in a battle to shore them up before they swallowed more of the city the way they'd taken Market Street.

Oddly, she didn't see the steel beams or support structures she would have expected from an operation to shore up the tunnels. Instead, there were a lot of holes in the walls and small tunnels. As if Royal Construction wasn't shoring up the tunnel at all but excavating a new one. But if that were true, why dig so many small tunnels instead of one large one?

"Maybe they're looking for gold," Mister E mused.

"Good luck with that," Val scoffed. "This peninsula was mined out a long time ago."

"A shame. Gold is the gift of the gods. There's not nearly enough gold in this city for my tastes."

Val rolled her eyes. ""I've never understood the fascination with gold. It's too soft to be good for anything. It's the most useless metal there is."

"That just shows the limits of your feeble human imagination. The value of

gold isn't in the physical realm. Gold is for higher purposes."

"Whatever, King Tut."

She hesitated, unsure where to go from here. The tunnel was huge, and the trail of footprints were swallowed up by the churned tracks of the digging machine. She bent low, trying to pick out the claw-toed marks she'd seen at the top of the crevice.

Something caught her eye, and she picked up a tuft of black fur. It felt coarse and wiry between her fingers. She looked for more and found another tuft several paces down the tunnel.

Moving slowly and carefully, she followed the trail of fur back toward the established underground tunnels. Interesting. She had expected the creature to come from some natural cave. But instead it seemed to live closer to the finished part of the tunnel system.

It took a while -- she kept losing the trail and having to double back to find it again -- but she eventually traced the creature to a narrow access tunnel. The work lights were dark here, but the beam of her flashlight found claw prints in the dirt outside a green metal door. The word "electrical" was stenciled on the surface in white. The door was rusty and bent, sagging on its hinges. It had clearly been forced open.

Val squeezed the handle of her knife so hard her fingers ached. This was it, she could feel it. Answers lay behind the door. Would there be another monster? A whole pack of them?

Only one way to find out.

Keeping the flashlight trained on the opening, she reached out with the toe of her boot, every muscle tense, pulse hammering in her throat, ready for anything. Hinges squealed as she kicked the door open.

Nothing jumped out at her. Nothing screamed and tried to chew her face off. Inside, the room was darkness and dust and silence.

The thin beam of the flashlight illuminated a rusty old generator draped with cobwebs. A thick layer of dust covered the floor and a purple and gold uniform hung on a hook on the wall. It was a Royal Construction shirt, torn open along the seam down one side. There was a name tag sewn over the breast pocket: Josh.

Val fingered the patch thoughtfully. Was Josh just a worker who stored his uniform in here? Or was he the monster? Either way, Royal Construction might know something about it.

She snapped a few pictures and did a quick scan of the room. Nothing but rags and dirt and a pile of gnawed bones in one corner. She was relieved to discover they were chicken bones, not human.

She was just about to leave when she noticed the dust on the floor around the generator was disturbed. There were scrape marks in it, like the generator had been moved. She knelt and checked the base of the machine. Sure enough, the bolts were missing from three of its four corners. The generator could be pivoted.

She pushed at it tentatively. It didn't budge.

"Oof. That thing's heavy."

"*You should figure out how to move it.*" Mister E slipped out from behind the generator with dust on his whiskers. "*There's a hidden passage back there.*"

Val eyed the generator doubtfully.

"Any suggestions?"

"*Yes. Push hard.*"

"Thanks, you're a big help."

She tried scooting or lifting it by hooking her fingers under the base, but it was too heavy. Her back almost gave out in the attempt.

She finally sat on the floor and put her back against the side of the generator. Wedging her legs against the wall, she was able to push with the larger muscles of her calves and thighs. The generator groaned, and Val groaned along with it. But it moved. Inch by inch, metal screeching over the floor, the generator slowly pivoted away from the wall.

Finally, a waist-high passage lay exposed. Panting and covered in sweat, Val shone her light into the darkness. A low, clay-walled tunnel led off through the earth. It was too low to stand in. If she wanted to go that way, she'd have to crawl.

Val groaned. "This idea is getting worse by the minute."

Mister E strolled into the tunnel, his tail straight up in the air. The tip of it just brushed the tunnel's ceiling.

"*Seems pretty straightforward.*" He turned and grinned his crescent grin at her. "*Just follow me.*"

Val sighed and got onto her hands and knees.

"Fine, but if you fart in my face I'm making a rug out of your hide."

"I'd like to see you try." Mister E laughed as he strolled away into the darkness.

12

The girl's name was Amber, and the first thing she showed Valora was how to fake taking her meds. She hid them beneath her tongue, then spat them out after the orderlies moved on. As the drugs passed out of her system, Valora felt like she was waking up from a long nap. Surfacing beneath the waves.

The two of them took to whispering on a battered couch in the corner of the lounge. Mister E sat on the arm, puffing on his candy cigarette. Despite her claims of magic, Amber could not see or hear Mister E. Against the wall, the TV played old sitcom reruns.

"What do you mean, I'm a witch?" Valora asked this question first. Everything else could wait.

"Come on, you know what I mean." Amber was sitting cross-legged with a cushion on her lap, worrying a loose thread with her fingers.

"Do I?" Valora challenged.

Amber rolled her eyes. She jabbed a finger at her sternum.

"I can feel it in here, same as you. Don't lie. I know you can."

Valora didn't bother to deny it. Amber was the first person she'd ever met who seemed to know what was going on inside her. She wanted answers.

"And that makes me a witch?"

"Witch, wizard, Sorceror Supreme, whatever you want to call it. It all amounts to the same thing."

"Magic?"

"Magic," Amber agreed, her green eyes glowing.

"How do you know? Do you have a teacher? Are there others like us out there?"

"Slow down. One question at a time," Amber laughed. "Yes, there are others out there. I was part of a coven back in Brooklyn."

"A coven? So you had spell books and did rituals and stuff? Like in the movies?"

Amber blew out a puff of air.

"I wish it was that easy. No, we don't have spell books. We don't draw circles and light candles and chant magic words. As far as we can tell, most of that stuff doesn't work."

"As far as you can tell? Don't you have a teacher? A cranky old mentor who makes you do chores and study scrolls by candlelight?"

"I wish," Amber said, cracking her knuckles one by one. "There are no wise elders. We've had to figure it out as we go along."

"No elders? So what, you're all teenagers?"

"No, there are some older women. But even they came into their magic within the last decade. We think that magic was missing from the world for a long time, and it's only recently started to come back."

"Maybe you just haven't met the right people."

Amber nodded.

"That's possible. But we've been looking pretty hard. We've been in contact with witches all over the world, and none of them have had their magic longer than two decades. The ones who claim to be lifelong practitioners usually turn out to be fakes. Wiccans and New Age spiritualists and goth girls wearing pentagram necklaces. People who wish they had magic, but really they're just normies putting on a show."

"Usually?"

"Well, we have discovered one or two who actually have power, but my guess is they're lying about how long they've had it. They may have wanted magic their whole lives, but it's only recently that they've actually gotten it."

"How do you know?"

Amber shrugged. "I don't, not really. But I can guess by how skilled they are, which is to say not very. I've never met anyone who knew any more than we do when we really questioned them, which means they're just as uneducated as we are."

Valora chewed on this.

"So, if magic was gone from the world, why is it coming back now?"

"That's the six-million-dollar question, isn't it? I wish I had an answer, but the truth is we don't know. Some people think it's intentional, like there's some secret society out there working to bring magic back. Some think it's a natural phenomenon, like climate change or the thawing of the polar ice caps or the switching of the Earth's magnetic poles."

"Climate change is not a natural phenomenon."

"Not currently, no. But if you look at the history of the planet, there have been plenty of ice ages and periods of tropical Earth. Just because human actions are driving the change this time doesn't mean it's not a natural phenomenon."

"Maybe that secret society you mentioned is behind climate change," Valora said, cocking her head to the side.

Amber turned her palms up.

"It's possible. Maybe magic was locked away in the permafrost and it's now being released. Maybe the old gods have woken up from a really long nap. Or maybe it's aliens."

A startled laugh burst from Valora. "Aliens?"

"Is the idea of aliens any crazier than old gods or secret societies or climate change? Believe me, we've talked about every wacko idea you can think of. This is magic we're talking about. Real honest-to-god magic. I don't think we can dismiss any theory on where it comes from, no matter how insane it sounds."

"*Old gods are nothing to scoff at,*" said Mister E. His tail twitched in agitation. "*They have no sense of humor.*"

Valora scrubbed her hands over her face.

"This is a lot to take in."

"I know," Amber agreed. "But don't worry, we'll have plenty of time to debate the origin of magic after we complete step one."

"Step one? What's step one?"

"Step one: We get you out of this dump."

Valora gaped at the tall girl.

Mister E's golden eyes shone. *"Now we're talking. Finally, somebody with ambition."*

"Did you really get yourself thrown in here on purpose?" Valora asked.

"Is that so hard to believe?"

"Well, it's not the craziest thing you've told me, but I don't see why anyone would get themselves committed."

"To find you, of course." Amber grinned. "Almost everyone touched by magic has been labeled as crazy. Most have been locked up at some point. The odds are in your favor if you look for witches in institutions."

"So what did you do to get thrown in here?"

"You're asking the wrong questions."

Valora arched an eyebrow at her. "Oh yeah? What are the right questions?"

"The right question is: How do we get out of here?"

"Like that's going to happen."

"O ye of little faith."

"I'll believe it when I see it. Speaking of believing it, how do I know you're really a witch?"

Now it was Amber's turn to raise an eyebrow. "You don't believe me?"

"I haven't seen any proof."

"You don't need proof. You already know."

This was true, Valora did know. She didn't know how, but she could sense Amber's magic swirling inside her. The hairs on the back of her neck stood whenever Amber entered the room. But she was feeling stubborn, so she crossed her arms over her chest and lifted her chin.

"I don't know anything. Prove it. Do some magic."

"This should be good," said Mister E. He blew a big smoke ring and shot a smaller one through the center.

For a long moment Amber just stared at Valora, her green eyes smoldering. Finally, her mouth quirked up at the corner and she nodded.

"All right, you want to see something?" She glanced around to make sure no one was watching them. No one was, everyone's attention was on the TV.

Amber made some furtive movements with her fingers and Valora felt a surge of power. The TV emitted a shower of sparks and the screen went dark. The room erupted in pandemonium, patients jumping and yelling for the orderlies. Bill barreled into the room, pushing patients down and cursing up a storm.

Valora gaped at Amber, who started giggling. Valora's lips quirked and within seconds both were rolling on the couch, cackling like Macbeth's crones. Bill shouted at them to be quiet, but for once Valora didn't quail in front of him.

For the first time in her life, Valora knew she wasn't alone.

13

Crawling through tunnels sucked. Crawling through tunnels made of damp clay that stuck to your hands and knees was awful. Crawling through damp clay tunnels while staring straight into a cat's asshole? Infinitely worse.

Mister E sauntered ahead of Val as if he did things like this every day. His golden eyes laughed at her as he glanced back into the light of her flashlight.

"You humans are very slow on all fours. I think your ancestors choosing to walk upright was a very poor decision."

Val glowered at him but could say nothing in response. She was holding her flashlight between her teeth.

After an interminable stretch of crawling, the tunnel roof finally rose high enough for Val to stand. She groaned as she got to her feet.

"Next time, I'm going first. Staring at your pucker for half an hour is not my idea of a good time."

"I'll have you know I have a very nice ass, thank you very much. All the other cats say so," Mister E huffed.

"Do you really talk to other cats?"

"Of course. Why wouldn't I?"

"Well, I mean, you're not really a cat. And you're invisible to other humans. So I just assumed..."

"*We both know what happens when you assume. How does the expression go? You make an ass out of u and me? Not the cleverest saying, but the point is spot on.*"

Val grimaced as she bent, stretching her aching back.

"So other cats can see you?"

"*When I wish them to.*"

"When you wish them to? Does that mean you could show yourself to other people?"

Mister E smiled and yawned, revealing his sharp fangs. He started cleaning himself.

Val rolled her eyes. "Fine, be enigmatic. See if I care."

She shone her flashlight down the tunnel. Crumbling clay walls rose on either side of them. Down the center of the floor was a trail of unmistakable clawed tracks.

"Do you think we're wasting our time down here?"

Mister E turned questioning eyes on her. Val continued.

"These tracks clearly lead back the way we came. We're tracking that thing back to its lair, but is that really going to do us any good? I mean, the monster is out in the city right now. How is discovering where it lives going to help us?"

"*I don't know. But I do know that knowledge is power. This particular piece of knowledge may come in handy if you want to exact revenge.*" Mister E stretched languorously, digging his claws into the earth.

Val's sigh turned into a huge yawn. "I suppose you're right. I just don't know how much more exploring I can take right now. It's been a long night."

"*I think we should at least see where this tunnel takes us, don't you?*"

"You do know what they say about curiosity and cats, right?"

Mister E smiled his crescent smile. "*Then it's a good thing I'm not really a cat, isn't it?*"

He sauntered away, leaving Val no choice but to follow.

"Are you ever going to tell me what you really are?"

"*No. I've got a bet with some friends over how long it will take you to figure it out on your own.*"

"Wait, you have friends?"

"*I have many things. Perhaps someday you will discover some of them.*"

"You could just tell me, you know," Val huffed.

Mister E's smile grew until it seemed wider than his face. "*Now, where would be the fun in that?*"

The tunnel had been growing gradually lighter as they talked. Val gaped as they rounded a final bend.

"I'll be damned."

The earth fell away in front of them while the sky opened above. They were standing on the edge of a deep ravine, or a canyon. Far below Val saw crumbled asphalt and crushed cars.

"We're in the Market Street Chasm," she breathed.

Mister E twined his body between her feet. "*Your powers of observation are truly astounding. You will have this mystery solved in no time.*"

Val ignored his sarcasm and took stock of the situation. They stood about a hundred meters down inside the chasm. Above, the jagged edge of asphalt and half-crumbled buildings left behind by the great quake framed drifting fog in the early morning light. Below, a narrow path wound down the side of the chasm. It disappeared into jumbled debris at the bottom. Val followed it until her eyes found a matching path winding up the chasm wall opposite them.

"All the way down just to climb all the way back up? Why don't they cross the bridge?"

"*If you were a giant, hairy monster, would you cross the bridge with all the normal people?*"

"Good point. But do we really want to keep going? It seems like an awfully long way to go for an uncertain reward."

"*That sounds like a perfect summation of life, to me: a long way to go for an uncertain reward,*" Mister E smirked. "*We've already come this far. We might as well see where this particular trail leads.*"

Val sighed dramatically.

"Fine. But if this turns out to be a waste of time, I'm making you carry me home."

She turned and started picking her way down the wall.

An hour later she emerged, sweating and filthy, on the far side of the chasm.

Val groaned and sank onto her haunches. "Remind me never to take your advice again."

Mister E sat and began cleaning himself. "*I never said it would be easy.*"

"Then I guess you weren't wrong. That climb was brutal. My ass muscles are on fire."

"*That should help you get more tips at work.*"

"Har-har."

Val peered around sourly. They were surrounded by half-collapsed buildings and cracked streets. Rusty shopping carts and abandoned vehicles littered the curbs and sidewalks. This section of the city had been hit hard by the quake, and most of it had been left that way.

"Great, now we're in the abandoned zone. Nobody sane lives around here."

A voice interrupted them, "Which makes your presence here all the more puzzling."

Val whirled to find a trio of women approaching. They had hard faces and held weapons in their hands. Their stride was purposeful, their steps sure. They fanned out in a semi-circle facing her. The leader spoke again.

"What are you doing here? Why did you cross the chasm?"

"Um, to get to the other side?" Val said.

The woman's eyes narrowed. She was a dark-skinned woman with big eyes and a flat nose. A thick metal collar encircled her neck. She spoke with an accent Val couldn't quite place. French? Caribbean?

"Is that supposed to be funny?"

"If you can't laugh at life, what can you do?"

Val subtly shifted her stance as the women encircled her. She kept her hand close to her knife.

"Why are you here?" the leader asked.

"Well, you see, once there was a man and a woman. And they loved each other very much..."

"Enough," barked the woman to Val's left. She was a big woman, with arms as thick as a bear and shaggy brown hair. She stepped forward and reached for Val. "You will answer our questions!"

Val batted the woman's hand aside with her forearm -- which felt like blocking a telephone pole -- and spun away from her grasp. The woman's eyes widened, then her face darkened with rage.

"*Oh boy, this should be fun,*" said Mister E. He hopped onto a low section of broken wall and sat down like a spectator at a sporting event.

"You know, you could help--" Val started to say. But then the bear-woman charged her and there was no more time for words.

The woman was big and strong, but her attack was clumsy and untrained. Clearly she was used to simply overpowering her opponents and thought she could do the same here.

Val disabused her of that notion. She grasped the woman's arm and stepped aside, using a judo throw to leverage her attacker's own momentum and send her sprawling in the street.

She had less than a second to congratulate herself before the other two advanced upon her.

These women had learned from their companion's experience and did not rush in. They spread out, flanking Val so they could come at her from both sides. They also did not come empty handed. The leader bore a long, smooth quarterstaff, while the third held an ugly-looking baseball bat that was splintered and jagged at the end.

Val drew her knife and backed away. The blade wouldn't do her any good against those weapons. She was outnumbered and outgunned.

She didn't want to bring her magic into the fight if she could help it. Her power ran on pure emotion, and once she let it out of its box, it tended to spiral out of control. Things could get messy in a hurry.

"Maybe you could try using your words to solve your problems," she suggested. "Like a big girl."

In response, the woman with the bat swung at her head. Val ducked and the woman stepped forward and swung again, clipping Val on the shoulder with a backhand swing. The splintered wood tore at her leather jacket.

Val's face darkened as she inspected the damage.

"All right, that does it."

Her magic surged as she lunged forward, inside the woman's reach. She slashed her knife across the guard's forearm, causing the woman to drop the bat. Before the wood even hit the ground, Val was driving her fist into the woman's stomach. The air whooshed out of her. As she doubled over, Val stepped forward and brought her knee up into the woman's face. Her nose broke with a satisfying crack.

"Don't scratch the leather," Val advised. "It makes me angry. You wouldn't like me when I'm ang--" The rest of her sentence was lost as the quarterstaff hit her across the jaw, snapping her teeth together and sending her sprawling.

"I advise you to stay down," the leader said.

Val spat blood and smiled. Her power rose like a storm as she pushed herself to her feet. Wind began to swirl around her.

"Lady, you just made a big mistake."

When her emotions were up, Val was fast and strong. Her magic boosted her strength and reflexes, making her a match for just about anyone in a fair fight. Even though her opponent's quarterstaff gave her an advantage, Val expected to end this fight quickly.

She was wrong.

Val lunged forward, using her speed to repeat what she'd done to the guard with the bat and get inside the leader's reach. To her shock, the dark-skinned woman reacted just as quickly, snapping the quarterstaff across her ribs. Val grunted but kept coming, and the leader pivoted and pushed, using Val's momentum to shove her past.

Val's surprise made her hesitate, and the leader used the opening to jab the end of her staff into Val's stomach. Val grunted and stumbled, but recovered in time to dodge the follow up swipe as the woman swung the quarterstaff at her face again. Val thought her attacker's face looked longer than it had, and had the hair on her arms always been so thick and black? Then she launched herself at the woman, and the time for looking was over.

The fight became a blur. Val and the leader both moved inhumanly fast, stabbing and dodging, blocking and rolling. Their battle was beautiful and deadly. As Val's adrenaline rose, the wind howled around them, picking up debris and bits of broken wood. A jagged aluminum can whirled through the air like a blade, slicing a red line across the leader's cheek. The woman stepped back, staring as her fingers came away from her cheek wet with blood.

"What are you?" she asked.

"I've been asking myself that question for years," Val replied. "Let me know if you come up with an answer."

As she crouched to renew her assault, a new command rang out behind her, *"Stop fighting!"*

Val and the dark woman turned to face the newcomer.

14

The man stood at the edge of the chasm, the wind whipping his dark hair around his black-bearded face. Clearly, he'd just come up the same trail Val had climbed. He was thin, grotesquely so, with sunken cheeks and ribs that stuck out like railroad ties. Val knew this last part because his white shirt was unbuttoned, exposing his emaciated torso above filthy brown pants. His hair was coarse and black, curling down over his shoulders.

Something in his eyes seemed familiar to Val, but she couldn't put her finger on what it was, exactly. She decided he was probably one of the Alley Cat's customers. She saw a lot of scruffy men in her line of work.

Eyeing the newcomer warily, she stepped back, angling her body so she had space to react if either of them tried anything.

"Stay out of this, Alain," said the leader. Her face was covered in a sleek layer of black fur now as well, and her green eyes seemed wider. "This woman attacked us."

"I think you've got that backwards," Val snarled. "You started this fight. But I'm going to be the one who finishes it."

"I don't think this woman is our enemy, Nouhaila," Alain said. He had the same accent as the dark-skinned woman.

"You don't think? I'm so glad you are thinking, Alain. Her actions say otherwise." She nodded toward the two guards on the ground.

"They came at me, lady," Val repeated. "I just gave them what they had coming."

"You followed my trail across the chasm," Alain said. "Why are you seeking me?"

"Seeking you? I'm not seeking you, I'm looking for a ... oh." Val tensed as she realized why the man's eyes looked familiar. "You're the shifter from the alley. Did you kill my friend?" The last came out as a snarl. She stepped toward the man, bringing up her knife.

"No! I did not harm Ruby!" He held his hands up in a calming gesture.

"If you didn't harm her, what were you doing in that alley?"

"The same thing it seems you were. Trying to find her killer."

"Well, isn't that convenient. But I have it from a good source that her killer was a monster. How do you explain that?"

The man bobbed his head. "Yes. Her killer was a monster. But that monster was not me."

"And I'm just supposed to take your word for it?"

"No. Come with me. I will show you the truth."

Val clenched her jaw, considering her options. She was badly outnumbered. Her eyes went to the sleek black fur now covering the leader's face. The immense bear-woman. Now that she knew what to look for, it was easy to tell they were all shifters. She'd been lucky they only came at her one at a time. If they'd decided to attack her together, she'd have had no chance. And if the man had wanted her dead, he could have joined in the fight instead of stopping it.

She lowered her knife. "Fine. Enlighten me."

They led her into the tumbled-down neighborhood. This part of the city had been hit hard by the quake, and every building they passed showed signs of damage. Many were partially collapsed, and some were little more than heaps of rubble. Debris blocked the streets, and they wound around mounds of broken lumber and bricks on narrow trails.

"Kind of hard to get delivery vehicles in here," Val said. "You should get these streets cleared."

"We do not wish them cleared," the lead woman, Nouhaila, said. Her fur had retracted into her skin, and she now looked fully human again. "It is easier to protect ourselves if our enemies must come at us on foot."

"You have a lot of enemies?"

The woman snorted. "Everyone is our enemy. People fear and hate each other because of their race or where they are from. How do you think they react to us?"

"Good point. If I had fur and a tail, I wouldn't be too keen on hanging out with my neighbors either." Casually, she added, "How many of you are there, anyway?"

The woman gave her a withering glare.

"I am not so foolish as to answer that question."

They led her to a block that had been leveled and cleared. Tiny huts had been made using the debris of larger buildings, mostly bricks and wood, creating a little community within the wreckage. At least a dozen houses ringed the block, with a large open space in the center. Barefoot children chased each other around a garden plot full of tomatoes and squash. Solar panels sat on most of the roofs, and a pair of windmills turned overhead.

In the center of the square stood something that clearly did not belong. It was a large bronze sculpture of Lady Liberty. It stood taller than Val, and looked old and weathered, as if it had stood outside for a long time. It was attached to a makeshift wooden base, and jagged bits of metal suggested there had once been more to the sculpture than only Lady Liberty.

"Ruby found that," Alain supplied. "She was always finding beautiful things and bringing them home."

Val nodded, taking it all in, her eyes wide. "I had no idea this community existed."

"Most people don't," Alain said.

"We want to keep it that way," Nouhaila added. She glared at a Royal Construction bulldozer parked half a block away. A barricade of burned-out cars blocked the road leading into the camp. A pair of shifter sentries kept watch behind them.

"I can see why you would," Val answered. "Your own little slice of paradise. Is this what you wanted to show me?"

"No," said Alain. "Come this way."

He led her to a little hut on one side of the square. It was a cement dome, with colorful glass bottles embedded in the walls.

He gestured to the low doorway. "Go in. See for yourself."

Val hesitantly poked her head in the door. Inside, it was beautiful. The sun shone through the bottles in the walls, painting the interior with a multi-colored mosaic of light. It was a simple dwelling, with a table and chairs and a small kitchen. Doorways in the back opened into a pair of bedrooms. Wilted wildflowers sat in a jar on the table. A child's drawings hung on the wall, simple crayon portraits with blue skies and a smiling sun. Beside the drawings was a framed photograph.

Val's breath caught in her throat. The photograph showed a young woman and a little girl, beaming, arms around each other in a tight hug. The little girl had blond curls and eyes as big as the moon. The woman hugging her was Ruby.

Val flashed back to her first weeks in the city, when Ruby had shown her around. The woman in her memory was the Ruby in these pictures. This was not the green-sequined Ruby she saw at the Alley Cat. There were no haunted eyes. No nervous insecurity. The Ruby in the photograph looked happy.

"Ruby lived here?"

"*Apparently.*" Mister E flopped down in a sunbeam on top of the table. "*Your powers of observation are astounding.*"

Val ignored him and circled the small hut. It was warm and simple. Clean. Not at all what she would have expected based on the Ruby she saw at the Alley Cat.

"Momma?" The girl from the photograph burst into the room, little legs pumping in denim overalls with an embroidered sunflower beaming from the front pocket. She skidded to a halt when she saw Val, her blue eyes wide.

"Maddy!" A young woman pursued the girl into the room, her round cheeks flushed from the chase. She seized the child by the arm and grimaced up at Val and Alain. "Sorry. She saw you come in here and slipped away."

"It's no trouble," Alain said. "Val, this is Shanna."

"Nice to meet you," Shanna held out her hand.

She was a short, round girl, with sleek brown hair and a wide smile. Her hand was soft and warm, and as they shook her soft brown eyes ran up and down Val's body in frank assessment.

Heat rose in Val's cheeks. She cleared her throat. "Yeah, you too."

Alain squatted to the child's level. "Your momma hasn't come home yet, Maddy. I need you to stay with Shanna, OK? We have some adult stuff to discuss."

"OK." The girl was hiding behind Shanna's leg now, her big eyes shining up at Val like searchlights.

"Come on, let's go pick some tomatoes," Shanna told Maddy. "Grab your basket and let's give Alain and Val some privacy, shall we?" Maddy nodded and snatched a small wicker basket as she scooted out the door. "Sorry. Won't happen again. Let me know if you need help with anything, yeah?" Her eyes and smile flickered over Val once again before she turned and disappeared through the door.

Val swallowed and rubbed her sweating palms on her pants, trying to drag her mind back to business. "So, uh, Ruby lived here?"

"Yes, Ruby lived here." Alain joined her beside the small table. "She was one of us."

"One of you?" Comprehension dawned. "She was a shifter? How did I not know that?"

"Yes. And now you know why I did not kill her."

"But, if you didn't kill her, why were you in the alley? Why did you attack me?"

"I was in the alley for the same reason you were. I was seeking the identity of her murderer. As to why I attacked you..." Alain looked sheepish. "I'm afraid I panicked. I apologize. I did not wish to be seen."

Val considered him skeptically. She didn't think he was lying, but she could tell there was more to the story. Something he wasn't telling her.

"If you didn't kill Ruby, who did?"

"I do not know." Alain looked away.

"But you have an idea."

Alain hesitated. "No more than suspicions."

"Well, that's something. Let's hear your suspicions."

He grimaced and pulled out a chair, lowering himself onto the wooden frame. He pulled on his scraggly beard.

Finally, he sighed.

"Someone has been hunting our kind."

"Alain!" Nouhaila stepped into the hut, her face stern. "That is not this woman's business."

"Ruby was my friend," Val said, rounding on her. "I'm going to find her murderer. It might go faster if you share your knowledge with me."

"You are an outsider. We have shown you that we did not kill Ruby. That is enough. Our business is our own."

Val squared up to the woman.

"My friend is dead. If you know who the murderer is, you'd better tell me right now."

"Or what?" Nouhaila's fingers tightened on her staff. "We can continue this discussion outside, if you like."

Val snarled and clenched her fists. Before she could act, Alain's voice rang out again.

"Stop this! Both of you! You are like wild cats fighting over territory. Your posturing is not helpful."

Val and Nouhaila both glared at him. The sorrow in his dark eyes made Val feel ashamed. He was right. The important thing was finding Ruby's killer. Fighting amongst themselves was counterproductive.

She took a deep breath.

"Look. We both want the same thing here. Justice for Ruby. It makes sense for us to work together."

"No. You are an outsider. Our business is our own." Nouhaila folded her arms over her chest.

"Do not make hasty decisions," Alain said.

Alain and Nouhaila locked eyes for a long moment.

"Wait here. We must discuss this. I will return." Alain took Nouhaila by the arm and pushed her outside.

Val explored the small hut while she waited. It was so tidy and cheerful. So domestic. She fingered the dying wildflowers in their jar.

Memories of Ruby showing her around the city flashed through her head. Ruby leaning in close to make a snarky comment about a passing businessman who took himself a little too seriously. Ruby buying her mochi for the first time. Ruby doubled over with laughter after a pigeon shat on her shoulder. Val could imagine that Ruby living here.

But it had been a long time since she'd seen that version of Ruby. Like so many of the girls, Ruby was usually drunk when she was at work. Val had assumed she was like that all the time now. But standing in the multi-colored light streaming in through the bottles, Val realized she hadn't really known Ruby at all. The dancer had been friendly to her, but she'd mostly kept her personal life secret, and she'd worn a mask at the Alley Cat, just like all the girls.

Val wondered why Ruby had done it. Why cross the chasm to dance for strangers when she lived in such a perfect little community? Was it simply the money? Or was there a darker reason? Something worth killing for?

"You should get a little hut like this." Mister E stretched languidly. *"Your apartment doesn't get enough sun."*

"Sure, piece of cake. Looks like all I have to do is become a shifter. Which means what? I have to get bitten by a werewolf?"

"Superstitious nonsense," Alain said, ducking back in through the doorway. "Shifters are born, just like anyone else. It is not a disease you can catch."

"Well, that's disappointing. And here I had my heart set on becoming a furry."

"Oh, you can still become a furry." Mister E grinned. *"That's another thing entirely. I can introduce you to some people, if you like."*

Val rolled her eyes. "Why am I not surprised that you have connections in the furry community?"

"I'm sorry? Are you insulting me?" Alain said.

"No. Sorry. Just talking to myself." Val gave Mister E a final glare. The cat just smirked. "So, have you made a decision?"

"The community will not help you. Our business remains our own."

Val scowled. "You know that's not going to stop me, right? I'm going to find Ruby's killer with or without your help."

"I had a feeling you would say something like that, yes." Alain bared his teeth in a wolfish grin. "That is why I am going to help you."

"But you just said the community wasn't going to help me."

"And they are not. But we are a loose community, made up of strong individuals. Very few decisions are binding for all. In this case, while the community will not officially assist you, individuals are still free to do so. I am exercising my individual freedom."

"I bet Nouhaila isn't happy about that."

Alain gave her a sly look. "She is not. But I do not care."

Val chuckled.

"Good enough for me. You're hired." A gigantic yawn cracked her jaw. "But first I need to get some sleep. Meet me this afternoon? Sixteenth and Mission?"

Alain nodded. Val smiled.

"Excellent. I'll see you there."

15

────────

I t was well after midnight when Amber came for her. Valora was lying on her bed, fully dressed and gnawing at her fingernails, when the keypad beside her door beeped, sparked, and went dead. The door swung open and Amber gestured Valora out into the hall. The facility around them was dark and silent, the only illumination the green of the emergency exits and the red status lights on the keypad locks.

"That's a neat trick," Valora whispered.

Amber grinned, teeth flashing in the darkness.

"It's a good thing all the locks are electronic. Makes my job a lot easier. Ready to get out of here?"

"Hell yeah."

They padded swiftly down the hall, past the locked doors of the other inmates. Valora hesitated.

"Shouldn't we let the others out too?"

"Why? They're not witches."

"Sure, but they're just kids. They don't belong in this shithole any more than we do."

Amber sighed.

"Look, your heart is in the right place, but think about it. First, they didn't stop taking their meds days ago like you did. So most of them are going to be zombies, and zombies don't move very fast. Second, what are we going to do with them once they're outside? I don't have a safe space for fifty teenagers. Are we just going to let them wander out onto the street and become homeless? They're better off in here. At least in here they have food and shelter."

Valora scowled and crossed her arms over her chest.

"You might be right, but they should still get a choice. Open their doors and let them decide if they want to stay or go."

Amber got up in her face and hissed, "We don't have time for this."

Valora glared right back at her. She could feel her magic rising with her temper. A breeze tickled the back of her neck.

"Just fry their locks like you did mine. Let them out. What they do after that is up to them."

The two girls locked eyes. Fists clenched. Power rose around them like mist. All the hairs on Valora's body were standing on end.

"Fine." Amber flung her arms out wide, releasing her gathered magic in a wave.

All along the hall, keypads erupted into fountains of sparks. The emergency lights flared and went out, plunging the entire floor into darkness.

Valora ducked and covered her head with her arms. "Holy shit."

"Are you happy now?" Amber snapped. "Come on, we've got to move fast. That's going to attract attention."

They ran for the stairwell at the end of the hall. Valora could hear the overnight orderly shouting at the station. Her heart hammered in her ears as they pounded down the stairs and slammed into the emergency exit door.

The door did not open.

"What the fuck?" Amber frantically pushed at the bar. "I fried the keypad. This should be open."

"It's double-locked," Valora whispered. "One electronic lock and one old-fashioned dead bolt. We're screwed."

Amber's eyes went wide. "Oh shit. I didn't even think about that. Why would they do that?"

"To keep the witches from getting out," Valora said. She didn't smile at her own joke, though. It wasn't funny. Her panic was rising, stoking her magic like a furnace. A dust devil swirled across the floor. "There's got to be another way out."

"No, this is it. This door opens onto the north side, near the forest. Any of the others will dump us onto the lawn. We'll be seen. And thanks to your bleeding heart the orderlies are awake now. We'll never make it."

On cue, the stairwell door crashed open above them, the sound reverberating. Footsteps pounded down the stairs.

Valora seized Amber by the front of her shirt. "Are you telling me you don't have a backup plan?"

"No, I don't have a backup plan. This was the plan. You screwed it up," Amber shoved her away.

"Hello there, girls." Bill appeared on the stairs above them, his chest heaving. He held a taser in his meaty hand. "I should have known you were behind all of this." He started to descend toward them.

"Fuck you, Bill," Valora growled. "You're nothing but a..."

Valora's teeth snapped together as the taser hit her. She convulsed, her muscles cramping as electricity shot through her. It felt like a swarm of bees under her skin.

It was over as quickly as it began. She looked up to find Amber standing over her, her hand on the taser wires. Bill yelped and dropped the gun as it sparked in his hand.

"Leave us alone," Amber said.

"You little bitch." Bill came down the last two steps and punched Amber right in the face, dropping her like a stone. "You don't tell me what to do."

Then he turned to Valora.

Mister E snarled and spat, his eyes glowing like the sun. "*Fuck this motherfucker,*" he hissed.

Valora let all her frustration gather. The years of institutions and foster homes. The hurt of being unloved and unwanted burning white-hot within her. With a cry, she released it.

The wind lifted Bill off his feet, slamming him into the locked door. The door exploded out of its frame with a boom, clattering across the ground like a kicked can. A wave of cool air washed in through the open doorway. Stars winked above the dark silhouettes of trees. Bill's body was a limp silhouette on the grass.

"*Yesssssss,*" Mister E hissed.

Amber gaped at her. "Holy shit."

"Yeah. Wow." Valora giggled, just as shocked as her friend.

"Remind me never to make you angry."

"You wouldn't like me when I'm angry," Valora confirmed.

Amber looked at the motionless form on the grass.

"Is he?"

"I don't know. And I don't care either."

"Right." Amber winced as she got to her feet. Her left eye was swollen and already darkening from Bill's fist. "Well, if the rest of the orderlies didn't know we were here, they definitely do now. We'd better get the hell out of here."

"You don't have to tell me twice."

Hearts pounding, the young witches raced into the night.

16

Ruby was screaming. It was dark in the alley, and Val could only see her green sequins, shimmering like a waterfall in the distance. Val ran as fast as she could, arms pumping, lungs burning, but no matter how fast she ran, she couldn't get closer. Then Ruby's scream became wet and horrible, and something burst from her chest, ribs and viscera exploding outward. Green sequins fell like rain.

Val started awake, heart pounding, sheets twisted and damp around her. She sat shaking for a long minute, the nightmare vision still filling her head. Slowly, she realized it was something else that had woken her up.

Her phone buzzed on the bedside table. She groaned and rolled away from it, snugging the blanket around her neck.

It buzzed again. She pulled a pillow over her head.

It continued to buzz, and finally she grabbed it and thumbed it on.

"What?" she snapped.

There was an awkward silence, then Jack's voice came over the line, "Well, good morning to you too."

"Jack? What the fuck do you want?"

"Well, that's a pretty big question. I'd like some coffee and maybe a milkshake... Or a coffee milkshake! Some oatmeal cookies on the side. And--"

"You're not nearly as funny as you think you are."

"Naturally. No one is as funny as I think I am. It's a physical impossibility. The universe would explode."

"Are you going to tell me why you woke me up, or am I going to reach through the phone and rip your tongue out?"

"Well, somebody's grumpy." Val could hear his pout. "I was just calling to invite you to brunch."

"Brunch? What time is it?" Despite the objections of her still sleepy brain, Val's stomach growled enthusiastically.

"It's 2:30. You should be up by now."

"I had a late night."

"Does that mean you're ready for brunch?"

Val fought a smile. Despite her annoyance, Jack had actually woken her up at a good time. She needed to meet Alain at four, but filling her belly first sounded like a fine idea.

"OK. But you're buying."

"Of course I am, it's my invitation after all. Lee's Diner in half an hour?"

"Yeah, OK. I'll see you there."

Val stumbled towards the bathroom, almost tripping over a pile of moving boxes in the hall. Julie's, presumably. She scowled at them and maneuvered her way into the shower, burying her head under the water, letting the steam and heat drive away the last vestiges of the nightmare. She really shouldn't be encouraging Jack. But she was hungry, dammit. And if her time as a homeless teenager had taught her anything, it was that you never, ever turned down a free lunch.

Clean, dry, and a bit more awake, she threw on a basic black outfit and fluffed up her hair in the mirror by the door. Another letter from New York sat on the table underneath the mirror. She sighed. Yet another thing she needed to deal with. She pushed it aside and grabbed her keys instead.

Thirty minutes later she strolled into Lee's Diner. Lee's was a San Francisco landmark, open twenty-four hours a day since 1951. It looked like it too, with all the classic fifties diner touches you'd expect:

neon lights, shining chrome, and red vinyl seats. One of the waitresses even glided around on roller skates.

Jack was waiting for her in a booth, with two mugs of coffee already steaming on the table before him. He grinned at her as she slid onto the seat across from him.

"Good morning, sunshine."

Val held up one finger in a wait-a-minute gesture. "Caffeine before conversation." She wrapped her hands around the mug and took a long sip. Her eyes widened. "A butterscotch latte! How did you know?"

Jack smirked. "Word gets around. And the right coffee is essential."

"One hundred percent," she agreed. "Caffeine and butterscotch make the world go around."

"I'm pretty sure that's gravity."

"Is it, though? I thought gravity made things stick to the ground."

"It's the sun's gravity, not the Earth's."

"Right. I knew that." She took another long sip, feeling her synapses crackle and pop as the caffeine and sugar flooded her system. "So why does the Earth rotate then? I don't see how the sun's gravity could do that."

Jack pursed his lips, which made him look like a pouty underwear model. "I don't know," he finally admitted. "You'd have to ask someone nerdier than me."

"Come on. I know there's a secret nerd hidden inside that pretty package. You lose your shit whenever someone mentions *Star Wars*."

Jack snorted. "That shows how little you know about me. I prefer *Star Trek*."

"Which only proves my point, nerd."

The waitress interrupted them with a pair of steaming plates, piled high with pancakes.

"You sly devil," Val said. "You ordered pancakes for me?"

Jack shrugged, but his blue eyes sparkled. "Bon appetite."

Val caught the waitress as she turned away. "Do you have any butterscotch syrup?"

The waitress looked revolted for a second but covered it with a professional smile. "Nope, sorry. We've just got the regular stuff."

Val sighed. "Oh well, can't win them all."

She considered Jack as she ate. She wasn't sure why she was resisting his advances. He was gorgeous and he bought her butter-scotch lattes. The girls at the Alley Cat all swooned over him. He was a catch by anyone's standards.

Still, there was something holding her back. Val had serious issues with intimacy, especially after what had happened in New York. She'd never dated much, and she had a lot of secrets. The whole idea of letting someone inside her defenses freaked her out.

It was more than that with Jack, though. Something she couldn't quite put her finger on. Maybe he was too perfect. Val preferred people who had been weathered by life. Cracks and imperfections made people interesting. Jack was too polished. He was like a movie star: Someone you fantasized about, not someone you actually dated. Also, he liked to hang out in the Alley Cat, which was a huge red flag. Men who spent a lot of time in strip clubs rarely made good boyfriends.

Thinking of the Alley Cat made her realize something else.

"How did you get my number?"

Jack smiled sheepishly and looked down into his coffee. "I asked Lisa."

"I wouldn't give it to you, so you asked my barback? That's very stalkerish of you, Jack."

"It's just a phone number. It's not like I followed you home. Besides, you came, didn't you?" He grinned up at her hopefully.

"I came because you woke me out of a dead sleep. I wasn't alert enough to wonder how you got my phone number. Now that I've got some caffeine in my system, I'm not sure I like it."

"Oh, come on. You got coffee and pancakes out of it; I'd call that a win. And why are you so tired anyway? Late night?" Jack waggled his eyebrows suggestively.

Val scowled at the change of subject but decided to allow it.

"I wish. No, I've got some heavy things going on right now."

"Such as?"

She eyed Jack warily, unsure how much she was willing to share with him. Then she remembered how good it had felt to confide in Malcolm. She'd seen a therapist at the WTF psychiatric facility as a teen, and the therapist had told her over and over that she needed to stop bottling everything up. Talking was good. Letting things out so they didn't poison you from the inside.

"Ruby's murder hit me pretty hard," she admitted.

"I suppose I should have seen that coming."

"Didn't it affect you? I mean, you're at the club all the time. Didn't you have a connection with her?"

Jack shifted in his seat.

"Not really. I mean the girls are ... the girls. It's their job to pretend to be interested in me. I know this might sound callous, but I'm just a mark to them. We have a transactional relationship. I appreciate their dancing skills and their bodies, but I view them as objects more than people. I don't try to get to know them beyond that."

Val's hands tightened into fists. How dare he think that way about people she cared about? Dehumanize them like that? Especially Ruby? Her power stirred in her guts.

"That's pretty fucked up, Jack. A woman is dead. She had a life outside the club, you know. She had a daughter. Her murderer probably looked at her the same way you do."

Jack's face cycled through several emotions at once, anger and exasperation among them.

"That's not fair, Val. I'm just being honest with you here..."

"You know where you can stick your honesty, Jack." She slid out of the booth and stomped away. She needed to get out of reach before she punched him in his stupid, pretty face.

"Val!" Jack called after her, but Val didn't slow down. She was already gone.

As she pulled the Ural out onto the street, a flash of silver caught her eye on the sidewalk. An ear comm, attached to a familiar face. Edward Hopkins.

"Hey, asshole," she yelled, slamming on the brakes.

Hopkins started at Val's voice, his eyes widening as he recognized her.

"Don't move," she shouted. She tried to back the Ural up into the parking spot she'd just vacated, but there was a scrap cart behind her piled high with rusting metal, pulled by a pair of donkeys, of all things. The driver gestured for her to get out of the way, cursing at her in some language she didn't recognize.

Hopkins started to run.

"Flaming toads," she growled, trying to keep one eye on Hopkins as she searched for another parking spot. There were none, so she finally just pulled the Ural half up onto the sidewalk and called it good.

By the time she got off the bike, Hopkins had disappeared around the corner.

"*Well done. Very subtle.*"

"Stuff it." She ran for the spot where she'd last seen the fleeing Black Knight.

But when she got to the corner, Edward Hopkins was nowhere to be found.

She sprinted down the street, hoping to catch a glimpse of him, but after two blocks she had to admit he'd given her the slip.

"Baboon babies!" She kicked a rusted-out metal drum someone had been using as a firepit, spilling its charred contents all over the gutter. It felt so good, she kicked it again.

"*Yesssss. Use your hatred.*"

"Oh, piss off."

Mister E just laughed.

Fuming, Val stomped back to collect the Ural.

17

V al was still steaming when she pulled up to Sixteenth and
Mission. Mister E echoed her agitation, stalking and spitting in
the sidecar, his fur all puffed out. They were throwing off so much
excess energy that the old Ural coughed and almost stalled twice on
the ride over.

She'd found Edward Hopkins. And she'd let him get away. Again.

Val felt as useless as a fluffy tail on a dolphin.

And on top of that, she was still pissed at Jack.

She didn't know why Jack had made her so angry. She knew how
things worked in the Alley Cat, and his assessment was right on the
nose. The girls and customers flirted and acted like they were interested in each other, but it was all an act. The girls were there for the
money. The customers were there to see naked girls. It was a business
transaction, nothing more.

If she knew all that, why was she so upset?

Maybe it was because she wasn't standing on either side of that
transaction. She was there to take care of both the girls and the
customers. She'd been a shoulder to cry on many times, comforting a
sobbing girl traumatized by a customer who saw her as nothing more
than a piece of meat. She supposed she'd subconsciously started

considering Jack a friend, and forgotten he was really a customer. To him Ruby was just one of the girls, her sexual attention no more than an economic transaction. And given how raw Ruby's death still was to Val, that was a cold truth she hadn't been prepared to face.

Alain was waiting for her inside the square on the corner of Sixteenth. A noisy market had sprung up around the boarded-up entrance to the old BART station. Vendors jostled for space with folding tables and temporary walls, selling everything from garden-grown fruits and vegetables to cheap cybernetic implants. The buzz of hawkers and hagglers created a wall of sound, and Val smiled as it engulfed her. The bustle reminded her of New York. The scent of the Indian spice merchants and taco trucks. The rapid-fire patter of the Egyptians selling incense. The sizzle of the woks in the Chinese food stalls.

She found Alain at a table in the shade, polishing off a monster burrito. He smiled when he saw her.

"You made it." He sounded mildly surprised.

Val slid onto the bench opposite him. "Did you think I wouldn't?"

He shrugged. "I figured it was a fifty-fifty chance."

"Do I look unreliable to you?" Val was indignant.

"No, it's not that. You just seem like the lone-wolf type. I thought you might have second thoughts."

"My word is good. When I say I'm going to do something, I do it."

"All right. Good to know," Alain said mildly.

Despite her indignation, Val had to admit he had her pegged. She was the lone-wolf type. Of course, being pegged only increased her irritation.

She examined the shifter. His dark eyes were gentle. Thoughtful. Not what she would have expected. By reputation shifters were wild and savage. Unpredictable. She wondered how much of that reputation was earned. She'd bet a good portion of it was simply stereotyping based on people's fear. Though perhaps much of that fear was deliberately nurtured by the shifters themselves. They seemed to value their privacy. If you wanted people to leave you alone, making them scared of you was a good way to go about it.

She didn't feel scared of Alain, though. He was too skinny, for one.

A strong wind would blow him away. And if there was one thing she was good at, it was creating strong winds.

His emaciated frame didn't look like the result of not eating, however. In addition to the burrito he was currently polishing off, his plate held the waxed wrapper of what looked like a second burrito.

"Tell me you did not eat two of those monstrosities," Val said.

Alain raised his eyebrows, all innocence.

"Is that so unusual?"

"I can't even eat one of those moose turds. I've never met anyone who could eat two."

"Moose turds?" Alain's forehead crinkled.

"Cause they're so big. Obviously. And you're dodging the question."

Now he smiled, exposing long, white predator's teeth. Despite the teeth, the smile didn't come across as threatening. In fact, it lit up his whole face, making him look improbably young.

"Sorry. Force of habit. My people don't interact with outsiders much. And we certainly don't answer their questions."

Val just stared at him, waiting. Alain laughed.

"Yes, I ate two whole moose turds. What can I say? I was hungry."

"You must have a metabolism like a jet engine."

"Indeed, I do. I burn a lot of fuel." Alain glanced around to see if anyone was listening, which was pretty absurd, considering the ambient noise levels in the market. He leaned close and lowered his voice. "Did we come here to discuss my dietary requirements? Or are we going to find my sister's killer?"

Val sucked in a breath.

"Your sister?"

"Yes. Ruby and I shared a mother. We weren't as close as I might have liked, but she was my sister, nonetheless." Pain shadowed his eyes. "For that reason, I would very much like to find the person responsible for her death."

"I'm sorry for your loss." Val held his gaze. "I cared for Ruby too. Revenge is a motivation we share."

"All right. So where do we start?"

"First, we need a list of suspects. I've got a couple so far. What have you got?"

"Royal Construction," he said immediately. "Ruby has been a thorn in their side for a while now."

"How so?"

"Did you notice the bulldozer parked outside our settlement? Royal Construction wants to clear out our community so they can build something there. We've been fighting them for two years. Ruby was one of our most vocal organizers."

Val blinked. That didn't fit her mental image of Ruby at all. Clearly the woman had kept her personal life far from the Alley Cat.

"Does Royal Construction own the land?"

"That's one of the main points of contention, actually. The previous owners disappeared during the quake years. Nobody knows what happened to them. We cleared the rubble from the fallen buildings and built a community on the vacant lot. We've been living there for almost ten years now. By right of occupation, the land is ours."

"But Royal Construction doesn't see it that way."

Alain shook his head in disgust.

"No. The city managers decided that the property title had reverted to them, and they put the lot up for auction. Naturally, no one bothered to inform us of this. Nor did they inform anyone else, it seems: Royal Construction was the only bidder. They purchased the property rights for a song."

"So they think you're squatters. You think you own the land by right of occupation. Sounds like a story as old as time. The natives who first settled this peninsula had the same issue with the forty-niners." Val drummed on the table with her fingertips. "But why would they kill Ruby? There are a lot of you living in that community. Surely killing one person wouldn't make that much difference. And why now?"

"I think things are coming to a head," Alain said. "The bulldozer drivers have been getting more impatient by the day. If I had to guess, I'd say maybe Royal Construction's investors are getting restless."

"Seems like a reasonable hypothesis," said Val. She stared up at the wispy clouds drifting across the sky. "But that still doesn't answer the question of why Ruby. How would killing one person change things?"

"No offense, but if you have to ask that, you really didn't know Ruby," said Alain with a sad smile. "In a lot of ways, she was the heart and soul of our community. The heart and soul of the protest groups, anyway. She was a real spitfire, a rabble-rouser. She led a delegation of our people to a meeting at the Royal Construction headquarters last week. They delivered a list of our demands. I wasn't there, but I heard it didn't go over well."

"So, what? Did she offend some high and mighty board member? Was it some kind of revenge killing? Or were they sending a message? Did they think that killing Ruby would make the rest of you fold?"

"All excellent questions," said Alain. "I think only Royal Construction would know the answers."

"Well, let's go ask them."

"Go ask them?" Alain gaped at her. "Ask them how? Do you think we can just waltz right into their building?"

"That's exactly what I think," said Val. "I'd like to see them try and stop us."

Alain stared at her for a long moment, unsure if she was joking or not. When he finally saw that she was serious, he shook his head and whistled softly.

"You are one crazy lady, you know that?"

"Yes, I'm aware. Believe it or not, it's the main thing that gets me through life."

Alain toyed with his burrito wrapper, his eyes thoughtful.

"OK, but before we charge off to Royal Construction half-cocked, did you have any other suspects? I mean, there is a chance that it wasn't Royal, right?"

Val looked at him for a long moment, measuring him with her eyes. Finally, she said, "Well, I guess you confided in me, so the least I can do is trust you back. Now that I've crossed you off the list of suspects, I have two others left on my list. First is a guy who was getting a little too friendly with her at the Alley Cat the night she was killed. A real prize. I had to peel him off her with a spatula and bounce him off a few walls to get him to understand that there are boundaries in our club. He was a member of the Black Knights. Do you know them?"

Alain nodded. "Religious fanatics right? Tattooed crosses on the backs of their hands?"

"Yeah, that's them. Anyway, the guy certainly had the temperament for murder, and he was plenty pissed off that night. But I think if he was going to murder anyone, it would have been me. I'm not sure why he would hurt Ruby, unless she just happened to be in the wrong place at the wrong time."

"Or maybe she looked like an easier target," said Alain. "Guys like that don't like to take on someone they consider a challenge. They like easy victories that boost their ego."

"True. I definitely know the type. Believe it or not, guys like that love to hang out in strip clubs. Nothing gets them off quite as much as having women take off their clothes to prove they are big, powerful men."

"I'm not surprised." He grimaced. "So that's suspect number one. You said there were two?"

"Yes, and the second one has got a pretty powerful motive. Ruby owed money to Vasilevski."

"The Russian mob? *Merde.* That's definitely a motive. Have you talked to them?"

"I questioned Vasilevski at the club the other night. He confirmed that Ruby owed him money. He's got a good poker face, though, and I couldn't tell if he had anything to do with Ruby's murder. Still, there were definitely things he wasn't telling me."

"Well, I'll have to trust your judgment on that one." Alain steepled his fingers on the table. "So, where does that leave us?"

Val squared her shoulders and tried to look confident. "The Black Knights and the Russians are both cans of worms I'd rather not crack open if we don't have to. Let's leave them for later. Right now, I say we pay Royal Construction a visit."

18

New York was cold and dirty, the people were abrasive, and everything moved at a thousand miles per hour all the time. The city was a living thing, people rushing through its arteries like blood.

Walking down the street, Valora felt like one cell in this vast body. It made her feel insignificant but strangely safe at the same time. You didn't get that in small towns where there was no foot traffic. People just drove from home to work to the supermarket and back home again. Insulated inside their little boxes. Moving around each other but never touching.

In New York there was plenty of touching. People smashed against you on crowded subway cars, brushed past you on the stairs and sidewalk, and pushed you out of the way so they could see what was behind the deli counter. There were more people living in a single block than there were in entire towns she'd been in.

It was overwhelming and scary. But Valora thought she might grow to love it.

Amber led Valora to an old brick warehouse on the outskirts of Brooklyn. It was vast and open on the inside, the cement floor cracked and stained with age. Huge rusty beams arched across the ceiling, and many of the tall windows were boarded up.

"Welcome to the Emerald City. It used to be a paper factory, but it's been abandoned for decades," Amber told her. "Fifteen people live here now, ranging in age from twelve to fifty." She raised her voice and called out, her voice echoing in the immense space. "Meeting in five minutes! Come meet the new girl!"

Valora cocked an eye at her. "Emerald City?"

"Sure, like the Wizard of Oz. It's a magical place, right?"

"I suppose that makes me a munchkin," Mister E remarked. *"Though I think I'd rather be a flying monkey."*

Only six people showed up to the meeting. Three teenage girls, two scruffy boys, and a smooth-faced old woman with a silver tiara and grey hair that hung in a braid down to her ass. They eyed Valora curiously.

For her part, Valora fought the urge to run. She didn't like being stared at. Making matters worse, the hairs on the back of her neck were standing straight up and the skin on the back of her hands was itching something fierce. Every single one of them was crackling with magic.

"This is normal," Amber assured Val as they gathered. "Everyone has lives. We're never all home at once."

Then she turned to address the group.

"Everyone, I'd like to introduce our latest stray. This is Valora..." She raised a questioning eyebrow at Valora.

"Keri," she supplied. "Valora Keri."

"Val Keri?" One of the boys smirked. He looked to be about Valora's age and was pretty in an old-world kind of way, with olive skin, soft lips, dark eyes, and black hair that curled down to his shoulders. "With a name like that, you must fuck some shit up."

Valora scowled in confusion.

"You know, Val Keri. Like Valkyrie. The Norse warrior women?" he explained.

Val shuffled uneasily. "I've never heard of them."

The boy gaped at her. "How is that possible? Have you been living under a rock or what?"

"OK, Silvio. We're getting off track," Amber interrupted. "You can

lecture Valora on Norse mythology later. Right now we're doing intro-
ductions."

The other teenage boy was as fair skinned as Silvio was dark, with
red hair and freckles.

"Colin," he said, bobbing his head in nervous greeting.

The teenage girls all had braided hair, big eyes, and tattered
sweaters. "This is Anastasia, Olga, and Maria. They're sisters from
Greece," Amber said by way of introduction.

"Welcome..." said the first.

"...we are pleased..." the second added.

"...to meet you," the third finished. The girls wore long skirts, and
they each curtsied as they spoke. The notes of their voices blended
together into a minor chord. Val suppressed a shudder. The sisters
were spooky.

"I'm Paula," the older woman said with a smile. She held out her
hand and Valora shook it gratefully. Her skin was dry and smooth, like
worn parchment paper. "I'm the geezer of the bunch."

"She'll try to tell you that makes her wise," Amber said. "Don't
believe the bullshit. Paula just likes to make stuff up. "

"I resent that," Paula said amiably. She winked a sparkling blue eye
at Valora. "This braid is made of pure wisdom. Don't let anyone tell
you different."

"Don't let her sell you any bridges and you'll probably be all
right," Amber advised. "Now that you've met some of the crew, let's
see if we can find you a bed. You'll meet the others in due course. Just
introduce yourself whenever you run into a new face and you'll be
fine."

Tiny cubicles had been constructed out of plywood, cardboard, and
tarps along one wall.

"It looks like a tent city." Valora wrinkled her nose.

"I mean, it is a squat." At Valora's shocked expression, Amber
laughed. "What, you thought we were renting this place? Get real. Do
you have any idea how expensive this much square footage would be?
No, the only reason we're here is because it's abandoned and nobody
else wants it right now."

Amber found her an empty cubicle with a stained futon on the floor inside. The cubicle was barely big enough for the futon and some cinder-block shelves along one wall.

"My, how we've come up in the world," Mister E said. *"This is even worse than that attic your aunt made us stay in."*

"Home sweet home," Amber said. "I know it's basic, but trust me, once you spruce it up, it'll be downright cozy. I'd tell you to drop your stuff off, but you don't have any stuff. So that's step one: Let's find you some stuff. There's a community pile of blankets and clothes left by some of our previous residents over there in the office. Some of it's pretty ratty, but if you dig, you can probably unearth some gems. Enough to get you started, anyway. After that, the city's great for free stuff. You can score just about anything if you keep your eyes open."

Valora claimed a blue sleeping bag, a pillow, a pair of black jeans, and a couple of tattered wool sweaters.

After she dropped them off in her cubicle, Silvio called out to her.

"Hey Valkyrie! You want to come on a food run with me? I'll show you the best spots to get a free lunch."

Valora looked at Amber uncertainly. Amber shrugged.

"Do what you want. There are a few ground rules we can cover later, but you're free to come and go whenever you want."

Amber smiled, and Valora hesitantly smiled back. New York, The Emerald City, it was a lot to digest at once, and she was feeling a bit overwhelmed. But in a good way. Being there felt right.

"Thank you," she said. "For everything."

"Hey New Girl, train's leaving. You coming or not?" Silvio yelled, his voice booming around the open space.

Valora hesitated for a minute, caught between shyness and curiosity. Then she swallowed and made her decision. If this was to be her new life, she was going to grab hold of it with both hands.

"Wait a minute," she yelled back. "I'm coming too."

19

Alain turned down Val's offer of a ride in the sidecar of the Ural with a grin.

"I prefer to run."

"After two burritos?" Val shook her head. "I'd puke all over my shoes."

"I'm a jet engine, remember? I'll see you there."

"He's just showing off," Mister E said as she kicked the Ural into gear. *"Trying to impress the lady."*

Val snorted. "Yeah, because I'm clearly a delicate flower waiting to be swept off my feet."

Mister E blew a smoke ring, undeterred. *"Maybe he likes his woman strong. It takes all types you know."*

"Uh-huh."

She saw no sign of Alain as she headed for North Beach, but she did glimpse a big black dog loping along their route a couple of times. It was a hound of some sort, long and lean, built for running. It seemed like the kind of shape that would fit Alain.

True to his word, Alain was waiting for her when she arrived. He watched her back the Ural into a narrow spot by the curb and put her helmet in the lock box. The Royal Construction offices were located in the wedge-shaped Sentinel Building, a copper-domed landmark at Jackson & Kearny. Pretty fancy digs, but she supposed with all the quake damage the construction business must be booming. Especially if they'd gotten the city's contract to shore up the underground.

Royal Construction's main office was on the fifth floor, and a young woman with black-rimmed glasses eyed them from behind the receptionist's desk as they pushed through the doors. A small placard on the desk identified her as Hillary Linscomb. Val flashed Hillary her best professional smile and deliberately started recording on her phone, pointing the microphone toward the young woman. Alain stayed a step behind her, content to let her lead.

"Hi, I'm Val Keri with the Bridge Bulletin. I'm doing a story on your company's efforts to bulldoze a community in the Mission District. Any comment?"

Linscomb's face paled.

"I'm afraid I don't know anything about that ... I mean, I don't know what you're talking about."

"Which is it, Miss Linscomb? Do you not know anything about it? Or do you not know what I'm talking about? Because those are two very different answers."

The kid opened and closed her mouth, "I ... Uh."

She was saved from further flailing when a sleekly dressed woman strode out of the office behind her. She was pale and thin with black hair cut in a razor line level with her chin. Her lips were the red of a winter sunset. The hair on the back of Val's neck stood the moment she saw her. The woman crackled with energy.

"What is going on here?" the woman asked, her voice low and smoky. "I don't recall seeing an interview on today's schedule."

The receptionist flinched and bit her lip to keep from yelping out loud.

"Ms. Pearl, I was, uh, I mean this..." the receptionist stammered.

Ms. Pearl raised a hand to silence the girl, and the receptionist shut her mouth so fast her teeth clicked together. The kid looked terrified.

Val frowned. She recognized an abusive relationship when she saw one.

She shifted to face the woman. Val fought to keep her expression friendly, despite the invisible Mister E hissing from his perch on her shoulder. This woman was dangerous. She was also someone who might have answers. But would Val be able to get them out of her?

"I'm Melinda Pearl. Please step into my office." She eyed Val like a cobra in a mongoose pit, before stopping Alain with a flat stare. "You will wait out here."

Alain bristled, but Val put a hand on his arm. "It's OK. I've got this."

He gave her a searching look, then nodded. "I'll be right here if you need me."

Melinda Pearl's office was not what Val was expecting. She expected a corner office with lots of windows and natural light. A great view of North Beach out the window. Instead, the interior was dim, the windows covered with thick curtains. A single lamp with a stained-glass shade stood upon an immaculate desk, lighting the space with a muted glow. It felt more like the interior of a church than an office.

"*Vampire*," Mister E hissed in her ear. "*Don't look in her eyes.*"

Val's spine turned to ice. She'd heard rumors that there were vampires in the city, but she hadn't run across any of them personally. Now that she had, she wished she hadn't. Power and menace radiated off Melinda Pearl like fog from the bay.

"The outside world distracts me. I find it easier to focus like this," Pearl said simply, her expression daring Val to disagree. "Please, have a seat."

Val lowered herself into an upholstered wooden chair, the green velvet giving slightly beneath her weight. The dark-stained wooden arms were smooth with polish beneath her fingers, curling downward into carved claws. Like the rest of the furnishings, it felt like an antique, and was probably worth more than anything Val had ever owned. She sat up straight and tried not to let her discomfort show.

Melinda Pearl leaned back in her own polished chair and focused her attention on Val. Something cold looked out of her eyes. "What can I do for you?"

Val cleared her throat and lifted her phone. "I hope you don't mind speaking on the record?"

Pearl regarded her curiously, her gaze intense. Val felt as if she was being weighed and measured, like a rack of ribs on a butcher's scale. She suppressed a shudder.

"I don't see why not," the woman said finally. "I have nothing to hide."

"Great." Val's nervous smile felt like a grimace. "I was wondering if you'd care to comment on the disputed lot at Alameda and Harrison?"

"Disputed lot?" Ms. Pearl's voice was all innocence, but her eyes flickered to a large map of the city pinned to the wall behind her desk. Several sites on the map were circled in red.

Val's pulse ticked up as she realized one of the red circles contained the shifters' settlement. She inclined her head towards the map.

"It's my understanding that your company is seeking to evict the current residents of that block."

Pearl didn't flinch, but her expression became even colder.

"The current residents are illegal squatters."

"Perhaps. But they've been living on that lot for over a decade. Don't you think that gives them some rights?"

"Not in the eyes of the law, it doesn't. We are simply playing by the city's rules." Melinda Pearl turned her palms up in a what-are-you-going-to-do gesture.

"And do those rules include murder?"

"I don't know what you're talking about." Despite her denial, Pearl didn't sound surprised by the accusation.

Val leaned in, and Mister E perked up as well. There was something here.

"Really? You didn't know that one of your most vocal critics at the settlement was killed? I find that unlikely."

"I am the head of this company. I do not need to be informed of every little thing that happens. That is why I have employees."

"So you'd characterize a woman being murdered as a 'little thing'?"

Pearl's mouth curled with distaste.

"I think this interview is at an end."

Val bit back a curse; she'd pushed too hard. She hastily tried to backtrack.

"Please, Ms. Pearl. The woman's family would really like to find her killer. Any help you could give me would be greatly appreciated. Have there been reports of strange activity at your worksite? Any accidents or other disappearances? This is your chance to cooperate with our investigation. Working with us now will let us paint you in a favorable light when we break the story."

Melinda Pearl made a feral sound deep in her throat.

"Who are you really, Miss Keri?"

Val's heart raced. She squeezed the arms of her chair and tried not to show her panic. Should she double down on the lie? Cut and run? Admit the truth?

Her eyes flicked back to the map behind the desk. She stared at the image, focusing on the locations of the red circles, trying to burn it into her memory.

An old black and white photograph tacked up beside the map drew her eye. It was a picture of a bronze sculpture depicting three figures on a pedestal atop a hill. Val's eyes widened. The central figure of the sculpture was Lady Liberty. It looked to be the same weathered Lady Liberty she'd seen in the center of the shifter community. A tiny caption read, *"The Triumph of Light."*

Melinda Pearl was still waiting for Val's response.

In the end it was Mister E who decided it. The cat-demon never backed down from a fight. He responded to Pearl's challenge in kind, puffing out his tail and hissing. Val's power stirred in response. She held her head high and met Pearl's question with a belligerent stare.

"You're right, I'm not a reporter. The murdered woman was my friend. Why don't you stop lying and tell me what you know about it."

The businesswoman leaned back, steepling her fingers.

"I'll give you some free advice, Val Keri. Stay out of my business. You're out of your depth here; this is where the big fish swim. A little thing like you could get snapped up in a single bite."

"I'd like to see you try. You might bite off more than you can chew." Val leaned forward, her hair stirring in a sudden breeze. "If you had something to do with my friend's death, I will find out. And I'll bring you down for it."

"Such strong words. I'm all tingly." Pearl smirked and waved her fingers at the door. "You and your swollen sense of self-importance can see yourself out."

"What about the Market Street tunnel?" Val said, remembering the digging she'd stumbled upon. She snuck another glance at the red circles on the map. "You're not just shoring up the old underground tunnel. What are you looking for down there?"

Melinda Pearl's face became a marble statue. "Don't make me call security."

Val held her gaze for a long moment before rising to her feet. "I'm going to get answers one way or another. You'd better hope I don't have to come back here to get them."

She straightened her leather jacket and left, slamming the heavy door behind her.

The receptionist jumped at the sound. Val regarded the young woman. She had that hunched-in, protective way of sitting that abuse victims had, and her eyes were always on the move, looking for danger. She couldn't be more than twenty.

"You don't have to put up with her shit, you know," Val told her.

"I'm sorry?" Hillary Linscomb squeaked.

"There's a big world out there. Plenty of jobs where your boss isn't an asshole."

The young woman's eyes shifted nervously to Pearl's door, then fixed on her desk. "I'm very happy here, thank you."

Val leaned in close and whispered. "When you're ready to escape, I can help you. Come see me at the Alley Cat. I'm Val."

The young woman sat so still she might have been part of her chair.

Val sighed. "Right. Well, it was nice meeting you, Hillary."

She motioned to Alain and they made their way out of the building.

"Was that a waste of time?" he asked.

"I'm not sure," Val replied. "Pearl is definitely hiding something. She had a map on the wall behind her desk. There was a red circle around your community, and other circles around a half dozen other locations. There was also an old photograph of a sculpture called *The Triumph of Light* that looks just like that bronze Lady Liberty sculpture in the center of your settlement."

"And you think that has something to do with Ruby?"

"Maybe. I don't know. But I know where we can find out."

20

The library sat on a small hill overlooking the Market Street chasm. The columned building was known as the Granite Lady, and it had been the San Francisco Mint until 1937, stamping out coins and holding millions of pounds of gold bullion. During the great San Francisco fire of 1906, the Granite Lady kept over a third of the country's gold reserve safe from the flames. She'd functioned as a museum for decades after her retirement in 1937, before being abandoned and falling into disrepair during the turbulence. Nowadays, she guarded a far more valuable treasure.

"Are you sure you'll find what you're looking for here?" asked Alain. He'd ridden over in the Ural's sidecar, and his coarse black hair was looking a little windblown.

"If it's magical in nature, we'll find information here," Val said.

"And if it's not?"

"Then we look elsewhere."

She felt the twin gryphons watching them as they walked up the steps to the entrance. The stone guardians were a recent addition; to the casual observer they appeared to be simply ornamental sculptures flanking the entrance on their pedestals. Val knew better.

The gryphons were magical guardians, ready to spring from their pedestals and tear into anyone approaching the library with the intent to do it harm. How they knew your intentions was beyond Val. That type of magic wasn't in her repertoire.

As she stepped through the doors, the smell washed over her. Books. Real paper books. Shelves and shelves of them, filling the massive space from floor to ceiling, stretching as far as the eye could see.

The library was one of the greatest caches of human knowledge remaining on the planet. The collapse had proven how fragile electronic storage systems were, with enormous databases lost in an instant. Decades of information lost forever. Paper books, which had been sliding toward extinction for years, suddenly became valuable again.

The library was a treasury of knowledge. More specifically, the library was a treasury of magical knowledge.

Behind the desk to Val's left sat the organizing force behind it all.

One might expect such a person to be an imposing figure. Powerful of stature and build. Ready to rain fire upon any who dared to invade their domain.

The Librarian was none of these things.

Her glasses drooped on the end of her nose. The bun of her hair was untidy at best. She wore two sweaters, and holes adorned the elbows of her burgundy cardigan. The handkerchief in her pocket was well-used. The Librarian looked like what she was: a small woman who spent all her time indoors, in the company of books. There was no hint that this was a woman of power. That this woman was responsible for one of the greatest treasures on the planet.

Until she glanced up.

Her eyes were a deep violet, like the gloaming sky between sunset and full dark. They glimmered with the cold light of a thousand stars. Looking into those eyes, Val felt like she was an astronaut falling through space, slowly being sucked into a black hole. Mister E flattened himself against her shoulder and pressed his face to the back of her neck, trying to escape that all-knowing gaze.

Then the Librarian blinked, and smiled, and became just a mousy, slightly disheveled woman once again.

"Can I help you?"

Val tried to return the smile, failed, and nodded instead.

"I hope so. I'm looking for information on *The Triumph of Light*. It's a big bronze statue. I think it might have been mounted somewhere in the city at one time."

The Librarian tapped a pencil against her lips, thinking. Her violet irises were huge through the lenses of her glasses.

"Yes, I believe there was a sculpture of that name commissioned by Adolph Sutro. There's some very specific mythology attached to it, though I can't recall exactly what off the top of my head."

"Are there books that can tell me more?"

"Of course there are." The Librarian snatched up a pencil and began to write in small, precise letters. "I recommend R. Pope's *Complete History of San Francisco Magic*. You may also be interested in T. Connolly's *Phantasms in the Fog*, and M. Weimer's *Hometown Tourism: Uncovering the Mystical in your own Backyard*."

Val eyed the list dubiously.

"Do any of these focus on *The Triumph of Light* specifically?"

The Librarian's expression turned frosty.

"You have to read them to find your answers. That's what books are for."

"Right." Val's cheeks grew warm. "Where..."

"Fourth floor. Up the stairs to the left."

"Got it. Thank you." Val forced a smile to show her gratitude, but the Librarian didn't see it. Her gaze was already turned back to her work.

Val made her way down the central atrium and up the wide staircase. Dim light shone in through massive skylights overhead. To both sides, several floors of library opened onto the space above her, like cutaway layers of a birthday cake. The carpet was dusty and worn, but still quite beautiful, with red and gold and silver designs swooping about. More like something you might find in a palace, not a library.

"This place is amazing," Alain breathed. "Do you mind if I explore a bit?"

Val's lips quirked at the awe in his voice, remembering how she'd felt the first time she'd entered the library. "Go ahead. I'll holler if I need you."

Alain wandered off and Val followed the Librarian's directions to a stairwell on the left. She found herself swallowed by a canyon of books. The shelves towered twelve feet high on both sides of her, groaning beneath the weight of their contents.

Much knowledge was lost when the great server banks died. The weight of human knowledge had been transferred to the cloud, and now the cloud was gone. Dissolved back into the component electrons from whence it came. Real paper books were once again humanity's most reliable way to store information, just as they had been for so many centuries before the Age of Information.

Val ran her fingers along the spines of the books, feeling the different textures. Smooth plastic and rough paper and pebbly hardcovers. Some books had come from other libraries and bore the bar codes and Dewey decimals of their former organizational systems like scars of another life. Some books were hardy survivors, their water-swollen pages straining against their covers. In the world before, these books would have been replaced. But not now. Now the industrial printing presses were silent, and every book was irreplaceable. Every book might be the last of its kind, the last repository of that particular bit of knowledge.

What the Librarian had done here was astounding. How she'd gathered so many books was a mystery; Val wouldn't have thought this many books still existed in the world. No wonder she guarded them so fiercely.

She found the recommended books one by one and sat down to read.

Adolph Sutro had been an eccentric millionaire and mayor of San Francisco. At one time he had owned roughly one twelfth of the land in the city, most of it in the Richmond and Sunset districts. His name still adorned various landmarks and sections of the city, including Sutro Tower, Sutro Heights, and the ancient ruins of the Sutro Baths at Land's End.

In 1887, Val read, Sutro donated a huge sculpture to the city called

The Triumph of Light, installing it on a pedestal atop Mount Olympus in what was at the time considered the geographic center of the city, above what would later become the Haight-Ashbury district. The statue depicted Lady Liberty standing tall above two other figures, symbolizing the victory of liberty over despotism. The monument stood for seventy years, towering over the city skyline, though its origins were largely forgotten over the decades. Eventually the sculpture was vandalized and fell into disrepair. It disappeared from its pedestal sometime during the 1950s. No one seemed to know what had become of it.

According to Connolly's book, what most people did not know was that Sutro was a sorcerer. Magic was hard to come by in his day, but he had struck a vein of power while excavating the Comstock Lode, where he first made his fortune. For the rest of his life, he had dedicated his considerable resources to the accumulation of magical power. Legend said he had stored his power in a single, immensely powerful object, the Scepter of Sutro. Whoever held the scepter could supposedly control all the magic in San Francisco.

"*Well, that would explain a lot about Sutro's life,*" Mister E purred. "*He was the King of San Francisco for a time.*"

When Sutro died, the scepter was lost. Rumor held that the scepter had been hidden inside one of the monuments that bore his name.

"Interesting," Val breathed. If the scepter had been hidden inside *The Triumph of Light,* that would explain why Royal Construction was looking for the statue. She thought of the bronze Lady Liberty sculpture in the Shifter's compound. Could that be *The Triumph of Light*? Had it been broken over the years so that the Lady Liberty portion was all that was left?

The next book she cracked had an even more interesting theory. M. Weimer suggested that Sutro had feared his scepter would be used for evil after his death. To prevent this, the Scepter of Sutro had been dismantled, broken into half a dozen pieces. The pieces were hidden in various places.

Weimer agreed with Connolly that the pieces had most likely been hidden inside Sutro's monuments. Weimer speculated that likely hiding places included the Sutro Tower, Sutro Baths, *The Triumph of*

Light, and the great Sutro Library, which was considered to be the largest individual library in the world in its day. Unfortunately, the library had been consumed in the great San Francisco fire of 1906.

Val thought of the map on Melinda Pearl's wall, with its red circles. Could the circles correspond to locations where they thought the pieces of the scepter might be found? It would explain all the digging they were doing in the underground tunnels.

She got a big map of the city and spread it open on the table before her. She marked the red circles from memory, then marked the locations of Sutro's most famous monuments using the books.

Her pulse quickened. They matched. Royal Construction wasn't shoring up the tunnels at all. They were looking for the scepter.

Val kept digging and was rewarded by a full-color artist's rendering of the Scepter of Sutro in R. Pope's book. It was about three feet long and made of gold. The shaft was finger-thick, flaring to a pair of heavily ornamented nobs at the ends, encrusted with jewels. Val stared at the illustration for a long time. Something about it tickled at her mind, but she couldn't quite put her finger on what.

Suddenly Mister E's fur puffed up, his golden eyes swiveling. Val felt the hair prickle on the back of her neck. Someone was watching her. She kept her head down, but raised her eyes, peering up through her eyelashes. She didn't see anyone at first and thought she might be imagining it. She was about to return to her reading when a flash of movement caught her eye. There, blue eyes between the shelves. Blond hair and an olive-green jacket.

The eyes widened. The person turned to flee.

"Stop!" Val leapt from her chair and shot off in pursuit.

The green jacket was halfway down the aisle when Val rounded the corner. Her jaw set with determination. She flung a hand out toward the watcher.

"I said, stop!"

A gust of wind hit the figure in the back, knocking them into one of the massive shelves. They stumbled and went down beneath an avalanche of books.

Val advanced down the aisle. The watcher lay still, almost

completely buried. All she could see was a scrap of green jacket and a curling blond lock between the mounded books.

"I don't want to hurt you. I just want to talk." She reached her hand out toward the jacket.

The pile of books exploded.

21

The warehouse was in an industrial area, and Silvio led Valora past block after block of old factories and shipping docks. The sidewalk was crumbling, with thick grass sprouting through the cracks. The streets were extra wide to accommodate the heavy delivery trucks rumbling up and down. Valora saw the tents, lean-tos, and cardboard boxes of homeless people beside steam vents and under bridges. It made her sad to see so many desperate people, and she shuddered to think how close she was to that herself.

"Why don't you let more of them into the warehouse?" she asked. "There's plenty of room."

Silvio looked at her like she'd lost her mind.

"They're normies. They'd freak if they knew what we can do."

"Would they?" She stared at an old woman in a yellow rain hat who was carrying on an animated conversation with an invisible companion. The woman was using an empty cable spool as a table, and she had a couple of plastic chairs and cracked plates set out with cloth napkins, as if she were having lunch in a restaurant. "They seem harmless enough."

"Some are, some aren't," Silvio said. "You never know which is which."

"What about her?" Valora pointed to the old woman. "She seems safe."

Silvio sighed and shook his head.

"Let me tell you a little story. There used to be a girl in the warehouse named Latisha. Sweetest girl you ever met, would literally give you the shirt off her back. She was like you, she saw all these people out here and wanted to help them. The difference is, Latisha actually could. She was a healer. I mean that was her magic, she could heal people. A kid named Brian broke his arm once and Latisha set the bone and healed it right in front of me. It was unbelievable. Craziest thing I ever saw. It stopped bleeding, the skin closed up, within half an hour Brian was walking around like nothing had ever happened. Truly amazing.

"Anyway, Latisha would go out and visit the homeless people around here and try to help them. She was cautious, never did anything overt. Helped close non-visible wounds, stop infections, fight fevers, that kind of thing. Nothing big and flashy like with Brian. She knew better than that. But one day she goes to visit this kid named Marcus, who lived under a blue tarp a couple blocks that way." Silvio gestured vaguely with his arm. "Anyway, Marcus had been sick a lot, he had HIV or cancer or something like that. Something real bad. Something you don't get better from. Latisha had been visiting him pretty regularly, trying to ease his pain and help him out in small ways. But he just kept getting worse, and watching him die and knowing she might be able to help him was driving her crazy."

Silvio had stopped walking as he told his story. He talked with his hands, and now he stood on a street corner, punctuating his words with wild gestures, like an orchestra conductor building to the climax. The wind kept blowing his hair across his face, and he brushed it away with his fingers over and over. Valora would have been annoyed by that -- she kept her hair tied back and firmly out of the way -- but Silvio was too wrapped up in his story to notice. Valora thought his focus was adorable.

"So one day, she goes to see him and Marcus cuts his hand open pretty bad. Blood all over the place and no real way to stop the bleeding. Now this is a guy who's already in bad shape. Anything extra could push him right over the edge. Latisha's heart's just breaking for the guy, and this cut is the last straw. She can't stand it anymore. She says, fuck it, she's going to help this guy. She's got to. She can't live with herself it she doesn't. So she reaches out and takes this guy by the hand and she heals him. But she doesn't just heal his cut, she figures if she's going to do it she might as well do it all the way. She heals him completely. Cleans out the cancer or HIV or whatever he's got eating him up inside. Now, doing this leaves her as weak as a kitten. It takes everything out of her. So she's kind of slumped against something or collapsed on the floor or whatever and this guy Marcus stares at his hand, where the skin is smooth and new, like he never cut it at all, then he stared at her, then he stares at the hand again. He does this for like five minutes, just staring back and forth, trying to wrap his brain around what happened."

Silvio looked off into the distance, as if he could see it all playing out again.

"And he can't handle it. He freaks out and snaps. Loses his shit. He beat her to death with a two by four. Can you imagine? She saved his life and he killed her for it."

His eyes glistened. His fists clenched in impotent anger. For a minute, the only sound was the rumble of the big trucks and the low moan of the wind. Valora groped for something to say, but found nothing. Her shock made her feel hollow. Like Silvio's words had scooped out her insides. She'd seen bad things in her life -- hell, she'd done plenty of them herself. But nothing like that.

Finally, Silvio looked at her. He forced a smile.

"And that is why we can never, ever bring any of the normies into the warehouse. If they knew what we can do, they'd lose their minds. It'd be like the Middle Ages or the Salem witch trials all over again. They'd burn us at the stake."

Valora looked at all the people camped out around them. The crazy old woman in the yellow rain hat. In the light of Silvio's story, she looked dangerous and unhinged. Val shuddered.

"Well, thanks for that image. Now I'm going to be paranoid and watching my back all the time."

"You should be. Even if you weren't a witch, this is New York.

Always watch your back," Silvio said. Then he grinned, his boyish smile lighting up his face, making him look improbably young. "But that's what I'm here for. Don't worry, Valkyrie. I've got your back."

Valora rolled her eyes at the name, but she grinned back despite herself. Silvio's enthusiasm was infectious.

They finally got out of the industrial area and found themselves in a rundown neighborhood. Exhausted houses sagged against their neighbors, paint peeling off in strips. There was a little commercial street full of shops. Silvio rattled off information as they passed each one.

"Pop's Coffee puts their old pastries on top of the dumpster every night around five. Isaac's Bagels does the same on Tuesdays and Fridays. The dumpster behind the mini market is a great place to score stuff that's past its expiration date."

"Past the expiration? But doesn't that mean you're not supposed to eat it?"

Silvio gave her a pitying look.

"I can see you've got a lot to learn. No, the expiration date is just a legally mandated guess as to when something might go bad. It's only a guideline. You can eat lots of things past their expiration date, no problem. Just use your eyes and nose. If something looks or smells off, don't eat it. If it seems fine, it probably is fine."

Valora wrinkled her nose. "So you eat food out of dumpsters?"

"Sure, there's nothing wrong with it. It's perfectly good food. Why let it go to waste? Look, I'll show you." He led her into an alley and fished a package of cheese wedges out of the supermarket's dumpster. He brushed coffee grounds off the cardboard. "It's unopened. Which means it's double sealed. Perfectly clean." He peeled open the cardboard, revealing the neatly foil-wrapped wedges inside. He opened one and popped it in his mouth. "Mmmm. I love soft cheese. Here, have one."

Valora's stomach rolled as she took in the rainbow sheen of oil spilled on the asphalt, the old plastic bottles in the gutters, the flies swarming a pair of rotting apples.

"No thanks. I'm not hungry."

Silvio smirked at her. "You are such a noob. Give it a few days.

When you get hungry enough, you'll realize what a good deal free food is, no matter where it comes from."

"If you say so."

"I do. Stick with me, kid. You'll see."

As they rounded a corner, Silvio bumped into a pair of tough-looking Italians in suits.

"Watch where you're going!" One of them said, shoving Silvio aggressively.

"Woah, woah! Sorry man. My bad," Silvio bounced off a parked car and tried to back away, his palms out. The guy shoved him again.

"Hey, leave him alone," Valora yelled, stepping between them.

The guy looked at her like she'd come from another planet.

"What're you supposed to be? The world's smallest biker gang?" The guy laughed and stepped forward. He towered over Valora, and she had to crane her neck back to meet his eyes. He reached out and cupped her chin. "Believe me, you don't want to get involved here, sweetheart. I suggest you walk away."

Valora's anger surged. The wind started to swirl around her.

"Or what?" she snarled. This guy had no idea who he was messing with. What she could do. She slapped his hand away from her face.

The big guy's face darkened.

"Just because you're a girl, doesn't mean..."

Silvio grabbed Valora's arm and yanked her back.

"What she meant to say was, 'We're sorry, and it'll never happen again,'" he said, pulling her down the sidewalk away from the tough guys.

"What are you doing? Let me go!" Valora struggled, but Silvio just tightened his grip and walked faster. He didn't release her until they'd put a full block between them and their antagonists.

"Why'd you pull me away? I could have taken that guy," she growled.

"A couple of tough Italians in suits in New York City. Think about it. Who do you think that was?" he said.

Her eyes went wide.

"The mafia? Really? I thought that was just in the movies."

"Art imitates life. Trust me, the mob is very, very real. You do not want to get on their bad side."

"I still could have taken them," she muttered.

"With what? Your magic? What did I tell you about that? You can't use your magic out in the open. If anyone sees what you can do, they'll burn you at the stake. Remember what happened to Latisha."

She scowled and pulled away from him. Even if what Silvio said made sense, she still hated backing down from a bully. Valora sulked for the rest of the afternoon.

22

Val flung her arms up against the wave of books. A heavy hardcover clipped her on the chin and she staggered, lights dancing before her eyes. By the time her head cleared, the spy was up and running. She could tell from the shape of his shoulders that it was a man now, with a green jacket and blond hair. Val stumbled after him.

"Stop," she shouted.

The man ignored her, rounding the end of the massive bookshelf and heading toward the exit. Val pushed power into her legs, putting on a burst of speed. She couldn't let him get away.

She followed him around the bookshelf, throwing another gust of wind at his back. The man stumbled but didn't go down this time. If anything, the wind seemed to push him forward, helping him run faster. He hit the stairwell, vaulting down the first flight in a great leap.

Val growled and redoubled her speed, legs pistoning beneath her.

She too vaulted down the first flight of stairs, but couldn't control her momentum when she landed and crashed shoulder-first into the granite wall.

"Flying roaches," she swore, pushing herself off the stone. Her shoulder screamed in protest. It felt like she'd torn something in there.

She didn't leap down the next flight, opting to take the stairs two at a time instead. It was marginally slower, but it saved her a lot of pain on the next landing. The guy in the jacket continued to leap down each flight, but there was something odd about it. He didn't fall the way he should, instead he kind of glided in the air, almost as if he had...

"Wings," Val breathed. "The fucker's got wings hidden beneath a glamour."

"If he gets outside, you'll never catch him," Mister E added. He was perched on her shoulder, claws digging into her skin.

"Tell me something I don't know." Val pounded down another flight of stairs, skidding across the landing. "Can't you do something more useful?"

"Such as?"

Val could feel the cat's grin. It was infuriating. "I don't know. Maybe stop him?"

"Oh, I couldn't do that. You know I'm not allowed to directly interfere with the mortal plane. My role is an advisory one only. You're on your own here."

Val cursed again. "You're worse than useless, you know that?"

"All right, fine, there is one thing I can do."

Val sucked in a sharp breath as the guy's wings suddenly became visible, stretching out to both sides of him in wide, sweeping arcs. They were covered with white feathers and looked pillow soft, just like Val had always imagined an angel's wings would be. As she watched, they spread wide, billowing upward as he glided down another flight of stairs.

He was almost to the bottom floor. From there it was a straight shot out the front exit. With those wings, she'd never catch him once he got outside. She had to stop him now.

She gathered her will as she watched him scoot across a landing. He hit the top of the next flight of stairs and launched himself into the air -- just as Val released a howling gust of wind. The wind caught him like a kite in midair and flung him into the wall. He cried out and crashed onto the stairs, bouncing down the rest of the flight in a painful tumble.

He came to rest on the shining marble of the ground floor and lay still, moaning.

Val grinned in triumph, her blood singing within her. That'd teach the fucker. You can't fly away against someone who controls the wind.

She dashed down the last two flights and grabbed the guy by his jacket. She sucked in a breath as she saw the tattoo on the back of his hand: the inverted cross of the Black Knights. She adjusted her grip on his jacket and turned his face up toward her. He was beautiful, with a chiseled jaw, an arrow-straight nose, and ice-blue eyes that shone like the interior of a glacier. She'd seen him earlier that day at brunch.

"Jack?" she gasped in surprise. "Were you following me?"

His eyes traveled over her face, as if he were having trouble focusing. Wonderful. Maybe she'd given him a concussion.

It served him right for spying on her. But it was decidedly not helpful if she wanted to get information from him.

"Jack, focus." She slapped his cheek lightly. His eyes got a little sharper. "Why are you here? Why were you watching me?"

"I like watching you," he slurred. "You know that."

Val growled and slapped him again, a little harder this time.

"Not funny, Jack. Seriously, what are you doing here? Are you spying on me? Are you one of the Black Knights? Why have I never seen that tattoo before?"

He had the good grace to look embarrassed.

"Guilty as charged. I usually keep the tattoo covered with a glamour, the same as my wings. But you seem to have dispelled both of them." He narrowed his eyes at her. "I didn't know you could do that. You're full of surprises today."

"I'm full of surprises? Jack, you have wings! Like real angel wings. I'm not the one who's been hiding things."

He shrugged and gave her one of his dazzling smiles. "Everybody's got secrets."

"Yours are a little bigger than most." She gave his wings a pointed look.

"Says the girl who controls the wind."

Heat rose up her neck.

"OK, fine. We've both got secrets. That still doesn't explain what you're doing here, and why you were following me."

He let out a dramatic sigh. "All right, I'll tell you. But you need to let me up off the floor first, this marble is not what I'd call comfortable."

"You will leave this library NOW," the Librarian loomed up above them, her voice like a thunderclap.

Gone was the mousy little woman from the front desk. Now her eyes crackled with blue lightning, her hair writhing like a nest of snakes. Val shrank away; she could feel the electricity in the air.

"I'm sorry. This guy was watching me through the stacks and--"

"I do not care to hear your excuses. You have broken the sanctity of the library. You will leave. NOW." The building seemed to shake around them as the last word rumbled through the air.

Val swallowed. "Yes ma'am. Sorry ma'am."

Alain was waiting for them outside by the gryphons.

"What happened in there? I was browsing the shelves when all hell broke loose."

"It's kind of a long story," Jack broke in. Val noticed his glamour was back, his wings once again invisible. "Hi, I'm Jack."

Jack extended his hand, and Alain took it.

"We should go somewhere to talk, yeah?" Jack suggested. "Who's hungry?"

23

The place Jack took them wasn't exactly a dive bar. It wasn't exactly not a dive bar either. It was dingy and dark inside, with walls the same shade of black as the walls of the Alley Cat. It wasn't until they had walked all the way through the place and come out the back that Val understood why he had brought them there.

Behind the unassuming interior was a magical walled garden. Green and gold lights illuminated eucalyptus trees from within, and paper lanterns were strung over the cobblestoned walking paths. The tables were set back into the bushes and plants, each one hidden in its own living alcove. Above, the evening fog was rolling in, golden in the glow of sunset, billowing and grasping as it ate up the blue. The air was cool and moist and smelled of eucalyptus.

"This place is amazing." Wide-eyed, Val followed Jack to a table tucked away in the far corner.

His smile was dazzling. "I'm glad you like it. It's one of my favorite places in the city."

They took their seats at the table. Alain was silent, his dark eyes drinking in every detail. Val was careful to put her back to the wall. Jack was being charming again, but that didn't erase the fact that he'd been spying on her. Or that he was secretly a ... what? An angel? That would certainly explain why he was so pretty.

She shook her head at the ridiculous notion. Angels didn't exist. But whatever he was, she wasn't going to trust him any farther than she could throw him. Not until he gave her some answers.

"So. Why were you following me?" Val said.

Jack laughed and flashed her a smile.

"Right to business, eh? I suggest we order drinks and appetizers first. And don't worry about the cost. It's my treat."

Val pressed her lips together at that. Jack was trying to charm her and buy their good will. Even if his smile still made her heart race a little, it wasn't going to work. She wouldn't let it. She glanced at Alain, who was staring around the garden in wonder. Well. It wasn't going to work on her, anyway.

Jack ordered them a bruschetta appetizer and the waiter brought them their drinks. Jack got a White Russian, as always. Alain took a glass of red wine. Val settled for ginger ale.

Jack raised an eyebrow at her. "Ginger ale?"

"I don't drink," she said stiffly.

He kept his blue eyes on her, a small smile on his lips.

"Former alcoholic," she snapped. "Are you happy now?"

He raised his hands in mock surrender. "I didn't say anything."

"No, but you were thinking it."

"You wound me, my lady. All I was thinking was that you must have Herculean self-control to work as a bartender."

"It's not that hard. Watching people get drunk and make fools of themselves on a regular basis doesn't make me want to join them."

"So you're the judgmental type then? Better than the rest of us?"

"Don't do that."

"Do what?" He arched his eyebrows, all innocence.

"Twist my words. People are free to do as they like. If they need a few drinks to have a good time, that's their business. Just because I don't want to join them doesn't mean I despise them."

Alain cleared his throat. They both glared at him, but he gamely continued. "Not to interrupt this lovefest, but why are we here?"

"An excellent question." Val glared across the table. "Why are we here, Jack?"

"Well, it's such a lovely evening..." he began.

"Cut the bullshit," Val interrupted. "Why were you spying on me? And what are you?"

Jack's smile turned sour.

"Fine. If that's the way you want to play it." He took a sip of his drink and sighed dramatically, staring up at the paper lanterns. The light played along his strong jawline, dancing in the highlights of his hair. Val's breath caught in her throat. He was mesmerizing, chiseled like a Greek statue.

After a minute, Val managed to tear her eyes away. She cleared her throat loudly.

"Fine." He sighed again. "If you must know, I was keeping an eye on you for your own good. I was trying to protect you."

"Protect me from what?"

"From yourself, mostly. You're poking your nose in places it doesn't belong. You're annoying dangerous people, Val. I don't want to see you get hurt."

"Uh-huh." Val didn't believe his bullshit for a second. "And is your sudden concern a private affair, or did the Black Knights order you to keep an eye on me?"

He raised one perfect shoulder and let it fall. "A little bit of both. You really pissed Edward off the other night. I thought it would be a good idea if someone kept an eye on you, in case he decided to exact some revenge."

"Revenge? If that creep wants revenge, he's welcome to try. I wiped the floor with him once already. If he comes at me outside of the Alley Cat, I won't be so gentle the next time."

"Well, I can certainly attest to that," Jack winced as he rubbed the lump on his head left by the library floor. "But Edward can get a little crazy sometimes. And we prefer to keep such things in-house."

"So you admit you were following me."

"Yes, I was following you. What's the big deal?"

"The big deal is that it's creepy, Jack. I'm starting to wonder if you Black Knights are all just a bunch of creepers. Are all the Black Knights angels? Is Edward?" Val cracked her knuckles one at a time. If that entitled asshole was an angel, she was going to have to reassess her conception of what an angel was. "Which brings me to another thing. How long have you been a member of the Black Knights? And why do you hide it?"

Jack raised his hands, palms out. "Slow down, that's too many questions at once."

"Fine, let's start with: Is Edward Hopkins an angel too?"

"First, there's no such thing as angels," said Jack. "We are seraphim. People commonly mistake us for angels, but there are no angels. It's all just human mythology."

"What's the difference?" asked Alain.

"Well, we don't live in Heaven for one," Jack said with a grin. "There is no Heaven, at least not in the way humans imagine it. For another, we're not shining examples of goodness here to pass judgment on earth. We are creatures like any other. Some of us are good, some of us less so."

"Are all the Black Knights seraphim? And why do you hide your tattoo?" Val pressed.

"No, not all Knights are seraphim. And I'm not hiding anything," said Jack. "There are simply some things that need to be done in the open and some things that need to be done more quietly. I'm one of the quiet members, you could say. And we're not the Black Knights either, we are White Knights. Black Knight is a slanderous term that's been put on us by our enemies."

"White Knights?" Val narrowed her eyes.

"We White Knights try to keep an eye on our kind. We like to keep our good reputation intact."

"So no Heaven? No Hell? No God, Jesus, or Satan? None of it's real?" asked Val.

"Well, what's real and what's not depends on your point of view, doesn't it?" asked Jack. "Just because you or I haven't personally experienced it, doesn't make something not real. Before today you would've said there was no such thing as seraphim. And now you probably have a different opinion on the matter."

"You're dodging the questions," said Alain.

"Am I?" asked Jack. His smug grin was back. Val wanted to punch it off his face.

She tried a different direction. "Why were you really following me? And don't give me some bullshit about wanting to protect me; I don't believe that for a second. And what does all this have to do with Ruby? And Sutro?"

Jack's expression flickered, his eyes going dark. It was just a moment, there and gone so quickly Val wasn't even sure she'd seen it. But, no, it was definitely there. Then his dazzling smile was back, twice as bright as before.

"Sutro was quite the character. Why do you bring him up?"

The artist's rendering of the Scepter of Sutro flashed in her mind. The thin golden shaft. Right behind it came an image of Ruby at the bar, toying with a finger-thick golden tube. Her good luck charm, she'd called it. Val's mouth went dry.

"I think Sutro might be the reason Ruby was murdered," she whispered.

Jack raised an eyebrow. "What does old Adolph have to do with any of this?"

His face didn't give anything away. Maybe he really didn't know anything about Sutro. Maybe he was only there for her protection. The only thing Val was certain of at this point was that Jack must be a damn fine poker player.

She decided to take a risk and trust him with the truth. She took a deep breath, meeting his ice-blue eyes.

"I think Ruby found something that some very powerful people want to get their hands on."

"And you're saying this thing has something to do with Sutro?"

"Have you heard of the Scepter of Sutro, Jack?" This time, she was sure she saw a slight widening of his eyes.

He realized she'd noticed his reaction and threw her another dazzling smile.

"The Scepter of Sutro," Jack mused. "There's a name I haven't heard in a long time."

"But you have heard of it."

"Of course, who hasn't? It's a popular myth in this city."

"A myth," Val said. "So you don't believe it's real?"

"I've never seen any evidence to suggest that it is," said Jack. "If it was real, I figure it would've turned up by now."

"Maybe it has. Maybe the scepter is the reason Ruby was killed."

Jack's sardonic mask didn't slip this time. He merely raised an eyebrow, encouraging her to go on.

Val told him about the map in Royal Construction's office, and the theory she'd read of the scepter being broken into pieces. When she mentioned Ruby's lucky charm, he pursed his lips, his face growing serious. When she finished, he steepled his fingers and sat staring into space, considering.

Alain broke the silence.

"So you think Royal Construction killed Ruby?"

"It makes sense," Jack said. "Do you know where the sculpture in your community came from?"

"No." Alain's mouth turned down at the edges. "But I do know that Ruby was one of the ones who found it."

Val's golden eyes shone. "There are others?"

"Sure. You don't think Ruby could move that thing by herself, do you? It must weigh five hundred pounds."

"We need to talk to them." She jumped to her feet.

"Oh, come on. We haven't even gotten our food yet," Jack protested.

"You can eat. I've got a murder to solve." She turned and strode toward the door.

Alain and Jack shared a look.

"Is she always this impatient?" Jack asked.

"In my experience, yes." Alain pushed his chair back from the table. "I'm going too. Sorry. Thank you for the drink." He strode off after Val.

"Oh, for fuck's sake," Jack grumbled. He downed the rest of his White Russian and followed them out of the bar.

24

The sea was easy to find in Brooklyn. Turn a corner and it was there, dirty waves rolling up the center of the street, lapping at the buildings. When the sea level rose, the city erected a massive seawall, surrounding itself like some ancient medieval castle. Billions of dollars were poured into protecting one of the greatest cities on earth. It had been a massive undertaking. A marvel of modern times.

But as with everything, making something and sustaining it were very different things. Devastating hurricanes ripped up the coast year after year. Angry waves pounded the wall, undermining the foundations inch by inch, like a prisoner patiently digging an escape tunnel. The seawall was breached and repaired, breached and repaired, again and again. Rebuilding was a constant, exhausting, expensive struggle. It wasn't so much that the city decided to abandon certain neighborhoods as that they eventually just focused their limited resources elsewhere. Like a kid with a sandcastle, they could only fight the waves so long before the sea had its way.

The old warehouse district was one such neighborhood.

Valora didn't realize just how close the sea was to their squat until the rainy season hit. After a week of driving winter rain, she woke one morning to find the floor of the Emerald City covered in cold water.

The air smelled like a freight ship, full of brine and rust and decaying organics. Mister E leaped up onto the top of her cubicle wall and perched indignantly, scowling down at the flood.

She stood in the doorway, unsure what to do. The water lapped against the plywood floor, almost touching her toes.

Amber sloshed by in big yellow rainboots.

"Good morning. Welcome to the rainy season."

Valora peered out at her uncertainly.

"Is it always like this?"

"Depends on the rain. When the sewers get too full to drain, the seawater creeps right in."

"I wondered why my cubicle had a raised wooden floor. Now I know."

"Yup," Amber agreed. She seemed irrationally chipper about the whole thing. "You'll want to raise your mattress up a little more. The water's probably going to get higher."

Valora felt dismayed.

"Higher than this? How will we get in and out? Boats?"

"Don't be so dramatic," Amber laughed. "It's only a couple of inches deep. The deepest I've ever seen it was a foot."

"A foot of water? I didn't realize I'd moved into Atlantis."

"You get what you pay for. Dry land's at a premium these days."

"Obviously. So how do I keep my mattress from getting soaked?"

"Pallets usually work. There are stacks of them in the old freight yard next door. Throw a couple underneath your mattress and you should be fine."

"What about my feet?"

"You need to get some boots." Amber lifted a foot to show off the bright yellow rubber.

Valora scowled. "Where do I get boots?"

"Do I have to do everything for you? Check the storage room. See if you can find a pair that fits."

It turned out there was not a matched pair, but Valora did manage to find two boots that fit, more or less. She sloshed back out with a pink boot on her left foot and a green boot on her right foot. They were ugly, but at least they kept her feet dry.

She sighed. "OK, now for the pallets."

Outside, low clouds brooded over the city. The rain splashed down in fat drops, rippling the flooded street. Brown waves lapped along the curb. The breeze smelled like rust and salt. Valora shivered and pulled her jacket tight, burying her fists in her pockets. She could already feel the water soaking through the shoulders, frigid on the back of her neck. This was not a day for being outside. She needed to get her pallets and get back to the Emerald City before she caught pneumonia.

She hurried down the block toward the freight yard. Rusted-out train cars leaned drunkenly, windows broken and boarded over, their rails overgrown with weeds. Just as Amber had promised, there were stacks of rotting pallets by the loading dock. Valora hurried over and dug through the stack, trying to find one that still seemed sturdy.

A sound froze her in her tracks and made the hair on the back of her neck stand on end. It was a rising, keening sound. As if the wind were singing. She turned her head toward the dark maw of the loading bay. Something moved deep inside, back where the gloomy light didn't reach.

The song tickled her ears, calling to her. It spoke of warm blankets and hot meals. Bathtubs and doors that locked. Unaware she had decided to move, Valora found herself walking toward it. Moving into the darkness.

An indistinct shape swayed in the depths of the loading dock. Dancing to the music. Or was that the singer? Valora's feet moved her forward. She had to find out.

As she got closer, the shape began to pulse. Waves of color lit the darkness. The crumbling walls disappeared around her. The sound of the rain was gone. The cold vanished.

Valora now stood in an open field. The sun was warm on her face. Long grasses tickled her legs. The song floated on the breeze, a lullaby rising and falling, full of strange harmonies that tickled her eardrums.

The singer stood beneath a willow tree at the edge of the field. She was draped in green, and swayed as she sang, her otherworldly voice embracing Valora's mind like a lover. As she moved closer, Valora saw the singer was wrapped in vines of broad-leafed ivy instead of clothing, the foliage as lush and formfitting as a ball gown.

As Valora stepped into the shade beneath the willow, the singer held out her arms. She didn't interrupt her song to speak, but her intention was clear. She wanted to embrace Valora. Hold her close, as no one had since her mother died.

Tears of joy slid down Valora's cheeks as she lifted her arms. Finally, she was home.

She stepped into the singer's embrace.

Cold pierced her spine, spikes of ice driving deep. She gasped, too shocked to draw breath.

Then the pain came.

She tried to scream but found she couldn't move. Couldn't breathe. She was frozen in place. Unable to do anything but watch in horror as the singer began to feed.

A sudden impact knocked her out of the thing's embrace. Her cheek slammed against the wet cement. The singer released an inhuman cry of rage, piercing her like a siren. Valora clamped her hands to her ears, but they did nothing to block the sound. The thing's rage was finger-nails scratching at the inside of her skull. Valora writhed, unable to escape the sound.

Then came a kicked-dog yelp of surprise. The sound changed to one of pain. The singer's wail retreated into the distance.

Valora shivered on the cement as normal sounds returned to the loading dock. Rain drumming on the roof. The wind whistling through broken windows. Her body was cramped and sore, as if she'd just run a gauntlet.

Someone spoke just above her.

"Looks like you've got a lot to learn."

She looked up to find Silvio standing over her, a wooden baseball bat in his fist. He extended his other hand to her. "Come on. Let's get you home."

25

Tracking down shifters was harder than Val expected.

"I thought these were your people?" she grumbled to Alain.

They'd spent the past hour circling the city, following traces of the other shifters who had helped Ruby bring the remains of *The Triumph of Light* into the settlement. Discovering the names of her collaborators was easy. Discovering their current whereabouts was not.

"I believe we have already discussed the phrase lone wolf?" said Alain.

"Sure, but they're not all wolves, are they?"

Alain rolled his eyes at her.

"Of course they aren't. But the maxim still applies. We shifters like our space."

They'd just left a bookstore off Geary, in the inner Richmond district. Shanna worked there on the weekends. But they'd arrived to discover that she'd already finished her shift, leaving them empty-handed once again.

"So now what do we do?" Val said, pulling her jacket tight around her. They were standing on the sidewalk in front of the bookstore, the cold bay wind tearing the fog into streamers around them.

Alain shrugged.

Jack put up his hands. "Don't look at me. I'm just tagging along. You're the one driving this bus."

Tagging along in Jack's case apparently meant following them overhead, where his flying form was obscured by the dark and the fog. He'd swoop down and land in some unobserved spot around the block, then come strolling up as they got off the Ural, grinning as if he'd just performed a party trick. Val supposed he didn't get to unveil his wings to many people, and he was enjoying the chance to show off.

A pale teenager poked her face out of the bookstore.

"Hey, did I hear you're looking for Shanna?"

"Yeah," Val answered. "Do you know where she is?"

"I heard her talking about a party at the old Sutro Baths. You might check there."

"OK, thanks."

The teenager disappeared back inside the shop. Alain nodded.

"That's right, I heard about that. Some kind of equinox gathering, I think."

"Well, what are we waiting for?" Val said. "Looks like we're going to Land's End."

Land's End was precisely what it sounded like. The Outer Richmond district met the sea in a steep cliff face, falling into the embrace of the frigid waves. Adolph Sutro had built an extravagant bath house here on a narrow strip of beach, using an ingenious system of tunnels to bring fresh seawater in and out. It had been a big hit in his day, enticing bathers to make the six-mile trek beyond the western edge of the city, over what was then nothing but barren, windswept dunes. Today the dunes had all been swallowed up by houses and the vast expanse of Golden Gate Park. Sutro's Bath had likewise been transformed. Like so many of Sutro's accomplishments, it had fallen into disrepair in the decades following his death in 1898. In the 1960s it had finally been consumed by a fire, leaving nothing but the blackened foundation to show there was ever anything there at all.

Nowadays it was mostly forgotten, but the little strip of beach was still easily accessible by a short hike down from a parking lot at the top of the cliffs.

Val could see the orange light of the bonfire reflected on the cliff

wall before she saw the flames themselves. The revelers had built a
stack of wooden pallets almost ten feet high. The flames shot into the
air in a roaring pyre. The sound of conversation and music echoed
over the constant roar of the breaking waves. The wind coming in off
the ocean was cold and damp, and Val was glad of the immense heat
kicking off the fire as they reached the bottom of the trail. The crowd
was predominately twenty and thirty somethings, but Val was pleasantly surprised to see a few grey hairs sprinkled here and there,
drinking beers and having animated conversations. One old shirtless
guy was even fire dancing, spinning poi as if they were extensions of
his own flesh and bone. Val watched him for a moment, mesmerized
by the effortless flow of his movements.

They found Shanna by the ruined foundation of the baths. She
wore a long brown cloak, but her shoes were off, and she was dipping
her toes in the freezing water that filled the old burned-out foundation.

Shanna beamed when she saw Val.

"Hey! Nice to see you again!" Her brown eyes caught and held Val's
golden irises.

"Yeah, you too." Val hoped the darkness covered the flush she felt
creeping up her neck.

She tore her eyes away from Shanna's and cleared her throat.

"I understand you were a friend of Ruby's?"

Shanna frowned and sadness entered her gaze. "Yes, she was my
sister."

Val gave Alain a look. "Are all of you related?"

He shrugged his thin shoulders. "Maybe not by blood, but we are
all brothers and sisters."

Val made a face. "No offense, but that sounds a little culty."

"One person's cult is another person's family."

She couldn't tell if he was joking. She decided she didn't want to
know.

"I understand you helped Val bring *The Triumph of Light* sculpture
into your settlement?" she asked.

Shanna nodded. "Yeah, what a monster. Damn thing nearly broke
my back."

"Did you find anything else with it?"

Shanna's expression became guarded. "Like what?"

"A golden rod perhaps?"

Curiosity filled the girl's eyes. "How did you know that?"

Val felt a surge of elation as Shanna confirmed her suspicions.

"What happened to that rod?" Jack stepped forward, his blue eyes blazing.

Shanna stumbled back, caught off guard by his intensity. "I don't know. The last time I saw it, Ruby had it. The rod disappeared when she died."

"Do you know what that rod is?" Jack pressed.

Shanna's smile was sly. "We've got an idea."

"Do you have any idea where it could be now?" Val asked

Shanna shook her head. "No. But"--she leaned forward conspiratorially--"I have a hunch where I might find another piece of the scepter."

All the hairs on Val's body stood on end.

"Can you tell us where it is?" she breathed.

Shanna winked. "I can do better than that. I can show you."

With that, the girl shrugged her shoulders and her cloak fell away. She stood naked in the firelight, her skin all sleek brown flesh and soft curves. Val's jaw hit the floor and Jack's eyebrows were so high she thought his hair was going to eat them. Only Alain seemed unsurprised. Shanna stepped out of her clothes and plunged into the still black water that filled the ruined foundation of the baths.

Val gasped as the frigid water closed over the girl's head.

Alain put out a hand. "It's all right. She'll be fine. "

Long seconds passed and Shanna did not surface. Val stared at the inky surface of the water. How long could the girl hold her breath? That water had to be freezing. Could someone survive in that kind of cold without a wetsuit?

She watched the reflection of the flames dancing on the surface of the water. A single star poked out of the fog, shining brightly for a moment, before being swallowed up once again. The wind gusted and Val shivered, pulling her jacket tight.

"This is ridiculous," she said. "We can't let her drown."

Alain put his hand on her shoulder. "She's not going to drown. We are shifters, remember? Some of us are aquatic."

Val's eyes widened. "Oh! She's a ... what? A fish?"

Alain laughed. "Something like that."

Ten minutes later, Shanna came strolling out of the darkness. Her dark nipples were erect, but her skin was covered with a sleek brown pelt, and she appeared completely unbothered by the cold. She calmly pulled her cloak back over her naked form.

Val gaped at her. "Where did you go?"

"Sutro created tunnels so the baths could be drained, and fresh water brought in from the sea. They're still there. I swam through one of them out into the open sea, and then climbed back up onto the beach over by the cliff."

"Did you find anything?" asked Jack.

Shanna shook her head. "No, but there are several tunnels down there. It's going to take me some time to explore them all."

"And you think there's a piece of the scepter hidden down there in the tunnel somewhere," Jack continued.

Shanna smiled. "I'd bet my life on it. "

Hours passed, and the party ebbed and flowed around them. Shanna made several trips down into the tunnels and back up again, without success.

Despite her heavy leather jacket, Val became chilled in the damp sea breezes. She looked at Jack, standing there with nothing more than a sport jacket.

"Aren't you cold?" she asked.

"Wings are surprisingly good insulators," Jack said with a wink. "Just because you can't see them, doesn't mean they're not wrapped around me right now."

Val laughed. "I'll have to try that sometime."

"You could try it right now if you like." Jack held out his arm, inviting her to step close so he could wrap it around her shoulders.

Val hesitated, but curiosity got the better of her.

"Don't get any ideas. I'm only doing this for the warmth. "

"Wouldn't dream of it," Jack said, smiling his dazzling smile.

As she stepped up beside him, she felt feathers brush against her cheek. Warmth enveloped her as Jack's wing cut off the wind entirely. It felt like he'd wrapped a down comforter around her shoulders.

"That's amazing," she breathed.

"That's only the beginning. You wouldn't believe the things I can do with these wings." Jack leered at her, wiggling his eyebrows.

"And now you've gone and ruined it." Val pushed away from him.

"What did I say?"

"You are entirely too confident, Jack. That's not always a good thing, you know."

Jack put on a wounded pout. "It's not? That's news to me."

Val patted his cheek. "Yes, I can see that it is. Maybe something for you to think about."

She walked away from him and headed for the bonfire to warm herself up properly.

The vibe around the fire was entirely different than it had been in the quiet little corner by the ruined foundation of the baths. Here people were pleasantly drunk and buzzing with conversation. Some roasted marshmallows or hotdogs on sticks, and bouts of laughter were frequent. Faces were ruddy from the heat of the flames and the bite of the wind.

The bonfire felt amazing. Val closed her eyes, soaking it in, feeling the heat seep beneath skin and muscle, warming her bones layer by layer. She hadn't realized how cold she really was until she started to thaw out. Her fingers and toes tingled painfully.

"Geez," she muttered to herself. "I didn't know you could get frost-bite from sea breezes."

"*Only in San Francisco,*" said Mister E, appearing on her shoulder. "*As Mark Twain once said, 'The coldest winter I ever spent was summer in San Francisco.'*"

"Where do you go when you disappear like that anyway?" Val asked him.

"*I don't go anywhere,*" he said. "*I am like your new friend's wings. Now you see me, now you don't. Just because I may be a grin without a cat, that doesn't mean the cat isn't still around.*" He blew lazy smoke rings at the fire to emphasize this point. Val rolled her eyes. He enjoyed playing the Cheshire Cat entirely too much.

Her eyes flipped around the fire from face to face. She wondered how many of these people were normies who had no idea that the person they were flirting with might in fact be a monster. Then her eyes lit upon a familiar middle-aged balding face, and she shuddered despite the heat of the bonfire.

What the hell was Edward Hopkins doing there?

The sharp-suited man hadn't noticed her, and she studied him quietly. He had crow's feet at the corners of his eyes and jowls under his chin. His bald scalp gleamed in the firelight. If he was a seraphim, why wasn't he gorgeous like Jack? Was the beauty of all angels just another myth? She watched him glance off into the darkness, then he turned and walked towards the shoreline.

Val followed him. Jack had assured her that Edward wasn't the killer, but Val wasn't convinced. He was still the person with the clearest motive and opportunity in her book. And he was definitely a violent asshole.

Pebbles crunched underfoot. Spray from the waves filled the air. As her eyes adjusted to the darkness, she stopped. Edward was nowhere to be found. The night had swallowed him whole.

"Fog spit," she whispered. Then a thought occurred to her. "I wonder if they can make their whole bodies disappear, not just their wings? Mister E? Do you know?"

The cat did not appear, but his voice whispered in her ear, "*It wouldn't surprise me. It's no more difficult to glamour your entire body than it is to glamour a part of you. In fact, I'd say it's more difficult to only glamour part of you. The specificity requires a certain degree of skill.*"

"Great," Val whispered. "So he could be standing right in front of me, watching me, and I wouldn't even know it? "

"*Yes, he could,*" Mr. E sounded pleased with the idea, almost as if he were laughing at her. "*Being invisible has all kinds of perks.*" He was definitely laughing at her.

Val scanned the shoreline nervously, making sure she hadn't simply overlooked Edward in her haste. No, the beach was empty. Reluctantly, she turned to go back to the fire. Halfway there she changed her mind and returned to the ruined foundations of the bath instead, where Alain still stood, watching the silent water.

"Anything yet?" she asked.

Alain shook his head. "No. I haven't seen her for almost thirty minutes."

"What about Jack?"

"I haven't seen him either. He wandered off right after you did. He's probably around here somewhere."

"He's probably charming the pants off some college girl," Val grumbled.

Alain looked at her out of the corner of his eye. "What's going on with the two of you anyway?"

"Nothing is going on with us."

"Uh-huh." The corner of Alain's mouth quirked up. "You keep telling yourself that."

Val glared at him.

"You don't know what you're talking about. There's nothing going on with me and Jack. Besides, how do you know I even like boys. Maybe I've got a crush on Shanna."

Alain laughed. "Well, she certainly has a crush on you. But something tells me it's not reciprocated."

"You don't know. I think she's kind of cute."

"Yes, but I'm not sure that cute is your type."

"Are you saying I'm not cute?"

Alain held up his hands. "I didn't say that. Don't go putting words in my mouth."

Their heads jerked up as a scream pierced the night. Val and Alain whirled toward the shoreline, peering in the direction of the sound. As one, they took off running.

26

They found Jack kneeling beside the waterline with a young woman standing over him. She was the source of the screaming.

As they got closer, they saw that Jack was bent over a dark shape lying on the wet sand. It wasn't until they were standing beside him that the shape finally resolved out of the darkness. It was Shanna.

The girl lay curled on her side, waves lapping against her bare feet, head pillowed on the sand, almost as if she were napping. Brown fur covered her sleek and round body like she'd paused mid-transformation. But the dark tangle of her intestines told another story, twisted and dark on the pebbled beach, stretching away from her like ropes of seaweed thrown up by the tide.

She'd been disemboweled. Just like Ruby.

More screaming filled the air, and it took Val a minute to realize it was her. She was kneeling on the sand beside Shanna, beating her fists against the wet sand. Unlike the other woman's, Val's screams were not screams of sorrow or horror. Hers were pure rage.

"He was here. That motherfucker was here!"

She whirled on Jack, her golden eyes shining like lamps. The seraphim's blue eyes were subdued by contrast. Downturned.

"Jack, Edward Hopkins was here. He used a glamour to turn invisible. He might still be nearby. Can you see him? Can you find him?"

Jack started at Edward's name, his head snapping up. He peered sharply around the beach, jaw set with suspicion. Then he sighed and shook his head.

"No. I don't see him. Not even a hint of glamour. If he was here, he's fled."

Alain was kneeling beside Shanna's head, stroking her wet fur.

"Alain, is she still alive?" Val asked. It was an absurd thought, but the way he touched her was so gentle it gave Val hope.

Alain's soft words killed it.

"No. She is gone." He bent and kissed Shanna on the forehead, then gently closed her eyes. "My poor, sweet sister."

"Motherfucker," Val hissed. "We were right here. This asshole's got balls."

"He is arrogant," Alain said. "He believes he has nothing to fear from us. He thinks we cannot touch him."

"Oh, I'm going to touch him all right. I'm going to rip his wings off and shove them up his ass one feather at a time."

Alain's eyes widened at her words, then he set his jaw and nodded. "She will be avenged. Both of my sisters will be avenged."

Val started to pace.

"Jack, were you the one who found her?"

The seraphim shook his head. "No, she did." He indicated the distraught young woman. "I came running when I heard her scream."

Val turned her attention to the woman. She was young, average height, maybe twenty years old. Her choppy brown hair was shoulder length, except for a single long bead-strung dreadlock behind her left ear. She had her arms wrapped around herself and her teeth were chattering. Val didn't know whether that was from cold or shock. Either way, she took off her jacket and draped it over the woman's shoulders.

"Hi, I'm Val. What's your name?"

"M... Marie," the woman stammered.

"OK, Marie, can you tell me what happened here?"

"I... I don't know."

"Just tell me what you saw. What were you doing right before this?"

"I was... I was over there. By the tidepools. There were glowing jellyfish. Blue and green." The woman's pupils were dilated, her responses sluggish. Either she was in shock or on drugs. Maybe both.

"OK. And then what happened?"

"I saw something blue on the beach. I thought it was more jellyfish. When I got closer, I saw it was a man with... with blue wings."

Val raised her eyebrows, glancing at Jack. He looked as surprised as she was.

"That shouldn't be possible," he said. "Nobody can see through a glamour."

Val turned back to Marie.

"And then what happened?"

"The man was struggling with something on the shore. I thought it was a fish, or a seal. Then I saw her stand up and realized it was a woman. She was holding something shiny. Something gold. Then a knife flashed and the woman fell. I yelled." Marie hugged herself tighter. "The man looked at me. His eyes were glowing. Blue like his wings. Then he just... vanished."

"Could you describe him? Was he dressed in a sharp suit? Balding?" Val asked.

Marie shook her head.

"I don't know. It was dark. All I could see were those eyes. Glowing." She focused on Val and jerked back, as if really seeing her for the first time. Her gaze took in Alain and Jack as well. "Like yours! Your eyes are glowing gold! And his are blue! What the fuck are you people?"

"Take it easy, we're here to help. We're not going to hurt you," Val placed a hand on Marie's shoulder.

"No! Get the fuck away from me! Help!" Marie screamed and spun away, leaving Val holding her jacket as the terrified young woman sprinted toward the bonfire.

More people were heading their way now. Dark silhouettes against the flames. Val saw the flash of a phone. The murmur of a man calling 911.

She looked at Alain and Jack.

"The cops will be here soon. You guys can get out of here. I'll stick around and deal with them."

Jack nodded, his chiseled face hard. "I'll see if I can track down Edward."

"I will come with you," Alain said.

"No. I can cover more ground by myself." Jack leaped into the air and disappeared, his glamour covering all but the sound of massive wings.

Alain scowled and looked at Val.

"You sure you do not want company?"

She shook her head and sighed. "No. It's going to be the same mind-numbing bullshit I went through after Ruby's death. Hours of pointless questions."

"Why stick around then? Why not leave?"

"Because somebody should be here for Shanna."

Alain's lean face drooped. His eyes fell on his sister's body. "Yes. You are right, of course."

Val lowered her voice.

"You heard what Marie said? About Shanna holding something golden?"

Alain nodded. "You think she found what she was looking for."

"And Edward killed her for it," Val finished. "Go ask around your village. There must be others who were working with Ruby and Shanna. See if you can find out anything else about the scepter. About where the other pieces might be hidden. Finding them is our best chance to catch our killer."

"OK. I'll see you tomorrow then?"

"If I can," Val scrubbed her hands over her face, suddenly bone-tired. "The cops might keep me overnight again. And I have to work tomorrow. I'll be in touch when I can."

"Right."

Alain strode away, a lean shadow against dark sand. Thirty yards farther, his outline shifted, becoming lower to the ground. Val watched him accelerate, shooting forward, a dark blur as four legs propelled him into the night.

She turned to face the fire and saw that revolving red and blue lights were already reflecting off the trees at the top of the cliff. Policemen with flashlights were picking their way down the trail.

Val shoved her hands in her pockets and pulled her jacket close against the biting wind.

27

S ilvio sat Valora down in the Emerald City's old office to clean up her wounds.

"Ow, that stings," she said.

"Such a baby," he mocked. "It's just hydrogen peroxide."

"It still stings," Valora insisted.

Silvio raised her hand to his lips and kissed her scraped knuckles. Valora jerked her hand away.

"What are you doing?"

"Kissing it better. Didn't your mom ever do that?"

"No, and I don't want you doing it either."

"Suit yourself." He smirked at her, his eyes twinkling with mischief.

Valora felt something inside her perk up at the look, a tiny flutter of butterfly wings in her stomach.

She pushed the feeling away with irritation. Her walls were high for a reason.

"Don't touch me."

"Why? What will happen if I do?"

"Trust me, it's for your own good. People get hurt if they get too close to me."

"Maybe I like living dangerously."

"It's not funny. You don't know what I've done."

Silvio's face turned serious.

"Hey, look at me. Look at my eyes. Everyone here has done things they wish they could take back. Do you think manifesting magical powers doesn't have consequences? A lot of the people in this warehouse have hurt people inadvertently. It's OK, you're among friends now."

Valora wanted to believe him, but she couldn't quite bring herself to do it. She'd spent too many years building up her defenses. Pushing everyone away. It was safer that way.

She shook her head. "Not like I have. You don't know what you're talking about."

"It takes time. You'll see." Silvio's mouth quirked. "Now, as payment for your rescue, I've got a job for you. Come with me."

He led her out the back door of the warehouse. On the high side of the yard, where the floodwaters didn't reach, there was a slumping stack of rotting pallets beneath a patched-together tin roof.

"Pallets, this is Valora. Valora, these are the pallets," Sylvia said with mock formality. "Now that everyone's gotten to know each other..." He handed her an ax. "Valora, chop up some pallets for me."

She eyed them dubiously. "Chop them up how?"

"In pieces, of course. How do you usually chop things?"

"I don't usually chop things. I don't think I've ever chopped anything in my life."

As the words left her mouth, she realized that wasn't true. A long-forgotten memory surfaced: Valora as a very young girl, trying to swing an ax as big as she was, while her father stood behind her and laughed. She remembered the smell of the pine, and the warm sun on the top of her head. It had been at her original home, in the little village in the mountains. Before she met Mister E. Before her mother died. Before her life changed forever.

When she didn't move, Silvio rolled his eyes and took the ax.

"Here, I'll show you."

He pulled one of the pallets off the stack and laid it on the gravel. He hefted the ax and swung it down in a clean arc. It hit the wood with a satisfying thwack.

"See? You pull it up over one shoulder like this. As you swing it down, let your hands slide down the shaft." He demonstrated again, this time cleaving completely through one of the slats.

He handed the ax to Valora. "Now you try."

Valora hesitantly hefted the ax. She was conscious of Silvio's eyes on her, and the ghostly eyes of her father in her memory. She could feel emotion welling up, and she gritted her teeth, swallowing it down. She was not going to cry. Not in front of this boy. Not in front of anyone.

She swung the ax. Though it didn't cut as deeply or cleanly as Silvio's cut had, it did at least hit the pallet, taking out a satisfying chunk of wood.

"Good. Now just keep doing that until that entire pallet is cut into pieces that will fit inside the fire ring." Silvio indicated a cut-down fifty-five-gallon drum and turned to go back inside.

"What are you going to do?" Valora called.

Silvio's answer carried a smile.

"I'm going to tune my guitar."

That evening they all gathered around the ring, sitting on empty milk crates and boxes. The fire was lovely, crackling and dry and warm. Paula even brought a package of hotdogs. They stuck them on the ends of sticks and roasted them over the fire, eating them charred and bubbling. Only Amber didn't partake.

"You don't want one?" asked Valora.

Amber shuddered. "God, no. You don't want to know what's inside those things."

"No, we definitely do not," Silvio laughed. He started strumming his guitar to drown out whatever Amber was about to say next.

The music was sweet and good. Silvio really knew how to play. He didn't just strum the melody, he added little flourishes too. Valora was impressed. She hadn't seen many people play music live in her life, and nobody who was any good.

He played a few songs to get warmed up, and then he started taking requests. Paula and the others shouted out the names of songs.

Apparently this was a common occurrence at the Emerald City, and everyone seemed to have their favorites.

Valora stayed silent, listening and watching with wide eyes.

Silvio sang on some songs, and on others he only played accompaniment while the others took their turns singing. Paula had a rich alto voice, and a fondness for sixties protest songs. Amber was a lovely soprano, and when she opened her mouth Valora thought it was like the heavens were smiling down upon them.

Paula noticed Valora's expression and leaned close to whisper in her ear.

"She used to be an opera singer. You should hear her when she really gets going."

Valora shook her head in amazement. If this was Amber not even going, she couldn't imagine what she sounded like when she sang for real.

Silvio's and Amber's eyes met as they performed, sparkling with some kind of secret musical chemistry. Valora's gut tightened with jealousy.

She pushed it away angrily. There was nothing between her and Silvio. She didn't even want there to be anything between her and Silvio. If there was something going on between him and Amber, that was their business.

She told herself these things, but she couldn't quite make herself believe them. The rest of the night her eyes flipped from Silvio to Amber, watching and weighing, trying to decode signs and body language. She never saw the look resurface when Amber wasn't singing, and after a while she almost convinced herself that she'd imagined it.

28

The quality of the coffee at the Tenderloin Station hadn't improved since Val's last visit. Detective Chen's mood, on the other hand, had gotten noticeably worse.

He sat across the examination table from her, tapping the end of his pen on his old-fashioned paper notepad. He stared at her, unblinking, eyes red and swollen from lack of sleep.

"This is the second time you've gotten me out of bed this week," he said. "It's also the second time you've brought me a dead body. I'm not a fan of this trend."

"Join the club," said Val.

She took a sip of the coffee and grimaced. It was four a.m., and she'd been sitting in the station for hours, as predicted. At least the cops had been nice enough to let her ride the Ural to the station, instead of taking her in one of their squad cars. She suspected they wouldn't be so nice a third time.

She really hoped there wasn't a third time.

"It's a pretty amazing coincidence, you being at the scene of both murders. Don't you think?" asked Chen. His eyes never wavered.

"That's one word for it," said Val. "Imagine how I feel. Usually I can go years without seeing a disemboweled body. This past week has given me nightmare fuel for the next decade."

"Yeah. So tell me again why you were on that beach."

Val sighed and took another sip of coffee. She'd already told her story half a dozen times, and she'd probably have to tell it half a dozen more before they let her go home. Cops didn't believe in coincidences. Her being present at two murder scenes made her suspect number one in their book. If she didn't cooperate, they'd put her in cuffs and throw her in a cell on general principles.

"I was there with a friend. He brought me there to introduce me to Shanna."

"Shanna was the victim?"

"Yes, Shanna was the victim."

"The report says her body was covered with fur. Which means she was a ... what?"

"A shifter."

"A shifter," Chen repeated, his mouth twisting sourly. He cracked his neck. "You know, my life was a lot simpler before the world was full of monsters."

"Yours and mine both."

Chen made a note in his notebook.

"Why were you going to meet her?"

"She was a friend of Ruby's. I was trying to find any clues that might lead me to Ruby's killer."

"See, that's the part that gets me right there," said Chen. "What the hell do you think you were doing investigating a murder on your own? I could book you on obstruction charges for interfering with an ongoing investigation."

"She was my friend, Detective." Val glared at the man. "No disrespect, but I know you've got a lot on your plate. And Ruby was just a stripper. I doubt your department is dedicating all of its resources to solving her murder."

Chen leaned forward in his chair. "Solving murders is my job, Miss Keri. I don't like your insinuation."

"Like I said, no disrespect intended, Detective." Val rubbed her temples. She could feel a headache coming on. Probably the combination of stress, lack of sleep, and police-station coffee. "I just know you have a lot on your plate, and I have a personal interest in seeing this asshole brought to justice. I thought maybe I could help."

"A noble impulse, Miss Keri. But misguided. I suggest you stick to pouring drinks."

"Your suggestion is noted, Detective. I'll take it under consideration."

"See that you do. Because if I find you near another murder scene, I'm gonna throw your ass in a cell on general principle. Is that clear?"

"Clear as an unmuddied lake, sir."

Chen snorted. "Get the fuck out of my station, Keri. Go home. Get some sleep. And leave the investigating to the professionals."

"Yes, sir."

Chen held the door for her while she exited the examination room. When she was five steps down the hall he said, "Keri."

Val stopped. Half turned back to him.

"Yes, sir?"

"You're not the only one that can quote *A Clockwork Orange*. You're not as clever as you think you are. Now get out of here. "

"Yes sir. I'll keep that in mind the next time I'm in the mood for some ultraviolence."

Chen waved her away.

She woke the next afternoon to a text from Alain.

"I may have some useful news for you. Can you meet me at the taco stand?"

Val cursed. She hadn't even had her coffee yet.

"Sure," she replied. "Give me thirty minutes."

On the way to the bathroom, she noticed that Julie's boxes were gone from the hallway. Val poked her head inside Julie's bedroom. It was empty, but filthy, with packing peanuts drifting like snow and dust bunnies the size of hamsters gathered in every corner.

"Thanks for cleaning up on the way out, Julie."

A glance at the calendar told her she only had ten days left to fill the room if she didn't want to be on the hook for the rent herself.

"Right. Clean out the bedroom. Post an ad. Interview prospective roommates. Oh, and find the Scepter of Sutro and Ruby's murderer in my spare time." Val ground her knuckles into her eye sockets. "Fuck my life."

A short time later, she found Alain in the same spot as before, and plopped down on the wooden bench opposite him. She raised her eyebrows at the contents of his paper plate.

"Two burritos again? Don't you ever eat anything else?"

"Not if I can help it." Alain patted his stomach with satisfaction. "This is ninety-nine percent burrito."

"And you're proud of that? I really hope you don't have a girlfriend."

"And why is that?"

"Did you ever see the movie *Blazing Saddles*?"

"No, should I have?"

"There's a famous scene in there, where all the men are sitting around a campfire eating beans and farting. I'm pretty sure the same thing applies to burritos. I think your diet is hazardous to the air quality in this city."

Alain chuckled. "Your opinion has been noted."

Val leaned back in her chair. "So, what do you have for me?"

Alain lowered his voice. "I talked to some friends of Shanna's. You were right. Ruby and Shanna weren't the only ones involved."

"What did you find out?"

"There are supposed to be six pieces of the Scepter of Sutro. Two are sitting in a museum in Golden Gate Park. Have been for years. Ruby found one piece of the scepter inside *The Triumph of Light*. Shanna must have found another beneath the Sutro Baths. We can assume the killer got both of those."

"That means there are two more out there."

Alain put a finger on the side of his nose. "Bingo."

"Do your friends have any idea where?"

"According to legend, Sutro hid them in six places that bear his name. That is, six places that bore his name when he was alive."

"Meaning some of them no longer do."

"Exactly. "

"So how do we find them? I'm sure the killer is after them as well. If we want to catch him, finding those pieces before he does seems like our best bet."

"And why would that be?"

Val smiled. "Haven't you ever baited a mouse trap? First you have to have something the mouse wants."

She pulled a map out of her pocket. On it were six red circles, drawn roughly over the locations she recalled seeing in the Royal Construction office. They both leaned over the paper.

"So pieces have been found in *The Triumph of Light* and the Sutro Baths. Here and here." Val drew a red "X" over each of those locations.

"Mark off the Sutro Library and Sutro Heights too. That's where they found the pieces that are in the museum."

"OK. That leaves us with two left. Mount Sutro and The Cliff House." Val marked off the indicated spots on the map, then squinted up at the sun. "Unfortunately, I've got to get to work soon. I don't have time to go exploring today."

"Don't worry, I'll go take a look around," Alain said. "I'll let you know if I find anything."

"Be careful. That seraphim is dangerous."

Alain smiled, baring his canines in a wolfish snarl.

"That's OK. So am I."

29

Being at the Alley Cat felt wrong. Val kept catching herself staring at the door. She should be out there, helping Alain find the missing pieces of the scepter, not in here pouring drinks for assholes.

"Are you OK?" Lisa slid a rack of glasses onto the shelf underneath the bar. "You seem kind of out of it tonight."

Great. Lisa was known for being in her own world. If Lisa was noticing, Val's distraction must be really obvious.

She forced herself to smile. "I'm fine, thanks."

Lisa tucked her hair behind her ear with one hand. As usual, she was dressed in an old-school athletic jersey and skinny black jeans. She looked like a strong wind would blow her away.

"OK. But I've got some go juice if you need a little pick-me-up."

"Go juice?"

"It's something my roommate brews up. It's got green tea, kombucha, cayenne pepper, garlic, apple cider vinegar, turmeric, and a bunch of other stuff. It really gets your blood pumping."

Val tried not to make a face.

"Sounds interesting. I'll keep it in mind. Thanks."

"Anytime." Lisa drifted off through the kitchen door.

Val sighed and scanned the crowd again. It wasn't even mid-shift yet, and time was really dragging tonight. An irrational part of her brain kept hoping Edward Hopkins would simply walk in the door and solve all her problems. Her hands tightened to fists at the thought of him. If she caught that creep alone, there might not be much of him left for Chen to arrest.

If she hadn't thrown him out of the club that night, would Ruby still be alive? Could all this have been avoided if she'd kept her temper in check?

No. She had to remind herself that Edward was already after Ruby. He had her alone in the supply closet. He was probably intending to murder her all along.

A memory of Ruby's broken body flashed in her mind. Intestines unspooling over the asphalt.

Val shuddered and cleaned some glasses, trying to banish the images with work. But they wouldn't stay away. Nor would the nagging guilt.

She noticed a table watching her from across the room. Two boys and a girl. They looked like club kids, all shiny fabric and high-tech jewelry. Not the Alley Cat's usual clientele.

One of them looked familiar.

It took her a minute, but then she had it. The receptionist from Royal Construction. The girl with the black glasses.

She started to make her way around the bar to see what they wanted, but a man waved a credit card at her and she had to stop and make a pair of Bloody Marys first. A flurry of customers came in just then, and half an hour flew by before Val had a chance to breathe.

When she looked over at the table again, the club kids were gone.

She sighed and ground the heels of her hands into her eyes. Wonderful. Now she had vampires watching her. As if she didn't have enough to worry about already.

"Are you OK? I've got some aspirin if you have a headache."

She opened her eyes to find Jack sitting at the bar. He looked as perfect as ever, all blue eyes and chiseled jaw and careless blond curls. He quirked an eyebrow at her.

"No, I'm fine, Jack. Thanks."

"You don't look fine. You look like a shit sandwich."

"You say the sweetest things."

"Not an insult, just a comment. I'd still like to take a bite of you, if it makes you feel any better."

Now she laughed. This was the Jack she was used to.

"Mmmmm. Shit sandwich. Makes me hungry just thinking about it." She straightened and put on her professional smile. "What can I get you, Jack?"

He looked hurt. "You have to ask?"

"No, but it's my job to ask, remember? One White Russian coming up."

As she slid the cocktail across the bar, she leaned toward him and lowered her voice.

"Did you find out anything about our friend?"

"You mean Edward?"

"Of course I mean Edward. Who the fuck else would I mean? Has someone else been killing my friends this week?"

"Easy, Tiger." Jack put a hand on top of hers. His skin was soft and unusually hot, like he had magma running through his veins.

Val jerked away. "Don't touch me."

He raised his palms. "Hey, sorry. I didn't mean to offend you."

"It's not you, Jack. I just don't like to be touched, that's all."

He arched his eyebrows. "That must make it hard to get laid."

"You have no idea."

The truth was, Val hadn't gotten laid in over a year. She'd almost given up on it. Her emotional walls were too thick, and the cost of letting someone through them was too high. She'd tried a couple of one-night stands, but sex as a merely physical act felt pointless. It always left her feeling lonelier than she'd been to begin with. Her body might have needs, but that's why they made vibrators. She didn't need contact with another human to scratch her biological itch.

Jack was the first person who had tempted her in that way in a long time. And he came with his own complications. Like the fact that he wasn't human.

"Tell me about the seraphim," she said.

"What do you want to know?"

"I don't know. How many of you are there? Where do you live? Do you just have wings, or do you have other powers?"

"All right, I get the picture." Jack took a thoughtful sip of his White Russian. "Well, I'm not allowed to tell you much. We like our secrets, and I'd be in serious trouble with the council if I told them all to you."

"Come on, Jack. You've got to give me something. Especially if I'm going to confront Edward. I need to be prepared. I need to know what he can do."

Jack's face hardened.

"You need to stay out of it. We seraphim handle our own business."

"I can't do that, Jack."

"Yes, you can. And you will."

"Oh, will I?" Val glared back at him. "What, are you my father now? I've got news for you, pretty boy. I don't take orders from you. My friend was killed in the alley behind this bar, and I'm not going to stop until I bring her killer to justice. And there's nothing you or anyone else can do about it."

The air sizzled between them. Neither looked away.

Finally, Jack grunted and sipped his drink. "You can't possibly bring down Edward by yourself. I'm trying to keep you from getting hurt."

"I'm stronger than I look, Jack. I can take care of myself."

"With your magic?"

Her eyes narrowed. "What do you know about my magic? "

Jack shrugged. "I know that you have it. I don't know many specifics yet, but I can see the power shining beneath your skin. Why do you think I wanted you to go out with me?"

There was a lot to unpack with that, and Val felt several conflicting emotions at once. First, she felt fear. She guarded her secrets closely, and the idea that someone could discover her magic just by looking at her freaked her out more than a little. Second, she felt disappointment. Jack had only wanted to go out with her because of her magic. He wasn't actually attracted to her. Even given her personal issues with relationships, it was still nice to feel like you were wanted. Jack hadn't actually wanted her at all. He only wanted her magic.

"I don't think this is something we should talk about here," Val said.

Jack made a show of glancing around. "We're in a strip club, Val.

Have you noticed how loud the music is? Pretty sure nobody's going to overhear us."

"All the same, my secrets are my own."

"That's not fair. I showed you mine. Don't you think you should show me yours?" Jack's gaze smoldered.

Heat rose up her neck.

"I'm not going to play your little quid-pro-quo game, Jack. I never agreed to share anything with you. If you were looking for reciprocation, you should've made the agreement ahead of time."

Jack's gaze darkened, and for a second he almost looked angry. There was a hunger in his eyes that made Val uncomfortable.

"Oh, I see how it is. Other people can tell you their secrets, but you keep your own."

"I'm a bartender, Jack. That's the way it is. People come in and tell me their troubles. I don't tell them mine."

A customer flagged her down from the other end of the bar, giving her an excuse to walk away. When she looked back a few minutes later, Jack was gone.

The rest of the night passed uneventfully, except for a brief period around midnight, when Vasilevski came in with his crew. The gangster eyed her warily when she approached the table with their shots, probably remembering the drink she'd spilled on him the last time he came in. He didn't say anything, though, and she delivered the drinks without incident. Tommy Walker came down to their table as soon as they arrived. There was definitely something going on there. But Val didn't have attention to spare at the moment. She needed to find Edward, or the missing pieces of the Scepter of Sutro. Or both. Preferably before anyone else got murdered.

It was foggy and cold when she got off her shift, and it had been a long night. Despite that, Val wasn't tired. Her brain was racing, trying to fit all the pieces together. What did Edward really want? What did the Scepter of Sutro do? And how did Jack fit in? Was he only interested in Val because of her magic? Was he acting alone, or was he keeping tabs on her for the seraphim? Could she really trust him?

Her thoughts went around in circles as she crossed the Van Ness bridge over the chasm. There were few other vehicles out this time of night, and the streets were quiet and empty. In other conditions, she might not have noticed the fleet, silent shadows tailing her across the bridge. Not that she could hear anything over the roar of the Ural. But they looked silent anyway.

She kept an eye on them in her rearview mirror as she turned onto Fourteenth. There were three of them, on foot. But they were moving as quickly as she was on the Ural. Probably not human then. Great. Just what she needed, more supernatural complications.

Never one to run from a fight, Val pulled into a narrow alley between two buildings. Halfway down, she stopped and parked the Ural sideways, blocking the road. The shadows hesitated when they saw her waiting for them. She clicked off the ignition and climbed off the motorcycle. She stood with her hands at her sides, relaxed but ready for anything.

"*You're attracting admirers by the bushel these days,*" said Mister E. He yawned and stretched inside the sidecar, showing no inclination to get out and join the fun.

"Must be my charming personality."

The shadows had halted, conferring amongst themselves. Apparently they reached some decision, because they began to glide toward her. Val could tell from their silhouettes that they were young and thin: teenagers or in their early twenties at the most. Despite that, they gave her an impression of strength and age.

As they got closer, she understood why.

It was the three vampires who had been watching her at the Alley Cat. The club kids. Two boys and a girl. Their high-tech jewelry flashed, thin strings of lights flowing around their necks and limbs.

Val sighed. Just what she needed, more complications.

"Why are you following me? What do you want?"

The trio seemed taken aback at her aggressive tone. They fanned out, the boys flanking to either side of her, while the receptionist girl stayed in the center. Hillary Linscomb. She wore silver pants and a tight silk shirt that glowed like it was spun from moonlight. Her hair was pinned up in little twists and orange light spiraled around her right ear. She strode to Val, chin raised, trying to act unafraid.

"Ms. Pearl would like a word with you," she said.

"Another one? She assured me she didn't know anything about what I wanted to know. Has that changed?"

Hillary shrugged, an unselfconscious, feline gesture. "I'm just the messenger. She doesn't pay me enough to know such things. My job is merely to make sure that you comply."

Val reassessed the girl. Gone was the mousy, frightened thing from the office. Out here, away from the overwhelming presence of Ms. Pearl, Hillary was cool and in control. Comfortable in her own skin. Powerful.

"And if I don't?"

The girl smiled, revealing gleaming fangs.

"We were instructed to bring you by force if necessary. It doesn't make any difference to us."

Val considered the girl and her companions. They were vampires, which meant they were stronger and faster than they looked. She might be able to take one of them in a fight. Two if she was extremely lucky. But all three together? No chance.

She smiled tightly. "I guess I don't have a choice then. Will you pledge my safe passage?"

"If you offer no aggression, you will not be harmed," Hillary said formally. "I give you my pledge."

"All right." Val relaxed a fraction. Vampires were very formal. If they gave you their word, they would keep it. "Offer no aggression" still gave them some wiggle room, but that was probably as good as she was going to get. "Where and when?"

"The when is now. The where, I must show you. If you'll follow me?"

"On foot?"

The girl laughed. "On foot if you like, but I doubt you'll be able to keep up with us. I suggest you ride your motorcycle."

With that she bowed and turned on her heel.

Val kicked the Ural back to life. It was a good thing she hadn't been feeling tired. It looked like she had another long night ahead.

30

"This city is full of dangers. You need to learn how to fight." Silvio leaned against the doorway, standing nearly ankle deep in the brackish water flooding the warehouse. His sneakers were soaked, but he didn't seem to notice.

"I know how to fight," Valora said. She straightened the futon on top of the new pallets. Her bed was now over a foot above the water. Hopefully, it would be enough.

"Do you? Show me."

"What do you mean? Do you want me to hit you or something?"

"Or something." Silvio grinned. "Come up to the second floor with me. Let's see what you've got."

Valora rolled her eyes. "Fine."

"*This should be fun,*" said Mister E. He leaped to the top of her shoulder, his claws pricking her skin.

Valora followed Silvio up a set of creaking wooden stairs.

"What was that thing that attacked me anyway?" she asked.

"We call her the Siren."

"Like a fire alarm?"

"No, like the women from Greek mythology. They would stand on the rocks and lure sailors to their deaths with their song."

Valora digested this.

"So she's Greek?"

"No. Well, maybe she is. I don't actually know. That's not the point. We call her the Siren because she lures people in with her song."

"Then you've seen her before?"

"Once or twice. She moves around the city a lot. I haven't seen her in this neighborhood in months."

"Are there others like her?"

Silvio waggled his head and leaned on the rusty metal railing, looking out over the floor of the warehouse. "Could be. It's hard to say. Even if she's the only siren, there are plenty of other nasties you need to watch out for."

"Such as?"

"That's a long conversation for another time. Right now, let's see how well you can defend yourself." He reached out and grabbed her arm, twisting it behind her back, holding her helpless. Mister E abandoned Valora's shoulder for the security of the metal railing. "Hmmm, not very well."

"That's not fair. I wasn't ready!"

"Do you think the monsters are going to wait until you're ready?" Silvio released her and she stepped away from him, scowling and rubbing her shoulder. He smirked at her. "Are you ready now?"

Valora eyed him warily.

"What are you going to do if I say yes?"

"Say it and find out."

She brought her hands up to a guard position, her tongue flicking nervously over her lips.

"OK. I'm ready."

Silvio moved fast, lunging forward to grab her arm again. Valora yelped and batted his hand away, stepping back out of his reach. But he kept coming forward, forcing her to retreat again. She caught her heel on the rough boards and fell hard on her ass, skinning her palm.

"Ow, shit. I got a splinter."

"If that's all you get when a monster attacks, you'll be lucky." Silvio offered her a hand up. She winced as he pulled her to her feet.

"OK, you've made your point. I need to learn to defend myself better. So how do I do that?"

"I'll teach you."

Valora squinted at him. "What makes you qualified to be a teacher?"

"I've got black belts in jiu-jitsu, taekwondo, and aikido." He laughed at her astonished expression. "I wasn't always a mage on the run, you know."

"So you've got magic too?"

"Of course. Everyone in the Emerald City does. It's what binds us together."

"What kind of magic can you do?"

Silvio looked away, his cheeks reddening.

"It's not that impressive."

"Are you kidding? We're talking about magic, Silvio. It's all impressive."

"Not my magic."

"What is it? Tell me. Better yet, show me."

He shook his head. "That's not what we're here for. I'm supposed to be teaching you to fight."

"Show me some magic and then you can teach me to fight. Come on. Please?"

Silvio sighed and pushed his hair out of his face with one hand. "Fine. But don't say I didn't warn you."

He sat down on the weathered planking and crossed his legs. His face scrunched up in concentration.

Nothing happened at first. Then Valora jumped as a roach scuttled across the floor and hid beneath Silvio's knee. It was followed a few seconds later by another roach. And another. Soon, Silvio had dozens of roaches circling around him like he was their own private maypole.

His brows drew together in concentration. The roaches started moving in unison, forming straight lines on the floor. She realized they were making letters. V - A - L.

Valora burst out laughing. "You can control roaches?"

Silvio's eyes opened, and his blush rose all the way to his hairline.

Val thought it was adorable. He studied his shoes as the roaches scattered, running back to wherever they had come from.

"Yeah. I told you it wasn't impressive."

Valora felt bad for laughing.

"No, it's cool! It just caught me by surprise is all. I mean, I can see how controlling roaches could be useful."

"Oh yeah? How?" Silvio challenged.

"Um... I mean... Well, it's your magic. Why don't you tell me? They've got to be able to do more than make letters, right?"

"They are really good at sniffing out food," he conceded. "Though they're less good at telling me whether it's edible or not. They're just as likely to lead me to a garbage can as a full cupboard. Still, they helped keep me alive when I was on my own."

"Is that how you found all the spots you showed me?"

"Some of them. Some of them I learned about from the others."

"So what you're saying is that roaches are part of the Emerald City community."

He laughed.

"Yeah, I guess I am. OK, I've shared my secrets. Now are you ready to learn to defend yourself?"

Valora grinned. "Sure. Let's get to work."

31

The place Hillary brought Val to was definitely not the Royal Construction office. She followed the vampires all the way across town, to an old rundown mansion in the Presidio. It was a grand old Victorian palace, likely built for one of Sutro's peers in the late 1800s. Grand as it may have once been, now it was falling apart. In fact, Val didn't see how anyone could be living in it.

The windows were dark empty spaces, either boarded up or smashed in and glassless. Shutters hung crookedly from the frames. The house sat alone on a large parcel of land, overshadowed by leaning trees. The fog was thick here in the Presidio, dark shapes looming up out of the fog like ghosts, unseen then suddenly there before you realized it. The two boys took up guard positions out front while Hillary led Val around to what she assumed used to be the service entrance in the back of the house. Crumbling stairs descended into the basement.

Hillary tensed as they circled the house, reminding Val of how nervous the receptionist had been when they first met. Val eyed her guide thoughtfully. Clearly the girl was unhappy around Ms. Pearl. Maybe Val could use that to her advantage.

"You don't have to do this you know," Val said softly. "You can escape."

"Escape my master?" Hillary's laugh was cold and mirthless. "There is no escape. I'm her servant. Now and forever."

"Doesn't seem like much of an argument for immortality."

"It is the price I must pay. It's this or death."

Val found her own muscles tensing as she followed Hillary down into the cellar. She didn't like this at all. But, like Hillary, she didn't have a choice. The young vampire had made it clear that Val was coming with her, whether she wanted to or not. All she could do was go along and see what Ms. Pearl wanted with her. And pray that what she wanted wasn't Val's death.

The good thing about dealing with vampires is that they are generally polite in an old-fashioned way. They follow rules of civility that most humans forgot long ago. This makes them trustworthy, as far as monsters go. If they tell you they aren't going to harm you, they won't. Unless you yourself broach the agreement. Then you're fair game. The vampires had promised her safe passage. All Val had to do was stay civil and ensure they kept their word.

She hoped that was the way it would work, anyway.

"You have other choices," Val whispered. "You don't have to stay in her shadow forever. My offer still stands. If you need help, come see me."

"Silence, human," Hillary hissed. "You know nothing."

Hillary led her through a crumbled hole in the cellar wall that turned into a passage. They left the manmade structure behind, descending into a natural crack in the earth. A hundred steps later, Val found herself in a vast cave. It was pitch black, with the only illumination coming from a handful of stalagmites and stalactites which glowed with a soft inner light.

"Bats in a cave," she muttered to herself. "That's not cliché at all."

"We are not bats, Miss Keri," Pearl's voice rang out across the cavern. Damn vampires and their exceptional hearing. "I'll thank you to keep your harmful stereotypes to yourself."

Val searched the place for the source of the voice, but all she could see were the looming silhouettes of the nearest stalagmites, stretching up into the darkness above.

Ms. Pearl's voice came again. "Leave us, Hillary. Miss Keri and I have private business to discuss. Wait outside."

Private business. Val didn't like the sound of that.

When the young vampire was gone, Pearl's voice hissed out of the darkness. Val still couldn't tell where she was; her voice echoed around the cavern, making it seem as if she were everywhere and nowhere.

"It has come to my attention that you are poking your nose in my business, Miss Keri."

Val wished she knew where the vampire was. It was deeply disconcerting to not even know which direction to address her words. Still, she tried not to let her discomfort show. She stood up straight, pulling her shoulders back and lifting her chin defiantly.

"What business would that be?"

"The business of lost objects, Miss Keri." Pearl's voice echoed strangely, seeming to get closer and further away as she spoke. One moment it would sound as if she were on the far side of the cavern, the next as if she were whispering in Val's ear.

"Lost objects?"

Val was proud that her voice wasn't shaking. She was tough. There were few things in the world that she genuinely feared. Unfortunately, vampires were one of them. They tended to think of humans as cattle. And they killed them just as easily.

"Don't play coy with me. You know that of which I speak. The Scepter of Sutro will be found, and it will not be found by the Black Knights. We have retrieved two pieces. The seraphim have two others. You will help us get our property back."

"Why would I do that?"

Pearl's laughter rang through the cavern.

"Your attempt at bravado is adorable. Do you think your act impresses me? You will do my bidding, or I will squash you like the insect you are."

"You don't scare me," Val said. The sweat slicking her back gave the lie to her words.

"Who are you trying to convince with that statement? Trust me, human. You do not want the seraphim to assemble the scepter. It will be much safer in our hands."

"You expect me to believe that? You are a bloodsucking vampire. Literally. And they are literally angels. Why in the world would I believe anything would be safer with you than it would be with them?"

"Have you found the seraphim to be so angelic? Ask your dead friends how good the Black Knights are."

She had a point there. Edward had killed both Ruby and Shanna.

On the other hand, Jack was helping her track him down. He had told her Edward was a pariah within the seraphim. Institutionally, they were supposed to be the good guys.

"The murderer is a rogue element. The other seraphim are hunting him down as we speak."

Pearl's laughter was icicles cascading down a mountainside.

"Is that what they told you? And you believe them? Oh, that is rich. I'm tempted to let you go your own way. With that level of ignorance, you deserve whatever befalls you."

"Again, why should I believe you? Give me one good reason."

"Because I did not kill your friend. Because I have not killed you, even though I have had ample opportunity. Is that not basis enough for trust?"

Again, the vampire had a point. That was happening with disturbing regularity.

"Say I was willing to believe you. I'm not saying that I am, but let's assume I was for the sake of argument. What would that mean? What would our next step be from here?"

"The new moon draws nigh. The scepter must be reassembled by then to complete the prophecy. If it is not, all this effort will have been wasted. I need you to retrieve the two pieces stolen by the seraphim. You will bring them to me."

Now it was Val's turn to laugh.

"How am I supposed to do that? I don't even know where the seraphim are. Until yesterday I didn't even know they existed. Now you expect me to, what? Find their secret seraphim hideout? Do they like to hang out in caves too? No, they're angels, they probably prefer belfries and steeples. Places with bells."

"You see? You do catch on fast. I knew you were the right choice. Find the right steeple and you will find the seraphim."

"Why don't you go yourself? Or send one of your boys? Why me?"

"Our kind couldn't get within three blocks of the Black Knights' cathedral without starting a war. There are rules and treaties that must be followed. Pacts that cannot be broken. You, on the other hand, are a free agent. One they already trust. You have a friend, do you not? What are friends for if not helping one another?"

"That doesn't sound like helping. That sounds like using. I don't use my friends that way. No deal. You can get your scepter yourself."

Val stiffened as Pearl's voice came from right behind her. The woman's breath was cold on her ear.

"Have it your way. But by the time you discover who your friends are, it will be too late. When the seraphim kill again, don't say I didn't warn you."

Like a whisper of a breeze, Ms. Pearl was gone. A pressure shift in the air told Val she was alone in the darkness.

32

The Librarian lowered her glasses and gave Val a disapproving glare as she stepped through the front doors of the library. She had anticipated this reaction and brought Malcolm with her as a distraction. True to his nature, Malcolm started talking as soon as he crossed the threshold.

"Oh my god, how did you never bring me to this place before? Girl, you've been holding out on me. How could you not bring me here? I don't know if I'm going to be able to forgive you for this one." He stared up at the rising floors above the atrium, mouth gaping open and doing little hops of excitement. He looked like a teakettle about to explode.

Val had gone back and forth on whether to bring Malcolm to the library. Technically, it was a breach in protocol. Non-magical beings were not supposed to be brought into the secrets of the library space. On the other hand, Malcolm was a tried and true bibliophile who adored libraries. Throw into the mix the fact that Val had been forcibly ejected the last time that she was here, and bringing Malcolm along seemed like a smart idea.

Malcolm stood in the center atrium, turning in circles. He looked like he might do a cartwheel any second.

The Librarian cleared her throat. Her voice dripped ice.

"You are on probation. Any breach of protocol and you will be banned from the library for one year."

Val bobbed her head in what she hoped was a contrite manner.

"Understood. Thank you for giving me another chance. I promise what happened last time will not be repeated."

"See that it doesn't. Now, what can I help you with?"

"I'm looking for more information on the Scepter of Sutro."

The Librarian raised an eyebrow. "That's a popular subject these days."

"Really? Who else has been asking about it?"

The Librarian gave her a flat stare. "I can't give you that information. The confidentiality of our clientele is guaranteed. Our information is free to all."

Val scowled. She had a pretty good idea who else might have been searching for the information. But it would've been nice to have some confirmation.

She ground her teeth and said, "That's fine. I understand. So, where can we find information on the scepter?"

The Librarian jotted some notes on her pad, tore off the page and handed it to Val. "Top floor. All the way in the back."

As they walked away from the desk, Malcolm snatched the paper from Val's fingers.

"Oh My God will you look at that handwriting! She writes in perfect Victorian script. Look at those looping Ls. And the curve on that F. I think I'm in love."

Val gave him the side-eye. "I didn't know you swung both ways, Malcolm."

Malcolm looked offended. "I'm talking about platonic love. Not mashing our squishy bits together. Obviously that's something you would know nothing about. Philistine."

"How many different types of love are there anyway?"

"There are as many different types of love as there are people on the planet. Love is love, girl. You can find what you're looking for, if you just open your mind and accept what the universe sends your way. Oh, and speaking of the universe sending things, I think I might have found us a new roommate. I'm going to have them come by the house tomorrow so you can meet them."

"OK, great. I'll be there." Val took a deep breath and tried to smile. She really hoped this person worked out. It'd be great to be able to cross one thing off her list, at least.

She let Malcolm lead as they gathered the reference materials the Librarian had recommended. Malcolm had an incredible ability to hone in on the exact spot on the shelf where the book they wanted was located. It would've taken Val at least half an hour to find all the books on the list. Malcolm collected them in five minutes.

He dropped the stack of books onto a reading table with an audible thump. Val eyed it with dismay.

"This is going to take forever," she said.

"Leave it to me, girl."

For the next hour, Val twiddled her thumbs while Malcolm gasped and ejaculated random factoids.

"Did you know that Sutro was thought of as a populist in his day? A real champion of the people. He made his money digging a mining tunnel in Nevada. He got the miners to agree to reduced daily wages in exchange for shares of the company. He was like a tech CEO a hundred years ahead of his time."

"That's fascinating, Malcolm," said Val. "What about the scepter?"

"I'm getting to that. Patience is a virtue, darling."

"I don't have time to be patient. Whatever's happening, it's going to happen on the night of the new moon. That's in two days. We need to figure this out now."

Malcolm rolled his eyes.

"Why is it always hurry up and wait with you magical folks? There's always some prophecy, some big deadline that everything is going to happen on this date or else chaos and death and mass hysteria will ensue. But the deadline is always really soon. Even though it's a prophecy that's been around for hundreds or thousands of years, nobody ever knows about it until the last possible minute. And then everyone has to run around like chickens with their heads cut off trying to fulfill the prophecy or ensure that the prophecy is not fulfilled, depending on which side of the coin you're standing on."

"I don't know, Malcolm. I don't make a habit of beating my head against ancient prophecies. This is my first one, actually."

Malcolm gasped and put his hand in his mouth in shock.

"You're a prophecy virgin? You've invited me to be part of your prophecy cherry-popping ceremony? I don't know whether to be honored or horrified."

"I'd go with both," Val said. "Now, can we get back to work please? Your ironic, self-referential commentary aside, we really are running out of time. We need to know what the scepter is supposed to do, and why everybody wants to put it back together so badly."

"Knowing is half the battle," said Malcolm. He dutifully buried his nose back in the books.

"Are you quoting G.I. Joe now? I didn't think you were the type."

"Not the type for buff soldier boys in tight pants? Girl, you really haven't been paying attention."

It took a couple of hours, but Malcolm finally pieced together enough information for them to believe they understood the prophecy of the Scepter of Sutro, and why everyone was so desperate to get their hands on it.

Malcolm cleared his throat dramatically, sitting up straight in his chair like a newscaster. He made his voice deep and spooky.

"Whosoever holdeth Sutro's Scepter..."

"Whosoever holdeth? Are you making this shit up, Malcolm?"

He ignored her.

"Whosoever holdeth Sutro Scepter shall have dominion over all the souls of San Francisco. He shall be as a king among men, and the people shall obey his every command."

"All the souls of San Francisco? Sounds like what you'd expect," said Val. "Why do all these prophecies give people control over other people? That seems more like a curse than a blessing to me. Can you imagine being in charge of every dumbass in this city? I can't even keep houseplants alive."

"Well, god-emperors are a unique breed," said Malcolm. "I mean if you want to build yourself a pyramid, you're going to need a few thousand slaves. Though building pyramids is so cliché. Personally, I'd go with something a little more modern. Like the Gherkin in London."

Val made a face. "Is that the building that looks like a giant spiraling dildo?"

"Damn right it is. I know phallic symbols are passé, but it would be my phallic symbol, so that would make it all right with me. I don't have to give a fuck what anyone else thinks about it."

"I guess that is one of the perks of being a god-emperor. You can be as tacky as you want to be."

"Exactly. Think about all those rich egomaniacs that plaster their names all over their properties. That's tacky as shit, right? But nobody judges them for it because they're as rich as gods. Everybody loves you when you're beautiful and rich."

"Beautiful OR rich," Val clarified.

"Sure. But I want to be both."

"Capitalism is a disease, you know."

"Do I look like I give a fuck? God-emperors only have to worry about themselves. I'm not talking about social justice here."

Val shook her head. "We're getting off topic here. Does the research say anything about where and when this ceremony needs to happen?"

Malcolm pulled out another book.

"It says... midnight on the night of the new moon, of course. Why can't any of this magical shit ever happen during normal business hours?"

"Malcolm... "

"All right, all right. Let's see here, by the light of the new moon, midnight, etc. etc. etc... Oh, here we are. At the top of the city, right in the center."

"Top of the city. Right in the center. So, what? The top of Twin Peaks?"

"People might think that today. But back in Sutro's time, Mount Olympus was considered the geographical heart of the city."

Val's face lit up. "Of course! That's where Sutro built his Triumph of Light monument. Naturally, that's where the ceremony needs to happen. Malcolm, you're a genius."

"That's Super Genius God-Emperor to you, darling."

Val cracked her knuckles.

"So we know the when, the where, and the why. Now we just have to prevent it from happening by finding the remaining pieces before the vampires or the seraphim get their hands on them."

Malcolm blinked at her owlishly.

"I still can't believe you're talking about vampires and angels being real. I mean, I know a lot of freaky people in this city, but your crowd takes the cake. "

"Believe me, I'd rather be working with some nice, safe computer programmers." Val pushed herself to her feet, pulling her leather jacket on like armor. "Thanks for your help, Malcolm. I'll take it from here."

33

"**A**re you all right?" Silvio extended a hand to Valora.

They were in the vacant lot behind the Emerald City. The sky was grey and sullen, matching Valora's mood. Silvio had just flipped her to the ground. Again.

She eyed his hand skeptically.

"I'm fine. What do you think I am, a princess? I've taken worse falls than that at my grandmother's house."

He kept his hand extended and she finally took it, allowing him to pull her to her feet. His skin was warm and soft, and she could feel the calluses on the pads of his fingers, hard as coins.

"Those are some serious calluses," she said.

Silvio smiled. "Yeah, steel strings are no joke. I have to practice my guitar almost every day to keep them up. If my fingers get too soft, I won't be able to play."

"Where did you learn to play that thing, anyway?"

"My dad taught me." Silvio got a distant look in his eye. "We used to play together in the backyard. He dug a big firepit and lined it with rocks. Set up some big stumps around it for us to sit on. Most Sundays we would sit out there under the stars, build a fire, and jam."

"Sounds very wholesome. Was your dad secretly John Denver?"

He laughed. "No, but 'Country Roads' was one of my dad's favorite songs."

"Did you live in the country?"

"Nope. Pure suburbia. But my dad liked to go hiking. And camping. I always thought he would've liked to live out in the country."

"Why didn't he?"

"Work, I think. He was a teacher, and there are a lot more schools in the suburbs than there are in the country."

"That makes sense. So if you grew up in a healthy suburban atmosphere, how did you end up here?"

Silvio looked away, his hands twisting around one another.

"He died. Cancer."

"I'm sorry. That must've been hard."

"Yeah. My grandparents tried to take me in, but I was seventeen and didn't want anything to do with it. I took off right after the funeral. Haven't been back since."

"Do you think they're worried about you?"

"I doubt it. My grandfather was a real bastard. They only offered to take me in because they felt obligated to the memory of my dad or some bullshit like that. They didn't actually give a shit about me." He picked up a rock and threw it. It clattered off an old piece of sheet metal. "What about you? How did you end up in this magical wonderland?"

"Pretty much the same thing," Valora said evasively. "Except I got started a lot younger. My mom died when I was a kid, and I got shipped off to my aunt's house. They couldn't deal with me, so I ended up in the foster-care system. Bounced around from house to house, in and out of juvenile and psychiatric facilities. That's where Amber found me, in the WTF facility upstate. She busted me out and the rest is history."

Silvio's smile lit up his face, banishing the dark shadows in an instant. It made him look five years younger.

"Yeah, Amber is an angel. I don't think any of this would exist without her."

Valora pushed her hair out of her face, tucking it behind her ear. "Did she bring everyone here?"

"Most of us, yeah. I think Paula found the E.C. on her own, maybe one or two of the others."

"Did Amber find you?"

"Yeah, she did. Though not quite in the way you think. We both liked to dumpster dive behind the old Safeway, and we kept running into each other. At first I hated her; I thought she kept getting all the good scores before me. Eventually we started talking and I figured out she was pretty cool. One day she saw me do my thing with the insects when I thought no one else was around. That's when she invited me to the Emerald City."

"So if this is the Emerald City, who is the great and powerful Oz?"

Silvio spread his hands wide and spoke in a booming voice. "I am the Great and Powerful Oz. Can't you tell?"

Valora tilted her head at him. "I don't know. I think you're a little too public to be the man behind the curtain."

Silvio inclined his head. "Fair enough. I do like to get out and interact with the little people."

Valora's hair escaped from behind her ear, falling in front of her eyes again. She reached up to push it aside, but Silvio beat her to it. He reached out, his fingers brushing her forehead. She froze like a deer in the headlights. His fingertips brushed against her temple and down the back of her ear.

His touch sent electric sparks down her spine. Valora forgot to breathe. Silvio kept his fingers there for a heartbeat longer, his eyes questioning.

Valora opened her mouth to speak, but no words came out. Her brain seemed to be disconnected from her body.

Silvio's expression turned serious. He leaned towards her, and when she didn't pull away, he pressed his lips to hers.

She had never kissed anyone before, not really. Sure, she'd been caught up in a childish kissing game once or twice. But they had been more of the Truth or Dare variety. Quick kisses, bashfully stolen by boys who had no idea what they were doing.

This kiss was different. Silvio's lips were warm and soft, and they moved gently against hers. This was definitely not Silvio's first kiss.

At first Valora was rigid, unsure what to do. Then her body began to respond on its own. Her mouth softened, and she clumsily began to move her lips in response. Warmth suffused her body, her heart lurched painfully inside her chest. She was tingling from head to toe. Her breath came in short gasps.

When Silvio pulled away, she wanted to cry out. To protest. It was as if the thing she had been looking for all her life had suddenly been taken away.

"Um... wow," she stammered. Then she looked away, her cheeks burning bright pink.

"Yeah," Silvio agreed. "Wow."

He reached out and laced his fingers through hers. She could feel the calluses against the backs of her knuckles, smooth and round as pebbles. Nothing in the world had ever felt better.

34

"You know I could do this easier on my own right?" said Alain.

"If by 'do this on my own' you mean 'get killed', then yes, I do realize that," Val shot back. "However, I'm not in the habit of letting my friends get killed. I'm already over my quota of dead friends for this week."

Alain glanced at her. "Is that where we are now? Friends?"

Val shot him a look.

"Let's not get carried away. Maybe we can consider this more of a probational friendship."

Alain grinned.

They were stalking through the dark on Mount Sutro. The trail was narrow, undergrowth reaching out to clutch at their limbs as they moved. The fog was thick up here, flowing in over the low-lying Sunset District before butting up against the hills. Gathering like cotton candy on a stick.

It was the ideal place for an ambush.

Val just wished she knew if they were doing the ambushing, or if they were the ones being ambushed.

They had decided that one of the last remaining unclaimed pieces of the scepter had to be in this forest somewhere. There were too many people around to look for it during the day, so naturally the hunters would come at night. Which was why they were here now. Hunting the hunters.

"I can deal with that," Alain continued. "I've been on probation before."

Val cocked her head at him. "That sounds like a story."

"Less of a story than you might think. More a natural product of a misspent youth."

Val laughed.

"Oh, yeah. I've been there." Suddenly she froze, hissing, "Quiet."

She pressed herself against the trunk of a tree while Alain melted into the undergrowth on the opposite side of the trail. They stood silent, listening. The only sound was the wind through the trees, rattling the branches of the eucalyptus. Then came the sound of wings. Large wings, flapping overhead.

Only Val's eyes moved, tracking upward. She cursed the fog. She could barely see the top of the tree she was leaning against. If anything -- or anyone -- flew by overhead, she doubted she'd be able to see them.

No.

There.

A dark silhouette moved just above the tree line. Val sucked in a breath. It was a seraphim. Though with the dark and the fog, it was impossible to tell if it was Edward or Jack. Or anyone else, for that matter.

"They're heading for the crest of the hill," Val whispered.

Alain nodded, and they started jogging up the trail. They moved as quickly as they could without making a lot of noise. Alain had searched the eighty-acre forest earlier and identified a handful of locations that looked like places where Sutro may have hidden a piece of the scepter. One of them was a small cave near the crest of the hill. Val guessed the seraphim was heading there.

Her hair was damp, the trail muddy beneath their feet. The wind blowing in from the coast was as cold up here as if they'd been standing on the beach. Val glared at the little forest around them. All this moisture might be good for the plant life, but for mammals it was unpleasant at best.

They slowed as they neared the crest of the hill.

"Wait here," Alain whispered. "I'll scout ahead."

Val nodded. She stood silent in the dark, every sense on high alert.

Alain moved away up the trail, and as he did Val saw his silhouette shift closer to the ground. By the time he reached the limits of her vision, he was just a large black dog, slipping away into the night.

Val wasn't sure what she would do if they caught Edward in the act. She just knew it would be violent and swift. Despite the vampire's overtures and the things she and Malcolm had learned at the library, Val didn't care much about the scepter, or the stupid prophecy. All she cared about was getting justice for Ruby and Shanna. She was here to bring down a murderer.

The seconds ticked by, each feeling like an hour. Val ground her fingernails into her hands, clenching her fist so hard it hurt. She wasn't good at waiting. She was more of a hit-first-and-ask-questions-later kind of gal.

She was so focused on the trail ahead of her that she almost screamed when Mister E spoke up right beside her ear.

"*Well, isn't this all very exciting,*" he said. He floated just above her left shoulder, blowing smoke rings that disappeared into the fog. "*I must say, I never expected to be hunting angels.*"

"What do you want?" Val growled.

Mister E smiled his unnaturally wide grin. He flexed his claws.

"*I'm looking for a little action, that's all. It's been too long since we've really gotten to take a piece out of someone.*" His smile was predatory, his eyes gleaming gold in the darkness.

Val felt his excitement. Felt her own pulse tick up in response. Even as a part of her mind was repulsed by the prospect, a much larger part of her was excited by it. She lusted for blood.

Cats might be cute, but pound for pound, they were one of the deadliest predators on the planet. Val felt her lips curl away from her teeth. Yes, she was a predator. And tonight, she would finally catch her prey.

Alain came ghosting back out of the fog, having already abandoned his dog form.

"They went into the cave. The seraphim disappeared inside before I got there. I stood outside for a minute, waiting, unsure what to do. Then I decided to creep closer. But before I could, I heard more wings. Then another seraphim came down out of the fog."

"Was it Jack?" asked Val.

"I couldn't tell, it was too dark and foggy. I hope it was, because the prospect of going up against one seraphim is daunting enough. We could be pushing our luck with two."

Val narrowed her eyes at him. "What do you know that I don't?"

"I just know the seraphim are deadly. All the stories about the angels fighting and tearing apart the heavens and earth? Why do you think we have those stories?"

"Because some Arab out of his mind on hallucinogens wrote down his visions a couple of thousand years ago?"

Alain chuckled.

"Well, yes. But more than that. We have those stories because the seraphim are some of the fiercest warriors ever to walk the earth. They even killed a few gods back in the day."

"You're just telling me this now?"

Alain shrugged. "Would it have stopped you from coming?"

"No, but I might've brought more weapons. Like a tank."

"I thought you had everything you need inside of you already."

"Oh, I have a lot inside me, don't get me wrong. But there are always tools that make the job easier. Knives, swords, heat-seeking missiles."

Alain started to chuckle again, but his laughter died when he saw her eyes.

"Are you serious?"

"Dead serious. You don't get to kill my friends and walk away from it. If a heat-seeking missile is what I need to take that fucker down, that's what I'll use."

Alain swallowed.

"Well. Let's hope it doesn't come to that." He glanced meaningfully up the trail. "Shall we?"

Val nodded, and they crept upward once again.

The entrance to the cave was well hidden, no more than a tiny crack at the base of a small cliff. It was well off the beaten path, so the odds of casual hikers finding it were microscopic. Alain had only discovered it because he'd spent nearly ten hours crossing and recrossing the mountain, searching every square foot with his heightened canine senses.

Now he took the lead, ghosting between trees and past bushes with preternatural silence. Val did her best to follow, but she sounded like an avalanche in progress compared to Alain. She ground her teeth at every snapped twig and kicked rock. She might as well have brought a brass band with her.

Alain halted outside the entrance of the cave. Val joined him, crouching behind a large boulder.

"Do you see that?" he asked, pointing into the fog.

She followed the direction of his finger and found a tiny pinprick of light, shining through the cliff about a dozen meters to the side of the entrance.

"What is it?"

"It's light from inside the cave. It's far enough in that you can't see it shining out the entrance."

Val listened but couldn't hear any sound to go with the light. Just the mournful dirge of the wind.

"So what's our play?"

Alain glanced at her. "That's up to you. I'm just the scout."

Val grimaced.

"Fine, I'm going in then. You stay here and keep watch. Warn me if anyone else shows up. Be ready for anything."

Val drew her knife, took a deep breath, and slipped through the entrance of the cave.

35

Chill stone flanked Val on both sides as she crept into the mountain, the crevice barely wide enough for her to enter turned sideways. It was cold inside the rock, but slightly warmer than it had been outside, without the fog and the constant wind blowing. One thing to be grateful for, anyway.

She inched along the crack for a good thirty yards, before she rounded a corner and saw light ahead. She froze and listened, clutching her knife. There were voices, at least two of them. She couldn't make out what they were saying. Was one of them Jack? She couldn't be sure.

As she got closer, the voices became audible.

"I'm telling you, this is the only way."

"And I am telling you, it's not. This is madness. It's not too late to stop this. You haven't gone so far that you can't turn back."

"Madness? What do you know of madness? Was your mate hunted and killed? Did you lose everything? Do not speak to me of madness."

The voices echoed, oddly distorted by the acoustics of the cave. Val inched forward until she could see a wide cavern opening up ahead of her. The interior was lit by a soft yellow glow. The cavern was so large it seemed the entire interior of the mountain was hollow. The smoothness of some of the walls showed this might not have been entirely accidental.

Val moved forward, inch by careful inch, until the feathery tip of a white wing came into view. She froze as the figure moved, turning and striding across the cavern. She glimpsed a face as the seraphim passed by, and her knuckles turned white on the grip of her knife.

Edward. The murderer was here.

The voice continued. "I know you're upset. Grief does terrible things. But more death will not bring them back."

"Upset? Upset?" The other voice rose, echoing off the interior of the cavern. "Death can only be appeased by more death. You know that as well as I do. Everything has its price. Piercing the veil requires the ultimate price. Tomorrow, you'll see. Tomorrow it will all be worth it."

Val couldn't wait any longer. She stepped out into the cavern and snarled, "You're not going to live to see tomorrow, murderer."

The seraphim whirled toward her. There were two of them, Edward and Jack, just as she suspected. Edward's eyes widened. Jack's lips twisted into a smile.

"Well," said Jack. "Why am I not surprised?"

"I guess I'm just a predictable kind of girl, Jack."

Edward had dropped his glamour and was now an inverted mirror image of Jack. Gone was the balding, jowly man. His eyes were warm chestnut, his black hair thick over coppery skin. He was every bit as beautiful as Jack, an inhuman beauty that took her breath away, even as her anger took over. How could something so beautiful be so evil?

She advanced on him, her lips pulled back in a snarl.

Mister E perked up, anticipating violence. The wind stirred. Her blood lust rose.

"You're going to pay for those girls you murdered, Edward."

The seraphim held out his hands. "You're making a mistake. I'm not the one you want. Listen to me."

"I've heard all I need to hear." The wind curled into a whirlwind, gathering dust and stones as it whistled through the interior of the cave.

Val charged the angel.

The seraphim was fast, faster than she expected. Before she could reach him, he exploded into the air on powerful wings. Two quick flaps and he landed on a ledge halfway up the wall.

"Please, listen," he called out.

But Val had heard more than enough. She sent her cyclone spiraling up. It buffeted the seraphim, flattening him against the wall, then it picked him up and dragged him from the ledge.

He tried to fight it, flapping his enormous wings, but once he was airborne, he was at the mercy of the whirlwind. He tumbled across the cavern and slammed into the floor face-first, skidding and rolling in the dirt.

Val bared her teeth as she advanced, her golden eyes glowing like lanterns. She stopped over the angel and lifted her knife. Mister E purred with pleasure, whispering in her ear, "*Yes, do it. Make him pay with blood.*"

Val plunged the knife down.

The seraphim again proved faster than expected, hitting her with a flex of his powerful wing. Val went spinning, swatted away as if she weighed no more than an insect. The air huffed out of her, and her teeth snapped shut on the tip of her tongue. Sharp pain stabbed through her and she tasted blood. Mister E rumbled with satisfaction. Blood was blood as far as he was concerned.

"I told you to wait." The angel was angry now, his entire body glowing with fury. Val suddenly realized that the light in the cavern had been coming from the seraphim themselves. Now it was so great she had to squint to look at him. "You are meddling with things you do not understand."

"Oh, I understand all right. It's the same old story. You've lost some-one, you're in pain, and everyone else is going to pay for it. You're a selfish jerk with no empathy. Do you think you're the only one who's ever lost someone? Do you think you're the only one in pain? You don't know what pain is." She launched herself at him with a cry, slashing wildly with her knife.

The seraphim curled his wing in front of him like a shield, and Val's knife sank into muscle. Scraped against bone. Edward gasped and flung her away again. But this time, her knife stayed embedded in his wing.

Val hit back, using her power to send a gale shrieking toward the angel. The wind caught his wings and lifted him like a kite. He slammed into an outcropping of rock and crumbled to the ground. Val smiled, her teeth slick with blood. Mister E did the same. Their eyes were mirror images, golden orbs blazing as she closed in for the kill.

"That was magnificent," said Jack. "You really are something else, aren't you."

"Don't get in my way, Jack. This fucker is going to pay for what he did."

"I wouldn't dream of it."

She stalked toward the downed seraphim, Mister E chanting in her ear, "*Kill him. Tear him. Give me blood.*"

Her shadow fell across the seraphim's face. He looked so innocent lying there, with his eyes closed and mouth open. Like a child sleeping. It was hard to believe he had brutally murdered two young women.

"*Remember Ruby,*" Mister E hissed. "*Remember Shanna. Remember what he did to them. Tore them open. Spilled their blood.*"

Val saw them in her mind as he spoke their names. Their bodies rent open and bleeding. Lying cold and dead upon the hard ground.

She raised the knife.

Edward's eyelids flickered open. His warm chestnut eyes caught hers. They were shining, soft as velvet.

He raised his hand, "Don't..."

Val plunged the knife into his chest.

He cried out in pain and shock. Bright blood speckled his lips. Mister E laughed.

The angel gasped, "It wasn't me." He struggled to draw breath, to form more words. His eyes flicked to something behind Val, widening with panic. "It was him."

The last of his strength left him. The light fled from his eyes. His head flopped to the side, limp and dead.

Val had killed an angel. She had done it. Avenged her friends.

But what had his last words meant?

She turned to find Jack hovering over her, a smile curving his luscious lips.

"Oh, you are a vicious one, aren't you? You're everything I hoped you would be."

36

Valora's days passed in a haze of wonder. In the evenings she and Silvio would go scrounge food from the dumpsters behind the grocery stores and restaurants and pick up free bagels and day-olds from the bakeries. In the afternoons, Silvio drilled her in self-defense. He taught her the proper way to settle her weight into her hips, giving her power when she punched and kicked. He showed her how to use her opponent's weight as leverage, flipping them onto the floor.

But the nights were her favorite.

At night they would sit around the fire on empty milk crates, feeding it jagged boards and pieces of pallet. Silvio would pull out his guitar and they would all sing songs together and talk.

Afterward, Silvio would come back to Valora's cubicle, or she would go to his. They would kiss and touch, and hold each other close. It was warm and soft and good. Valora had never felt anything like it in her entire life. She was happier than she had ever been.

Months passed, and Valora discovered her fellow magical outcasts were an eclectic bunch, from wildly different backgrounds, and with wildly different abilities. Silvio's roach-magic was far from the strangest thing the community members could do.

As she'd seen in the WTF, Amber was able to short-circuit anything that ran on electricity. Which meant pretty much everything. Colin could generate intense heat with his hands, making him responsible for starting their nightly campfires. He also kept the warehouse warm by heating little piles of bricks and cinder blocks until they practically glowed. Like rocks baked in the sun, they would radiate heat for hours while they cooled. The Greek sisters were telepathic. They could communicate with each other instantly and would finish each other's sentences as if they shared one mind. Valora found it creepy, and she avoided the girls as much as she could.

They all treated their abilities as something unique. Something only they could do. All except for Paula.

"Magic has always been with us," she told Val. "From the earliest days of humanity. It went away for a while, but now it's back, stronger than ever."

They were sitting on the floor in Paula's cubicle, drinking tea while Paula flipped Tarot cards onto a low table. A thick Persian rug spread beneath their legs, while gauzy curtains covered the walls. Multi-colored crystals hung from bits of string overhead. Incense burned in a little golden bowl, lazy smoke curling around them. Valora felt like she was inside the Arabian Nights. In a harem.

"Why do you think that is?" Valora asked.

"Why what is?"

"Why magic went away. Why it came back. All of it."

Paula smiled without looking up from the cards.

"That has been a subject of much debate among the magical community. Some blame people. They think that centuries of persecution, things like the Spanish Inquisition and the Salem witch trials, systematically killed off magic. Others blame the Industrial Revolution. As Amber's power clearly demonstrates, magic and science do not get along. Others blame the gods."

"The gods? Plural?"

"The old gods. Those of Ancient Egypt and Greece. The Norse and Native American pantheons. Mayans, Aztecs, Africans. Japanese, Chinese, Thai. The Celtic gods. I could go on. People used to worship

thousands of gods all over the world. Often due to the aggressive pros-
elytizing of the Christians, these gods fell out of favor and were forgotten. Obviously the Christians weren't solely to blame, they're simply
the biggest culprit. I think of them as the Walmart of religions, aggressively pushing all of the local mom-and-pop religions out of business."

Valora watched the smoke from the incense curl and shift while she
thought about that." So you think the old gods were real?"

"I believe the old gods are real. Not were." Paula smiled. "I believe
everything is real. How can someone look at the things we are able to
do and not believe? There's so much more to this world than we
know."

"I guess I can't argue with that. Though seeing magic with my own
eyes is one thing. Believing in gods is something else."

"Ah yes, the ever-present burden of proof. I want to show you
something."

The older woman drew a piece of muslin from a bag and spread it
on the table. It was covered with arcane symbols and letters, and in the
center was an Egyptian eye. Dark brown stains discolored the fabric.
Paula drew a bone-handled knife with a curved blade from the bag
and placed it on the table beside the cloth. She lit five small candles,
placing them around the cloth. Then her blue eyes caught Valora's.

"Give me your hand."

Valora hesitated, eying the knife. Paula smiled.

"I promise I won't hurt you. I just want to show you something.
Trust me."

Valora licked her lips and nodded, putting her hand into the older
woman's. Paula's fingers closed around her wrist in a surprisingly
strong grip, turning her hand palm up. She grabbed the knife and
slashed the blade across Valora's palm, drawing a bright red line.

"Ow!" Valora tried to pull away, but the older woman held her fast.

"Hush, this will only take a moment."

Paula squeezed Valora's hand into a fist and tilted it to the side,
letting blood drip onto the muslin. She closed her eyes and began to
chant, the vowels and consonants heavy and unfamiliar to Valora's ear.
The candles flickered and jumped. The incense smoke began to gather
directly over the muslin, swirling into a tiny cyclone.

Valora felt her hand grow warm. Again she tried to pull away and again Paula held her firm. Her grip was like a vise, her bony fingers digging into the tendons of Valora's wrist. The heat grew until her palm was on fire.

"Let go!"

With a final jerk, she pulled her hand away from the older woman's. Paula opened her eyes, a sheen of sweat beading her forehead.

"Look at your hand," she said.

Valora scowled but did as she was told. She gasped. The cut was gone.

"How is that possible?" She ran her fingers over the smooth skin. It was as if she'd never been sliced at all.

"Old magic," Paula said. "Old gods. I found this design and ritual in a book on Isis, one of the primary goddesses of Ancient Egypt. As you can see, it works. The old gods haven't gone anywhere. They're still here, waiting for us to reach out to them."

"How do you know it's Isis and not the magic that we use?"

Paula smiled.

"First of all, we do not all use the same magic. Every one of us here in the Emerald City uses a different type of energy. But putting that aside for now, I know it is Isis because I feel her presence when I invoke the ritual. Her power comes from outside of me, and it feels very different from my own magic. Unlike you, I do not have a lot of natural power inside me. At least not the kind I can project onto other things. My magic is more of an empathetic, sensitive nature. I'm aware of the forces around me, and I can sense and intuit things that others are not aware of. But healing your hand? That is well beyond what I could do on my own."

"Is that why you try old rituals like this? Because your own magic is limited?"

"No. I seek old rituals because I'm curious. There is so much magical knowledge that has been lost from the world. I seek to reclaim as much as I can."

"That makes sense." Valora rubbed her palm, still marveling at the freshly healed skin. "Have you found other old rituals that work?"

Paula's smile became radiant.

"Several. And I'm always looking for new ones. Would you like to see some of them?"

Valora nodded slowly.

"Yes. Yes, I would."

37

Val stared at Jack, her forehead creased in confusion.

"Hoped I would be?"

He bent and plucked something from Edward's grasp. It was a finger-length tube of gold, glinting in the soft light coming from the seraphim's body. A piece of the Scepter of Sutro.

"Thank you for that. Edward was being quite unreasonable."

"Unreasonable?" Val looked from the scepter to Jack's face, uncomprehending.

"He was trying to keep me from getting what I want. I'd call that unreasonable, wouldn't you?"

"What you want? But ... he assaulted, Ruby. I saw it." Val felt like a parrot, repeating everything Jack said. Her thoughts moved heavy and slow in the aftermath of her killing fury. Thick as congealed blood.

"Oh, he was an asshole, there's no doubt of that. And quite the thorn in my side, personally. But a murderer he was not."

A new voice came from the entrance. "He played you, girl."

Val whirled to find Ms. Pearl standing in the entrance to the cavern. She wore a tight black business suit and low black heels. Her black hair was perfect. She looked for all the world as if she were in her office, not standing in a cave in the middle of Mount Sutro.

"Played me?" Shit, she was doing the parrot thing again.

"You were very helpful," Jack said. He turned to face Ms. Pearl. "Vampire, you are not welcome here."

Ms. Pearl smiled with her bloodless lips.

"That's never stopped me before. It's never stopped you either, has it Jack?"

The seraphim chuckled. "Fortune favors the bold. You know that."

"Indeed, I do. You've stolen something that belongs to me." Ms. Pearl shot across the cavern in a blur of preternatural speed.

But fast as she was, Jack was faster.

He shot straight up, his legs propelling him the first ten feet, before his powerful wings took over. Ms. Pearl skidded to a halt beside Val.

"Dammit, girl. Couldn't you have grabbed him? You were a lot closer than I was."

Jack circled up and up and up toward the distant crown of the mountain. Then he banked sharply, shot towards one of the walls, and disappeared.

Ms. Pearl cursed. "I should've known he had another exit. He's a crafty bastard."

Val's head was spinning. "What just happened?"

"What happened is you let your friends' murderer escape. And handed him the last piece of Sutro's Scepter in the process."

"I thought you had two pieces?"

"He stole them."

"That's not possible."

But in her heart, she knew it was. Jack wore a beautiful mask, but she had seen it slip at times. She recalled the glimpses of frustration and anger she'd seen, there and gone so quickly she'd doubted their existence.

"But, what about Edward?"

Ms. Pearl gazed down at the dead seraphim. "This poor bastard was trying to stop him."

Val staggered. "No. No, that can't be right."

"It can, and it is. Seraphim laws very clearly forbid them killing one another. But manipulating an outsider to do their dirty work for them?

That's just good form. Congratulations, girl. You killed an innocent angel."

Val's world was coming apart. A roaring sound filled her ears. She couldn't catch her breath.

"No!"

She screamed and fled, pounding out into the darkness.

Alain was waiting for her outside the cave.

"What happened?" He took in her blood splattered hands. "Are you hurt?"

"Get away from me!" Val shoved him off the path, hard, adding a gust of wind for good measure. Alain flew off and was swallowed by the underbrush.

She fled through the forest, heedless of where she was going. She could feel Mister E gloating, his purr slow and satisfied. Basking in the afterglow of the kill.

Val wanted to peel off her skin. She wanted to vomit. She wanted to run so fast and so far that she would never find herself again. Where no one would ever find her.

She had killed an innocent angel.

Edward's eyes followed her in her mind. Their soft velvet depths. The shock and pain in them as she plunged her knife into his chest.

She ran faster, but they still followed her. She knew she would never outrun them. The same way she could never outrun her mother.

"I really am a monster. I try to do right, but all I do is bring pain and death."

"*Don't be ashamed.*" Mister E purred. "*You are a warrior. A bringer of death. It is the oldest profession there is.*"

"I don't want to be this. You made me this."

"*I didn't make you anything. We have a bargain, honorably struck. I wanted freedom, you wanted power.*"

"I was a child. I didn't know what I was doing."

"*What is it you humans are so fond of saying? Ignorance of the law is not an excuse?*"

"You're a monster. I don't want it anymore. Get out of my head. Leave me alone."

"*I'm afraid that is not an option. The laws of the compact are unbreakable.*

We are stuck together, you and I. We need each other."

"I don't need you. I don't want you. Get out!"

Mister E sighed.

"Child, you may as well rail against the sun and the moon. I'll tell you again, we are inextricably bound. The only way to get rid of me is to get rid of yourself. As long as you draw breath on this planet, I will be your constant companion."

"I hate you. I hate this power."

"You might as well hate the wind for blowing. Power is neither good nor evil. It simply is. How you use it determines its worth."

"Then it's you that's evil. It's you that wants blood."

Mister E smiled.

"That is my nature. I'm a predator. Predators desire blood. It's the most natural thing there is. Is an owl evil for eating mice? Are wolves evil for bringing down deer? What about humans eating cattle? Nature is neither good nor evil. It simply is. To call me evil is to call yourself and every living thing on this planet evil. Life feeds on life. That is the way of things. Railing against it will accomplish nothing."

"It shouldn't be that way," Val sobbed. "Life shouldn't have a cost."

Mister E yawned.

"These are infantile arguments. You're better than this. You have power, whether you wish it or not. All that matters is what you do with that power."

Val stumbled out of the forest and onto the street. She stopped, gazing at the peaceful neighborhood surrounding her. Lights were on in the houses, people calmly going about their lives. Eating dinner, watching movies, reading books. Talking and laughing. Carrying on as if nothing had happened. As if an angel hadn't just been murdered.

The street glistened beneath the cheery glow of the streetlights. Pockets of fog bloomed in the illumination. The breeze smelled of the sea, and the frying fish someone was making for dinner.

And there it was. Fish for dinner. Life feeding on life. The proof of Mister E's argument.

Power was neither good nor evil. Power simply was.

Val turned east.

"All that matters is what you do with it? Well, what I'm going to do with it is get roaring drunk."

38

A single finger of sunlight touched the bar, streaming in through the dusty glass. Val winced and turned away from it.

"Fuck. Is it morning already?" she slurred.

She squinted at the clock on the wall, the numbers swimming before her eyes. Finally, she gave up and asked the bartender. "What time is it?"

"It's probably time for you to call it a night."

Val scowled at the man.

"I'm still conscious, so clearly it's not." She downed the rest of her whiskey and shoved the empty glass forward. "Give me another."

A hand came down on top of her glass.

"The man said you've had enough."

Val frowned at the hand, her eyes tracing a brown sleeve up to an elbow, and then a shoulder. When she reached the newcomer's hollow face, she cursed.

"Shit. What the fuck do you want?"

Alain held her gaze. "I want justice for Ruby and Shanna. I thought you wanted the same thing."

Val turned away from him.

"I'm not the person you want. You're better off finding someone else."

"I don't have time to find someone else. The new moon is tonight. I need you."

"Get used to disappointment." Val removed his hand from the top of her glass and pushed it toward the bartender.

Alain put his hand on her shoulder. "What are you doing, Val? We don't have time for this."

Val knocked his hand away and got to her feet, staring him down. The fact that she couldn't stop swaying somewhat spoiled the effect.

"I said leave me alone. Believe me, you don't want me involved. When I'm around, innocent people get killed."

Alain folded his arms over his chest.

"What happened last night, Val? What happened in that cave?"

Val sat back down on the bar stool. "I don't want to talk about it."

Alain put his hand on her shoulder again. "You have to. Tell me what happened."

"I said I don't want to talk about it," Val snarled, her anger rising in a sudden wave. She pushed Alain, hard, and he stumbled back. She rushed him, swinging a clumsy punch at his face.

Alain dodged the punch and grabbed her around the waist, pulling her to the ground. They wrestled on the sticky bar floor, cursing and growling.

Normally, Val would've mopped the floor with Alain, but she was very drunk, and the shifter ended up getting her face down on the ground, with her arms behind her back, pinned and helpless.

She struggled, snarling and kicking. But he refused to let go.

"It's OK," he murmured, his voice gentle. "Whatever happened in there, it's OK. It wasn't your fault. I believe in you."

Her snarls turned to sobs, and Alain went from restraining her to patting her back, whispering softly. She cried and wailed, banging her fists against the floor, releasing the tempest inside of her.

After what felt like an hour, her sobs finally slowed. She felt empty and drained.

"Better?" Alain asked gently.

Val nodded and wiped her eyes on her sleeve.

Alain offered her a hand up.

"Good. Let's get you cleaned up. Ruby and Shanna still need you."

And he was right. Goddamn it all, but he was right. She wasn't the hero they needed. Far from it. But apparently she was the only one they were getting.

That would have to be enough.

Val woke to the smell of pancakes. She rolled over and threw up into the trashcan next to her bed.

She felt a little better after that and managed to stumble down the hall to the kitchen. Malcolm was busy at the stove, humming away and flipping pancakes. To her surprise, Alain was sitting at the kitchen table. She blearily took the chair across from him.

"Good morning, Sunshine," said Malcolm. "I'm glad to see you're still among the living."

"Coffee?" Alain asked, offering her a cup.

"Please. Thank you." Val groaned.

"Hung over?" Malcolm smirked.

"I feel like something died inside my brain."

"That's because something did, darling." Malcolm slid a little plate of pancakes onto the table in front of her. "Many somethings actually. You wouldn't believe how many brain cells you killed last night."

"That's OK. I wasn't using them anyway."

Val stared at the pancakes doubtfully. Her stomach rumbled, but she couldn't decide if it was hunger or nausea. Probably both. She decided to risk it and cautiously dribbled some butterscotch syrup over them before cutting off a small bite.

She eyed Alain across the table. "What are you doing here?"

"He came by to check up on you," said Malcolm. "I invited him in for pancakes. Any friend of yours is a friend of mine. Especially when they're as cute as this one is." He winked at Alain. The shifter flushed beneath his beard.

Was Alain cute? Val considered him doubtfully. She supposed he could be considered cute. If scruffy and emaciated was your type. He definitely had that dark, sensitive look going for him. Like rock stars, poets, and heroin addicts.

"I wouldn't think he was your type," she murmured.

Malcolm laughed. "Girl, I've got all kinds of types. That brooding artist thing he's got going on is sexy as hell."

Alain's flush darkened. He studied his coffee.

"And the way he blushes when you talk about him? Absolutely fucking adorable." Malcolm walked over to the table and pinched Alain's bicep. "Sure, he's a little on the scrawny side. But that's nothing my pancakes can't fix."

Val put a bite of pancakes in her mouth, chewed cautiously, and swallowed. When her stomach didn't reject it immediately, she cut off another bite.

"How long have you been here?" she asked Alain.

"Not that long. Just long enough for a cup of coffee."

"Not long enough for any shenanigans, if that's what you're implying," Malcolm said. "Besides, shenanigans come after pancakes."

"I'm sorry about last night," Val said. "Or this morning."

"Don't worry about it," Alain said gently. "I've been there. I guess whatever happened in that cave didn't go well?"

"That's the understatement of the century."

Alain quirked an eyebrow at her, inviting her to elaborate.

Val took a long sip of her coffee and sighed.

"Edward wasn't the murderer. Jack was."

"That tall dream is a murderer?" Malcolm gasped. "I suppose I shouldn't be surprised. The shittiest gifts always have the best wrapping paper. Still. That's a damn shame."

Val grunted. "Yeah, something like that."

"So what happened?" Alain asked carefully.

"I didn't know. I thought Edward was the killer. He tried to tell me, but I wouldn't listen." A tear dripped off the point of her chin, soaking into her pancakes. Val didn't notice. "I killed him. I killed an innocent man."

"Oh, honey." Malcolm wrapped his arms around her shoulders and she leaned her face against his chest. He didn't say anything more, he simply held her while she sniffled.

"Thank you," she said as she finally pushed him away and sat up.

"Anytime, girl. If there's one thing I'm good at besides pancakes, it's being a shoulder to cry on. You would not believe how many broken hearts I've seen. In fact, the broken hearts came first. The pancakes came later."

Val smirked. "Broken hearts and chocolate pancakes. You should open a restaurant."

Malcolm put his hands on his hips.

"You know, I really should. Especially in this town. I'd have so many customers I wouldn't know what to do." He looked so serious for a moment that Val almost laughed. "You know, I really think there might be an untapped market there. Everybody markets to lovers, but nobody thinks about what happens when the Happily Ever After runs out. I'll sell chocolate pancakes and ice cream. I'll make a killing."

Val winced, and Malcolm raised a hand. "Sorry. Poor choice of words."

"No, it's OK. I'm working on it." She took a sip of coffee and look at Alain. "So, the new moon is tonight. What's our plan?"

"I was hoping you had a plan."

Val sighed. "I was afraid you were going to say that."

The doorbell rang. Malcolm's eyes widened. "Oh shit, I forgot! That's got to be the new roommate candidate!"

Val snorted. "Perfect. I always like to meet new roommates when I've been crying."

"I can tell them to come back another time."

She sighed. "No, let's get it over with. Maybe we can at least cross one thing off the list today. We should probably move out to the living room, though. This kitchen isn't big enough for four people."

The person Malcolm escorted into the living room was built like a brick wall. Wide shoulders, square jaw, biceps as thick as a telephone pole. Close-cropped sandy hair hugged their skull above grey eyes. However, the eyes contradicted the body. They were soft and expressive, and crinkled shyly as Malcolm introduced them.

"Val, Alain, this is Sandra."

"Hello." Sandra's voice was little more than a whisper.

"Ignore me, I don't live here," Alain said. "Talk amongst yourselves."

Val snorted. "And I don't always look like a raccoon. But it's nice to meet you anyway. Come in, sit down. Tell us a bit about yourself."

Sandra perched daintily on the edge of an armchair. "Um. What would you like to know?"

"Whatever you think is important. What's your schedule like? Where do you work? What do you like to do for fun?"

"Do you squeeze the toothpaste in the middle or roll it up from the bottom?" Malcolm interjected. "Cause there is a right way and a wrong way, and some of us do it the wrong way." He shot Val a meaningful glare.

She rolled her eyes. "Yes, important things like that."

Sandra studied her toes, looking like a deer in headlights. "Um... well..."

"I can answer those other questions for you," Malcolm jumped in. "Sandra is an artist, and she makes the most amazing animations. For her day job, she works at the coffee shop below my office, which is where we met. She's sweet and kind and always remembers to put exactly two and a half sugars in my latte. That kind of attention to detail gives me hope about the toothpaste question." He cocked an eyebrow at the big woman.

"Um..." Sandra blushed adorably, the flush rising from her collar all the way up her cheeks. "Yes, all that is true. I make animation and I make coffee and... I like to knit and... pet cats."

"*Well, she's got my vote.*" Mister E twined around Sandra's ankles, purring.

"So you work mornings?" Val asked. Sandra nodded. "We won't be seeing much of each other then."

"No, I guess not. Malcolm told me you tend bar?"

"Yes, at the Alley Cat over in Polk Gulch."

"Oh!" Sandra finally looked up and met Val's gaze. "I know someone else who works there too. Do you know Junior?"

Val sat up. "You know Junior?"

Sandra smiled sheepishly. "His sister works at the coffee shop with me. He's really sweet."

Val returned the smile. "Yeah, he is."

She caught Malcolm's eye and gave him a nod that meant, *she seems fine to me.*

Malcolm nodded back, then turned to face Sandra.

"Okay, you're doing great. But before we make any decisions I really do need to know. How do you squeeze your toothpaste?"

They invited Sandra to move in at the end of the week.

After she left, the three of them warmed up their coffee and had an impromptu war council at the kitchen table.

Val and Alain talked about seraphim and scepters and vampires, while Malcolm kept the mugs full and interjected jokes whenever things got too grim.

By sunset, they had a plan.

"It's not the best plan in the world." Val leaned back and stretched, the vertebrae in her spine popping one by one. "But it's the best we're going to do on short notice."

"No plan survives first contact with the enemy anyway," Alain said.

"That's right," Malcolm agreed. "You need to improvise. Be fast on your feet."

"Well, in that case we're doomed," moaned Val. "I feel about as fast as a sloth on opioids right now."

Malcolm obligingly refilled her coffee cup.

"Don't you worry, girl. As long as there's coffee, there's always hope."

39

Valora returned from dumpster diving one evening to find the Emerald City dark and silent. Silvio hadn't wanted to come scavenging with her again. He'd been distant lately, his smiles less frequent, the silences growing between them. It made Valora's heart ache, but she didn't know what to do about it. She had never been in a relationship before. Never been close with anyone, really. So she continued to go through the motions, pretending nothing was wrong, pretending she didn't notice the difference.

She tried to distract herself by spending more time with Paula. Learning more about the history of magic. Studying old rituals and spells.

But inside, she was screaming.

This night there was no fire burning in the drum, no guitar, nobody sitting around singing songs or talking. It was as if someone had tipped the Emerald City up on its side and dumped all the people out. Where was everyone?

Valora wandered through the empty factory, poking her head into dark cubicles. Finally, she heard a murmur of voices from an unused back office. A sliver of light from under the door crept across the scuffed floor of the hallway.

Valora knocked once and pushed the door open, poking her head inside.

"Hey guys? Where is..." She stopped as if she'd hit a wall.

There, on an old mattress in the corner, lay two bodies. They were naked. What they were doing was unmistakable. The motion of the boy's hips. The soft sounds coming from the girl's mouth.

The hair spilling across the pillow was red, and the upturned face belonged to Amber. Her eyes were closed, her mouth open. Her hands were locked around the shoulders of the boy above her.

The boy was lean and muscled, with shaggy black hair spilling down over his neck. His parted lips were plump and sensual.

Valora would know those lips anywhere. She had run her hand over those shoulders a thousand times.

Silvio.

And Amber.

A great rushing filled her ears. Pain like she had never felt before stabbed right through the center. A red haze filmed her vision. She couldn't breathe. She wanted to throw up.

Anguish and pain and power roared up within her. The world turned black. Distantly, she could hear someone screaming. She didn't realize until much later the screaming person had been her.

The wind was there in an instant, a black cyclone swirling faster than any she'd ever called before. It screamed out of her, the voice of the storm rising with hers. It picked up dirt and debris, rusted nails and metal filings, turning the air dark and sharp. As black as her despair. As sharp as the shock of betrayal.

The storm raged, obscuring everything. There were no walls, no floor, no people. Only the rage of the storm.

Valora couldn't say how long the storm howled. She had no sense of time, no sense of anything at all. She was lost inside the darkness. Lost inside the pain.

Eventually, after what could've been days, or hours, or only minutes, Valora collapsed. She had pushed past her limit, releasing all the pain in a storm unlike anything she had ever summoned before. She'd drained herself utterly, and now she collapsed like a marionette with cut strings. She lay unmoving, a silent heap on the floor.

When she woke, the room was dark and still around her. Nothing moved. There was no skitter of mice in the walls. No birds chirping up in the rafters. It was silent as a grave.

She fumbled around until she found the lighter in her pocket and flicked it on.

Chaos surrounded her. The whirlwind had swept up all the leftover debris from the factory's past. Rusty nails, bolts and screws. Little pieces of jagged metal. Splinters and stones. They had scored the walls, gouging long scrapes and scratches in the old bricks.

But the bed was the biggest shock.

The two figures lying upon it looked like they'd been put through a blender. The skin had been flayed from the bodies, exposing red muscle and organs, with bits of white bone showing through here and there. The walls around them were splattered red, as was the mattress they'd been lying on.

They were both very dead.

To Valora's horror, she felt a warm satisfaction rise within her. Even pleasure.

They'd gotten what they deserved.

A low rumbling sound filled her head. It took her a second to realize it was Mister E, purring.

"What have I done?" she whispered. "I killed them." The words sounded far away, as if someone else were speaking them.

"*You did what needed to be done,*" Mister E replied. "*Pain must be paid with pain. Blood with blood.*"

"No. Not like this." Her stomach lurched and she fell to her knees, vomiting all over the floor. Hot bile burned up the back of her mouth and the insides of her nostrils. She heaved for a long time, until she had nothing left, until she felt empty and wrung out.

"I have to go," she whispered. "The others..."

Mister E stretched and yawned, showing his sharp teeth. "*You will deal with the others just as you've dealt with these. You have nothing to fear. You are a goddess.*"

"No." Valora pushed herself to her feet, stumbling back into the hallway. "No, this was an accident. I don't want to hurt anyone else."

Mister E chuckled.

"You are a force of nature, child. You might as well say you will stop the rain from falling. You will do what you do, because it is what you are. If people get in your way, they will get hurt. It is the natural way of things."

"Valora?" Paula appeared at the end of the hall, holding a yellow lantern. Her long purple dress brushed the floor. Crystals sparkled around her neck. "What happened? What's wrong?"

"Stay away from me." Valora shoved past the older woman. "Just leave me alone!"

"Valora, stop. Tell me what's going on!"

Valora ignored Paula, her stumbling feet carrying her through the darkened warehouse. She gave no thought to where she was going; she just knew she had to get away.

She crashed through the rusty metal door and into the night. Stars shone. A light, warm breeze blew. Spring was coming.

It was a perfect night, as if nature were mocking her. Her stumbling lurch became a run.

The world was beautiful. And she was a terrible, dark stain upon it.

40

"I feel like a ninja," Alain whispered.

"What?" Valora started, snapping back to the present, her golden eyes haunted. She'd been thinking of New York. Of the Emerald City all those years ago. Of Silvio and Amber. Of past sins she could never atone for.

"I said, I feel like a ninja," Alain raised his arms, showing off his tight black clothing. "Do you really think this is necessary? I could just transform, and then I'd be covered in black fur. My senses would be sharper too. Much better for stealth."

"It's always best to be prepared," said Val, bringing her attention back to the present with an effort. As her old therapist would have said, she couldn't change the past. All she could do was try for a better outcome today. Try to be a better person.

"*I wonder how Edward feels about that?*" Mister E asked, his crescent smile shining slyly in the darkness.

"Oh, fuck you," Val growled under her breath.

"Excuse me?"

Val cursed. Damn Alain and his enhanced hearing.

"Nothing. Just talking to myself." She shoved aside her dark thoughts, making an effort to keep her voice light. "They say the clothes make the man. You may not need to look like a ninja, but because you're dressed in black, you now feel like a ninja. And that's important. If we're going to survive tonight, we need all the ninja powers we can get. Besides, it's hard to have a conversation with you when you're a dog."

"I can't argue with you there."

They were crouched behind a low wall at the base of Mount Olympus. Well, the base of the crest of the mountain, anyway. The top of Mount Olympus had been turned into a public park once upon a time, which had been crowned by a massive pedestal and *The Triumph of Light* statue. At the time, it had been considered the geographic center of the city, commanding an uninterrupted view of the entire expanse of San Francisco, from beach to bay. Over the years, the city had encroached, and the park had been swallowed up piece by piece by the surrounding neighborhood. Nowadays it was just a small square, and all that remained of the once triumphant statue was an empty pedestal. The park itself had become disreputable, full of worn grass, half-dead trees, and litter. Home to homeless people and drug addicts.

"At least it's clear tonight," said Val. "I don't think I've ever seen so many stars in the city before."

"It's almost as if they've all come to observe the ceremony," said Alain.

"That is not a reassuring thought." Val gripped her knife and surveyed the surrounding park. Like Alain, she was dressed in black. Her customary black leather jacket, of course, but also black pants and black boots. Unlike Alain, she did not feel like a ninja. More like a hung-over biker.

The park was silent and dark. Cracked paths wound their way through the underbrush. Twisted trees covered most of the park, blocking out the weak starlight. There were lights over the paths, but a number of them were burned out, leaving darkness in their wake.

Val shivered. "Not exactly a reassuring atmosphere."

"If you're looking for reassuring, I think you're in the wrong line of work," said Alain. "Vampires and seraphim and ancient magical objects of power don't come together on bright sunny afternoons."

"Yeah." Val sighed. "Times like these make me regret my life choices."

She had the eerie feeling that they were not alone; she could feel eyes watching her from the dark. It could be her imagination. Or it could be vampires.

Most likely it was vampires.

She scowled. "I wish we knew what the ceremony entailed. It would be a lot easier to stop it that way."

Despite Malcolm's excellent work at the library, he had been unable to come up with anything concrete regarding the ceremony. Only the location and the time: the top of Mount Olympus at midnight on the night of the new moon.

"How do you think Jack knows what to do, anyway? Do the seraphim have their own private library?" Val knew she was babbling, and that she should probably shut up. But nerves were making her mouth run.

To his credit, Alain didn't seem to mind.

"The seraphim have been around for a very long time," he said. "I'm sure they have access to many things we don't."

"How does that work anyway? I thought magic was missing from the world for centuries and had only returned recently. If that's true, how do we have ancient creatures like vampires and seraphim?"

"Magic was weakened, not missing entirely," corrected Alain. "Magical creatures were still around, but there weren't many of us. We had to be very careful. Humans could've wiped us out."

"You mean with silver bullets?"

"With regular bullets, actually. That's how weak we were. It's only since the cataclysm that we've regained what you would think of as supernatural powers. Twenty years ago shifters could never live out in the open as we do today. Humans would've exterminated us in an instant."

"Does that apply to vampires and seraphim as well?"

Alain shrugged. "I wouldn't know. But I would think so, yes. We survived a number of desperate centuries."

"Maybe that's why they're so eager for the power of the scepter now."

"Perhaps. But I doubt it. The seraphim and vampires have always been power-hungry. In medieval times they were royalty, lording over the peasants."

"Like Vlad the Impaler."

"Exactly. Many of them used their powers to start a reign of terror. A lot of the most famous despots in history were supernatural creatures."

"Oh yeah? Who else?"

"I don't know the full list, but I can give you some of the most famous names. Genghis Khan. Alexander the Great. Julius Caesar."

"Where they all vampires?"

"No, they were all kinds of supernatural creatures. I don't know exactly what they were. Some may have been seraphim. Some may have been demigods."

"Demigods? You mean the offspring of gods and humans? Like all of those ancient Greek myths of Zeus rutting with the common people? That was a real thing?"

"Absolutely. All stories have a basis in reality somewhere. Never having met them, I can't tell you what type of gods the ancient Greek pantheon really were. If they were actual gods or if they were merely powerful supernatural creatures of a type that was specific to that area of the world. But I can confirm that they bred extensively with the human population, producing a great number of what we would consider demigods."

"Jesus," Val breathed.

Alain grinned. "Yes, him too."

Val stared at him.

"You can't be serious."

"Why not? Do you think Christian mythology is more reliable than any other kind? Where do you think their obsession with angels came from?"

"When you put it that way, I guess not. I'd just never thought of Christianity and mythology in the same category."

"Christian creation myths may have become the dominant narrative of our day, but that does not make them truer than any other set of myths. The seraphim were the power behind the Catholic church during the Middle Ages. They were driven out at some point and had to start a new religion. They decided to keep things a little more low-profile and founded the Black Knights. All religions rise and fall in their own time. They change and evolve, consuming other religions and being consumed in their turn. When mainstream Christianity falls, I'm sure something else will rise to take its place."

"My money's on aliens," Val grinned. "We'll be sacrificing cats to our new alien overlords any day now."

"Sacrificing cats?"

"I figure goats and cattle were sacrificed back in the day because shepherds were common. Everyone had goats. Today, not so much. But what does everyone have now? Cats."

"*I am not amused by this line of thinking,*" Mister E piped up sourly.

"You shouldn't be," Val whispered back. "I guarantee you'll be the first one on the sacrificial altar."

Mister E bared his teeth, his smile wide and luminous. "*Keep dreaming. Where I go, you go. Remember that.*"

A sound made them pause and look up. The *whump-whump* of great wings was approaching the hill. A shadow passed across the sky, barely visible against the backdrop of stars.

"He's here," Alain whispered.

Val nodded and tightened her grip on the knife. This was it. If Jack was able to complete the ceremony and assemble the Scepter of Sutro, who knew what would happen. Given that he had already murdered two people to get it, she was sure it wouldn't be anything good.

"Let's move closer," she whispered. "Quietly."

They slipped through the park, a pair of twin shadows. They stayed off the paths -- despite the burned-out lights there was still far too much illumination on them. Val winced at every leaf and twig rustling beneath her feet. Beside her, Alain was completely silent, and she envied him his shifter abilities.

At the center of the park was an open square, one hundred feet on each side. In the center of that stood the empty pedestal where *The Triumph of Light* once reigned over the city. A flagpole was now mounted atop the pedestal, the chill Pacific wind snapping taut a flag displaying the seal of the city of San Francisco. Jack stood on top of the empty pedestal beside the flagpole, his pale wings ghostly in the dark.

Starlight glittered along gold in his hands. He raised the scepter over his head, tilting his head back to the heavens. He began to chant, a low murmur, rising and falling. Val wasn't able to make out the words, but they sounded off, as if he were speaking in some long dead language, not English.

Val caught Alain's eyes. "Now or never." She crouched, preparing to rush the pedestal.

An iron grip closed around her forearm. Val yelped, and another hand clamped over her mouth.

"Quiet, girl." Ms. Pearl stood beside her, her dark eyes shining like wishing wells filled with raven's feathers. Her hands were strong and cold as stone. "He must be allowed to complete the ritual. The scepter must be made whole."

Val struggled, but it was no use. The vampire was too strong for her. Another vampire held Alain motionless as well.

"Don't worry, it won't be long now," Ms. Pearl purred.

Anger surged within Val, heat shooting up her spine. The wind began to blow, picking up leaves and swirling them around the square. Ms. Pearl tightened her grip, forcing Val to meet her eyes. "None of that, girl. Behave yourself or I'll snap your neck like a twig."

Val wasn't good at controlling herself. Once her emotions were triggered, they built and built, growing hotter until she erupted like a volcano. There wasn't an on/off switch she could trip. She ground her teeth, fighting her own panic and rage. It took every ounce of control she had, but she wrestled the wind down until there was just a slight breeze, echoing the simmering cauldron of her anger. Her power was banked, like a fire burned down to the coals, but it was not extinguished. Not by a long shot.

Atop the pedestal, light was building around Jack. The scepter began to glow like iron in a forge. The seraphim's chanting grew louder, rising to a crescendo. Lightning struck out of the moonless sky, burning Jack incandescent. The noise was incredible, the explosion so loud the shockwave knocked them all off their feet.

Val tasted dirt. Her head spun. She gagged and spit, free of the vampire's grip at last. She raised her head, peering blearily toward Jack.

His whole body was glowing, illuminated in the pure light of power. His face was exultant, his beautiful smile stretching his face beyond the point where a smile should end. He started to laugh.

The light in his eyes was pure madness.

Then the shadows exploded, and the vampires were upon him.

They moved almost too fast for Val to follow. Dark arrows flying toward the light.

Jack did not seem surprised. He didn't even seem worried. Pulses of light shot out from the Scepter of Sutro, catching the vampires in motion. Everywhere the light hit, vampires burst into flames.

The square was alive with the crackle of flames and the inhuman screams of the vampires. And rising above it all, Jack's maniacal laughter.

Val hardly heard any of it. Her ears were still ringing from the thunderclap. She heaved herself painfully up onto her elbows, and then to her feet. The square around Jack was like a shooting gallery. Vampires moving so quickly their movements blurred, Jack sniping at them as if he were playing a video game.

Then the vampires curved, suddenly coming at Jack in formation. Five of them rushing him at once from one side of the square.

Jack focused his fire in their direction. Taking them out. One. Two. Three. Vampires transformed into roaring pillars of flame.

"What are they doing?" Val wondered. "He's picking them off like clay pigeons."

Then she saw it, a lone vampire sneaking in behind Jack. While his attention was on the others. Beside her, another silhouette moved, dashing from his other side. Alain.

"Alain! No!" Her words were too slow, or Alain was too fast. Gone before the words could escape her lips.

Alain and the vampire hit Jack together. The seraphim's light was snuffed like a candle as he fell.

Val watched the golden scepter tumble over and over, ringing as it bounced across the flagstones of the square.

41

I t was like one of those slow-motion moments in a movie. The
Scepter of Sutro, bouncing and rolling, ringing like a bell. Jack and
Ms. Pearl and Alain, struggling in a tangle of fists and feet and cries of
pain. Impossible to tell where one ended and the other began.

Val was frozen, unsure what to do. She wanted to help Alain. She
wanted to hurt Jack.

But the scepter called to her like a beacon. Its long, flutelike shaft
gleaming as it rolled across the square.

Strange to think such a simple thing could be the cause of so much
struggle and death.

The scepter rolled toward her as if drawn by her own personal
gravity. She couldn't take her eyes off it.

She didn't know she'd made her choice until she reached out her
hand and stepped toward it.

Val could feel the power radiating from the scepter like heat. She
hesitated, her fingers inches away. Unsure what would happen if she
touched it.

Would it burn her? Would lightning strike her as it had Jack?

"*Pick it up*," hissed Mister E. "*Pick it up, you stupid girl.*"

"Fuck you, cat." Val pulled her hand away. "I'll break it just to spite you." She raised her foot, intending to stomp down on the scepter, to smash it back into the pieces from whence it came.

"No!"

A freight train hit her, knocking her off her feet. She slammed into the flagstones, rolling over and over with her mysterious attacker.

Instinct took over and she struggled, throwing elbows and knees. Punching out at whoever it was that held her down.

The slap that hit her snapped her head to the side. Stars exploded across her vision. Her ears rang. Whoever it was, they hit like a brick.

"Idiot, girl," Ms. Pearl snarled. "You trifle with forces you cannot understand."

She left Val lying there, stunned.

As the vampire reached for the scepter, a huge black dog snapped at her hand, causing her to pull it back. Alain stood over the scepter, growling.

Pearl sneered. "You can't stop me, shifter. But if you've come to die, I'm happy to oblige you."

"You'll have to oblige me first." Jack rejoined the fray, shining like a star. In his hand he held... a sword? Val blinked. Where the hell had he gotten a sword?

Pearl bared her fangs. "With pleasure, seraphim. If you'd like to die today, that can be arranged." She gestured and more shadows came out of the darkness, surrounding them. A ring of hard-faced men, carrying guns.

Val scowled as she recognized the Russian mafia. Vasilevski was working with the vampires.

She also counted six shadows moving with liquid grace. The surviving vampires.

Val did a quick count. A dozen Russians. Six vampires. Not good odds.

Alain still stood over the scepter, though. If Val could somehow get to that, they might have a chance.

Of course, every other person in the square was thinking the exact same thing.

She tried to think, find some angle to act, but indecision caught her. She wasn't even sure what she wanted out of this.

No, that wasn't true.

She knew exactly what she wanted. She wanted revenge. Revenge for Ruby and Shanna. She wanted Jack's blood.

But things were more complicated now. Val also didn't want to let the vampires win. She would oppose Ms. Pearl every day of the week on general principles.

Then things started moving, and the time for thinking was over.

The Russians opened fire as the younger vampires charged Jack, darting and feinting, working in unison like a pack of wolves. Jack's sword became a blur, slashing and cutting, blocking and thrusting so fast he looked like a blender. The sword wasn't as effective as the scepter had been -- the vampires didn't burst into flames whenever he touched them -- but it still did good work. She saw part of an arm hit the ground, and a vampire's head go spinning off into the darkness.

Jack didn't escape unscathed, though. His torso jerked as a pair of bullets connected. Also, the vampires were almost as fast as he was, and there were six of them.

Well, five now.

He cried out as one latched onto his back, rending and tearing. Long white feathers filled the air.

While the gangsters and vampires kept Jack busy, Ms. Pearl went for Alain.

The shifter was incredibly fast, especially in his canine form. He snarled and snapped, staying just beyond the vampire's claws. He nipped at her, but his teeth only closed on air. Her return swipes missed him as well. Stalemate.

Val lay in the darkness, momentarily forgotten.

If she moved, she would be forgotten no longer. But she didn't have to move to be effective. If she could summon a small, tightly targeted gust of wind, maybe she could sweep the Scepter of Sutro towards her.

Of course, small, targeted magic wasn't exactly her thing. She was more of a big, dramatic gesture kind of girl.

Still, she had to try.

She summoned the power within her, channeling it and shaping it. Her nostrils filled with the remembered scents of honey and sage, the crisp air swirling around Mount Olympus. The memory blurred, becoming one with the cold, damp wind blowing in from the Pacific. She called to it, gathering it to her, trying to catch just a tiny piece of it. Focusing her power down and down and down. To create a tight gust that would hit the scepter and only the scepter, pushing it across the square, lifting it and bringing it to her waiting grasp.

What she got... wasn't that.

The wind came towards her all right, but she didn't get a tiny piece of the wind. She got all of it. Howling down out of the sky in a massive gale. Dust and dirt, twigs and leaves filled the air, pelting everyone in the square, forcing the combatants to close their eyes and cower before the blast. The wind howled and roared, ripping the seal of the city down off the flagpole, whipping the fabric across the square in an instant.

The loose flag twisted around the scepter like a live thing, and the wind snatched them both from the flagstones. The flag-wrapped scepter shot toward Val like a bullet. She reached out her hand to catch it, but the wind swirled again, pushing it up, lifting the scepter beyond her grasp.

"No!" Mister E hissed.

Val watched helplessly as the cloth-wrapped scepter went spinning off into the night.

42

V al hoped for a moment that no one else had noticed. That in the maelstrom of dirt and dust and flying debris, the quick flight of the scepter had eluded their attention like the darting of a hummingbird.

That hope did not last long.

"No!" Jack screamed, and launched himself straight up into the air, his great wings straining, angling to intercept the scepter.

The roaring wind shoved him back down. He struggled, flapping harder, and Val could see the tendons standing out like cables in his neck. After a point, the wind actually started to work with him, in a way. He had to fight against it to get up in the air, but once he was airborne, it bore him along in the same direction the scepter had gone. East towards the bay.

Val couldn't let that happen.

She reached out with her mind and turned the wind, bending it around her as if it were tied to the end of a long string, using her body as a fulcrum. The wind surrounding Jack curled to the south, toward Twin Peaks, carrying the struggling angel with it. His anguished scream rose and was borne away, disappearing along with his body into the night.

Unfortunately, the ground-bound vampires were not so easily manipulated. They darted off to the east, running impossibly fast, black streaks pursuing the distant glint of the scepter.

Val and Alain stared at each other.

"Go," Val snapped. "You're faster than I am on foot. Try to get to the scepter before the vampires."

Alain barked once and took off, his lean body accelerating low to the ground, long strides eating the distance. He was made for running, a thing of fluid beauty, born to pursue. In a blink he was gone, swallowed by the darkness beneath the trees fringing the square.

Val watched him go, cursing. The Ural was parked on the other side of the park, down at the base of the hill. By the time she got to it, both the scepter and the vampires would be long gone. She would have no hope of catching them.

And that's assuming that she could even locate the scepter again. Once it was out of sight, it would be gone forever. There was no telling where it would come down. It might disappear for another hundred years.

Also, there was the small matter of the Russians. With the supernaturals out of the picture, the gangsters were all staring at her.

Vasilevski stepped towards her. He did not look happy. "You are the bartender. Why are you here?"

"*Fly, you fool,*" Mister E hissed.

"What? I can't fly."

"*You are the mistress of the wind. Of course you can fly. Command the wind to bear you.*"

Val considered this. She had never tried to fly. It never even occurred to her that she might. She'd had dreams of flying, of course. Flying was every kid's dream. But the bridge from dream to reality had always seemed too great. She didn't have wings, or a parachute, or even skin flaps to extend like a flying squirrel. What was the wind going to catch on to lift her?

"*It will catch on your body, imbecile. Focus the air beneath you. Control your power for once in your life. You can do more than just call down cyclones.*"

Val's heart pounded in her throat. She had to admit, the idea was thrilling. Who wouldn't want to fly? But the practicality was daunting. Even if she managed to get herself into the air, how would she steer? It was dark, and she was in the middle of the city. She was more likely to slam herself into the side of a building than she was to catch the scepter.

"I am talking to you," Vasilevski was crossing the square, his gun held low. It wasn't exactly pointed at her, but it wasn't not pointed at her either.

"*You must act now,*" Mister E hissed. "*Are you so stupid that you cannot control your gifts? The gift paid for by your mother's blood? Are you so fearful that you will run from greatness when it is before you? I should've let you die on that hillside. Let the other children pick you apart like vultures. If you had died as a child, you would've saved us both a lot of time.*"

Val's anger flared. And with it, her power.

"I'll show you who's a waste of time, you pathetic little shit."

She called the wind to her, funneling it down, narrowing it in the way she had failed to do when she was trying to fetch the scepter. Fueled by her anger, she used her will to wrestle the power into the shape she wanted it to be.

There was no coaxing, no pleading. Just raw desire and aggression.

A cloud of grit swept across the square. Vasilevski cursed and turned away from the wind, covering his face with his arm.

The wind upon her back doubled, then doubled again. It roared like nothing she had ever experienced before, so loud she couldn't hear herself think.

So strong she felt her feet begin to slide over the flagstones.

Her surprise caused her concentration to falter, and the wind lost its focus, spreading out around her once more.

"*Dolt,*" Mister E growled. "*Incompetent girl.*"

Val growled right back and ground her teeth together. Annoying little shit. She'd show him.

She focused the wind on her back again, doubling and doubling and doubling in force, until it was no longer only wind but a live thing, a giant hand shoving against her.

She felt the hand shape itself against her back, becoming as solid as flesh. Between one breath and the next, she was airborne.

She didn't let her surprise rattle her focus this time. Good thing, too. Within seconds, she was thirty feet in the air, clearing the tops of the scrubby trees bordering the square. The slope of Mount Olympus fell away beneath her, and she was flying.

A cry of pure triumph and joy ripped from her throat. She was flying. Really flying!

A building loomed up before her, and her heart skipped. She pulled on the wind in a panic, willing it to lift her higher. The wind obliged and she cleared the roof by inches.

OK, altitude. She needed more altitude.

Fortunately, San Francisco wasn't a particularly tall town. Building codes kept most neighborhood construction between three and five stories, aside from the small pocket of skyscrapers downtown. Downtown was a long way away though, and she was starting from the top of the hill. Very quickly, she was soaring high above the rooftops, looking down at the grid of streetlights below. Lights in windows. Flashing headlights.

For a moment she was lost in the magic of it all. A six-year-old child, wide-eyed with wonder, gasping and grinning. She felt like she'd been sprinkled with fairy dust. Like Peter Pan had come and she was on her way to Neverland.

Then Mister E growled in her ear and the spell was broken.

"Focus, girl. Your quarry is getting away."

She looked up, and panic gripped her. She couldn't see the scepter. There were too many lights, and for a moment she thought it was all for nothing. That she'd managed to fly but lost the prize anyway.

Then she saw a distant glint of gold, tumbling end over end. Relief hit her and her control wavered. She started to fall, dropping twenty feet in a second. Val yelped like a scalded cat as the street rushed up to meet her.

43

R iding the wind was not easy. In fact, it was the hardest thing Val had ever tried to do. The wind was not used to being controlled. It was capricious and inconsistent, blowing hard and soft, this way and that. Darting and spinning. The amount of air pressure needed to keep a full-grown human aloft, especially one without a parachute or wings, was enormous. Val needed a steady wind supporting her, and that steady wind needed to be blowing hard. If it slacked off, even for a second, Val would fall. And if she fell, her landing would not be soft.

All these thoughts flashed through her mind as she tumbled down. Her fight-or-flight instinct kicked in. Hard. Though in this instant it was probably more accurate to call that instinct flight-or-death. Fortunately, that instinct seemed to have better control of the wind than her conscious mind did. The panicking, animal part of her brain reached out and grabbed the wind instinctively, forcing a hard blast to swirl underneath her, blowing straight up so that she hovered in the air, like the people in those indoor flying places.

"What the hell am I doing?" she moaned, trying not to hyperventilate. "I'm going to die. Why did I let you talk me into this?"

"*When did you become such a whiny adult?*" Mister E said dismissively. *"The girl I met in the attic would've flown without hesitation. She wouldn't have given a thought to her own safety. Only the thrill of adventure."*

"That girl was seven years old! Children are too dumb to have a sense of self-preservation. They don't realize they could die. Me, on the other hand? I realize it all too well."

"You are weak. You are a weak vessel. We could fill a library with all of the things you have yet to learn."

"If I'm a poor student, maybe that has something to do with my teacher. If you'd told me I could fly before this, I'd have done it already."

"Yawn. Are you going to stay here and complain all night? Or are you going to get that scepter? I'm sure the vampires aren't wasting time squabbling amongst themselves."

Val glared at him, her golden eyes shining. "Fine. But this discussion isn't over. If I survive this, we are going to have a long talk, you and I. And you are going to tell me all the things I can do with my power that you haven't bothered to mention until now."

Mister E laughed. *"That will be a very long discussion. I suggest you bring milk and cookies."*

Val huffed. Infuriating cat. She scanned the sky, trying to find the scepter again. A chill went down her spine when she didn't see it.

No. There it was. Spinning out over the Mission District.

She gathered her will and bent the wind underneath her, pushing herself forward. She flew in fits and starts, in quick bursts forward, heart-stopping drops, and stomach-churning rises. She felt like she was in an out-of-control elevator. Or a plane moving through insane turbulence.

When a downdraft caused her to plunge a hundred feet, and nearly ended with her dead body splattered upon Church Street, she bit her bottom lip clear through.

Spitting blood, she said, "All of this up and down is not good for my stomach. I'm going to be sick."

Mister E didn't dignify that with a response, but she could feel his scorn radiating.

Five blocks later, she vomited all over Sixteenth Street, the wind snatching the hot mess from her mouth and scattering it over several city blocks.

"Well, that's going to make a lot of people unhappy." She belched. "Seems to have helped my stomach, though. I feel a little better now."

"*I'm so glad to hear it.*" Mister E dripped sarcasm. "*Now, if you're done being a frail human, can you please focus? The vampires are getting ahead of you.*"

Val looked down and saw he was right. Three shadows on 16th, running straight down the middle of the street, dodging the sparse late-night traffic with ease. She watched as they shot across Valencia and then Mission Street. Past the now empty square where the farmers market set up in the afternoon. The taco truck was still up and running, though, merrily lit with strings of green and red lights. Pushing out late night burritos to drunk people.

Val cursed and set her teeth, urging the wind to carry her faster as she raced the vampires across Van Ness.

"How do they intend to get the scepter, anyway? It doesn't show any signs of dropping soon. Can they fly up there?"

"*What goes up must come down. All they need to do is keep it in sight until that happens,*" Mister E said. "*And where did you get the idea that they can't fly? Haven't you heard stories of vampires turning into bats?*"

"They can actually do that?"

"*Well, most of them cannot. But a vampire of Ms. Pearl's experience is another matter.*" His golden eyes glanced meaningfully to her left.

It took her a minute to pick out the dark shape against the night sky, but then she saw it. A bat. A really, really large bat.

"Holy shit. That bat's as big as I am."

"*Of course it is. Haven't you ever heard of the law of conservation of matter? Matter can be neither created nor destroyed. Therefore, a vampire turning into a bat must turn into a bat that has the same amount of matter as the original vampire.*"

"Stuff it, Professor. I can't believe you're mixing science and magic like that. Pick one, would you?" Val growled. She redoubled her efforts, urging the wind to greater speed.

Unfortunately, the vampire had become aware of her as well. Pearl picked up her speed to match. It was a race for the prize.

"I wonder if I can blow her away like I did Jack?" Val turned her focus on the wind to her left, where the dark silhouette of the vampire was closing in. She concentrated on turning the wind north, blowing the vampire off course.

To her surprise, it worked. The vampire squawked as a hard gust hit her, pushing her toward the skyscrapers of downtown.

Unfortunately, as this happened, Val started to drop.

"Shit!" Her heart surged with panic, trying to beat its way out of her chest. Val windmilled her arms and legs as the street accelerated toward her. She flashed past a rooftop. Then the windows of the third floor.

Instinct saved her again, a hard gust of wind coming up beneath her, arresting her in midair, less than ten feet above the asphalt.

She hung there, gasping, "Oh my god oh my god oh my god."

Mister E huffed. "*You're pathetic. You cannot even split your concentration in two. What have you been doing all these years? How do you not have better control over your powers?*"

"You'd better ask my teacher," Val gasped. She pinned him with a sarcastic smile. "Thanks for everything, Teach."

She soared back up into the air, skimming over the rooftops. Despite her sarcasm, she could feel her control getting better. Not that it was easy by any means, and she climbed high up to keep a hundred-foot cushion between her and the nearest rooftop and guard against sudden drops.

But she was definitely getting the hang of flying.

The wind felt less like a wild animal and more like water, flowing around her. She could sense its flows and curls, its rushes and eddies. She visualized herself cupping her hands around it, shaping it like clay on a wheel. Moving it into this channel and that.

She had to maintain a strong updraft pushing on her at all times to stay aloft, and she kept the wind tilted at an angle, moving both up and forward simultaneously. Getting the pressure just right to maintain a level flight was almost impossible, so she moved in long arcs, as if she were throwing herself forward and then falling slightly, before she caught herself with next updraft and threw herself forward again.

At first this up-and-down motion was terrifying, and she felt she was always on the verge of falling. But as she got the hang of it, it started to feel, well, not quite comfortable, but at least familiar.

The scepter still sparkled in the distance. How had it stayed aloft for so long? Especially without her concentrating on the wind that bore it. Shouldn't it have fallen by now? Even wrapped in the flag, it was still a long metal tube, after all. Objects like that weren't lighter than air.

"Maybe it's a magical floating scepter," she muttered.

"*Don't strain your little mind too much thinking about it,*" snarked Mister E. "*It is what it is. Accept that and move on. And speaking of moving on, I suggest you go a little faster. The vampire is coming back.*"

44

A glance to her left showed that Mister E was right. The dark silhouette of Ms. Pearl was arrowing back in her direction.

"Is it just me, or is she coming towards me and not the scepter?" Val said.

"*Oh, she's definitely coming towards you.*" Mister E seemed entirely unruffled. "*You must have pissed her off with that little wind stunt pushing her away.*"

"Great, just what I need. Aerial combat. As if just flying isn't hard enough."

"*Perhaps you can outrun her if you set your mind to it.*"

"Perhaps." But Val wasn't optimistic. She was already flying as fast as she could, and the giant vampire bat was gaining on her.

Still, she gamely gritted her teeth and tried to call more wind. To her relief, it worked. The gale around her grew, roaring like a lion. She shot forward, and for the first time she felt like she was actually gaining on the scepter.

A grin split her face. She was flying. She was a wind witch.

This was awesome.

Val shot past Potrero Hill and out over the industrial area bordering the bay. The scepter was only a couple of hundred yards away now.

She watched as it cleared the shoreline and drifted out over open water.

Almost there.

She closed on it, stretching out her hand. A little closer...

The world went sideways as Ms. Pearl hit her with the force of a mountain.

They tumbled over and over, the vampire slashing at her with giant bat claws, trying to sink her fangs into Val's neck. Val was thankful for the thick skin and high collar of her leather jacket. Bikers didn't call them armor for nothing.

She tried to fight back, elbowing and punching, but she didn't have a lot of leverage. The vampire was latched onto her back. Val elbowed and squirmed, but couldn't get turned around to get a good punch in. Also, fighting in the air was weird. There was nothing to push off of, no leverage except what you could create using your opponent. Most of Val's fighting techniques were useless in this context.

They fell in fits and starts. Val couldn't maintain her concentration to keep the wind pressure up while she was fighting. And it was difficult struggling against the vampire while also struggling against gravity.

For her part, Ms. Pearl seemed unconcerned about their plunge toward the freezing waters of the bay. Val figured the vampire must plan to drop her and soar away at the last minute, leaving Val to take the dunking.

"Not going to happen, bitch."

She pulled the knife from her belt and stabbed the vampire's body. A high-pitched shriek let her know she had hit home.

Pearl's grip didn't loosen, though, so she stabbed again. And again. And again.

Finally, between one breath and the next, the vampire released her, Pearl's weight disappearing from her back.

Val had no time to relax or rejoice. The dark surface of the bay was coming up fast. Desperately, she called to the wind, and it caught her just in time, skimming her across the tips of the waves. Salt spray wet her face as she sucked in the cold air.

She shuddered as she willed the wind to bear her back up. That was too close.

She swiveled her head around, trying to find the vampire as she shot toward the scepter once more. There was no sign of her.

"Maybe I scared her off," she muttered.

"*Or maybe she's just biding her time,*" offered Mister E.

"You're a ball of sunshine, you know that?"

"*Always happy to help.*"

Val flew up into the night, nothing below her now but the dark expanse of the bay. City lights ghosted the water, along with the sparkling of thousands of stars. The reflected city lights wavered beneath the waves, as if there were another city lurking down there, a wet city undiscovered by the surface dwellers. To her left, the bay bridge glittered, lights illuminating the graceful arches and swooping support cables.

She put on a burst of speed and closed on the scepter once again.

Fifty yards.

Forty.

Twenty.

Her hand closed around the golden shaft.

Another hand closed around hers.

45

Val looked up into the sculpted face of Jack. The seraphim smiled, his blue eyes full of starlight.

"Fancy meeting you here," he said. His smile was as flirtatious as ever. As if he were sitting across the bar from her at the Alley Cat, sipping a White Russian.

Despite herself, despite everything she knew about him, his beauty still took her breath away.

But beauty was only skin deep. And in Jack's case, it barely went that far.

She kicked at him, but the kick had no force; there was no ground to push off of. Jack blocked it easily, his smile never wavering.

"Is that any way to treat a friend?"

"You're no friend of mine," Val growled.

The corners of his mouth turned down in an exaggerated frown.

"No? I can't tell you how sad that makes me. Like the tears of a clown."

"The tears of a murderer, you mean. Crocodile tears." Val slashed at him with her knife, but Jack dodged it easily. He was much more comfortable in the air than she was, maneuvering reflexively.

Duh. He'd been born with wings.

"I never wanted to hurt anyone, you know. Least of all you." His eyes were so sad it almost broke her heart.

"Tell that to Ruby and Shanna," Val snarled. "Tell that to Ruby's little girl."

Jack sighed. "We all do what we must."

On the word "must" he yanked the scepter, hard, trying to pull it from her grasp. Val had been expecting this, and she held tight. He whipped her through the air around him as if she weighed no more than a child, but she clung to the scepter as if her life depended on it.

Which it probably did.

Jack hit her with his wing, a powerful flex that battered one whole side of her body. The air whooshed out of her. She felt like she'd been hit by a bus. His wings were strong. She slashed at him again, but again he avoided her attack easily. She was no match for him in the air. She needed an alternative plan.

Val called the wind from the south, creating a gust that pushed them north, toward the bridge. Jack didn't seem to notice or, more likely, he just didn't care. He was utterly confident in his superiority.

"Sacrifices must be made for the greater good," he said. "You don't understand what the Scepter of Sutro can do."

"I don't care what it can do. Those sacrifices are people. People I cared about. Nobody gets to hurt my friends on my watch."

"Your watch?" Jack quirked an amused eyebrow at her.

"That's right, Jack. My watch. My city. My people. My friends. And creeps like you don't get to kill them."

Jack laughed. "And you say I have illusions of grandeur."

"I'm not a ruler, Jack. But as they say in the comics, 'With great power comes great responsibility.' I've got the power and I'm going to use it responsibly."

"Sounds like somebody's got a guilty conscience. Overcompensating much?"

Val said nothing because he was right. She did have a guilty conscience. She had killed children. She'd killed her friends in New York. She'd even killed her own mother. Nothing she did could ever make up for that. She knew that.

Still, she had to try. Attempt to balance the scales in whatever small measure she could. Her power may be evil. Mister E may be savage and bloodthirsty and primal. But Val didn't have to be. She would fight those urges with everything she had. Fight to use her powers for good.

It was all she could do. It was her only hope.

The wind slammed them down on top of the bridge.

They hit the ground and slid. Val was ready for it and didn't let go of the scepter. Jack was caught by surprise, his hand opening reflexively as he tried to catch himself.

For a moment, Val held the scepter alone.

Time froze. She was lying on top of one of the support towers of the Bay Bridge. The platform was cold and hard against her back. The sky shone around her, lit by the lights of the bridge, the lights of the city, the lights of Oakland and San Jose in the distance.

Then came the greatest light of all. In an instant, she could feel every living soul in San Francisco. Millions of minds. Millions of spirits. Millions of hearts beating. The scepter touched them all.

She could see them, like bright points of light scattered upon a map. But more than that, she could feel them. Feel their energy, their spirits, the energy pulsing through their veins.

It was like nothing she had ever experienced before. It was like touching the heart of a star.

What did someone do with that kind of power? Could she communicate with them? Could she tap into that energy?

The thought was staggering. The power of millions of people. The possibilities were endless. She could be a god.

No wonder Ms. Pearl and Jack were so eager to possess the scepter. Back in Sutro's time, this would've been a powerful weapon. But back then the population of San Francisco was a tiny fraction of what it was now. Now... her mind reeled, unable to grasp the implications. She was like an amoeba trying to understand a human being. The scale was beyond her.

And then, as quickly as it had come, the sensation was gone. The air huffed out of her, the icy surface of the platform slamming against the back of her skull. There was someone else there. Another presence, wrestling for control.

Jack was back.

46

"Your human mind cannot comprehend the forces you are trifling with," Jack snarled. "Give me the scepter. Give it to me and everything will be better."

"Better for who?" Val shot back.

Jack smiled, and she saw the madness in his eyes, burning like a fire out of control.

"Better for everyone. There's so much waste in the world. Time and energy wasted. Humans working at cross purposes to one another. Building up and tearing down in a constant cycle. This earth could be a paradise with the right hand to guide it. The right vision. Someone with enough power and imagination to end all this needless conflict. All this working at cross purposes. I can make the suffering end. I can make all of humanity march to the same tune. Imagine what we could accomplish with millions of souls working in harmony."

He yanked on the scepter, but Val held fast, refusing to relinquish her grip.

"You're insane," she growled. "Delusional."

"No, I have a vision."

"You know who else had a vision, Jack? Every conqueror and petty tyrant in history. Genghis Khan had a vision. Alexander the Great had a vision. Hitler had a vision. They were all seraphim too, weren't they? Is that just what your kind do, Jack? Have visions? Visions that involve subjugating millions of people? You don't want humanity. You want ants. One giant hive mind, with you sitting at the top. Well, that's not what it means to be human. Being human is messy. It's chaotic. But that's the beauty of it, Jack. Love, passion, inspiration. All of these things are possible because we are individuals. If you kill our freedom, you kill the best parts of being human. The things that make us exceptional. There's a reason that dictatorships are drab and cheerless places. People aren't meant to be drones."

Jack's blue eyes shimmered with tears. His perfect lips curled down. He looked at her with such infinite sadness that Val felt her heart would explode.

"I'm sorry," he said. "I'm sorry you cannot understand."

And then he punched her in the face.

The back of her head cracked against the metal platform. Stars exploded before her eyes, a loud gong echoing in her ears.

She blinked, and he hit her again. And again. And again. The world went soft at the edges. Her body felt distant. Blackness closed in.

She felt her grip on the scepter start to slip. Jack hit her one more time and pulled the golden rod from her nerveless fingers.

From far away, Val heard him laughing. There was nothing sane at all in that laughter. But the sound was still beautiful. She could see how the seraphim had done it throughout history. How they'd always gotten people to follow them. Even in his insanity, Jack's charisma shone like a star.

"Just like every abuse victim. They know the fuckers are crazy, but they love them anyway," Val slurred. "I guess that makes me the beaten wife in this story."

The words sparked anger. Fury raged up inside her like a bonfire. She would be no one's victim. Never again.

A cyclone sprang up around them, wind whipping at her hair, plucking at Jack's wings. Swirling faster and faster. No, not just a cyclone. This was a full-blown tornado. A dark funnel stretching up, blotting out the sky, full of sound and power and fury.

Val felt herself lifted off the platform. Dimly, she could see Jack rise as well. He was still shining through the murk, like a light deep at the bottom of a pond. Despite all his power, despite the millions of lives he had to draw from, he was no match for the elemental fury of the storm. Jack might have the people of San Francisco on his side, but the winds spanned the globe. Wind was everywhere, and nothing could stop it.

The air buffeted Val, spinning her around, shaking her like a dog with a rag. She clung to a slim thread of consciousness as it tried to slip away.

She would not lose. She would not let Jack win.

"*You don't have to fight so hard,*" Mister E said. "*You are the mistress of the wind. Embrace its power. It is you and you are it.*"

"I can't," Val choked. "It's too strong."

"*Your lack of imagination is pathetic. Stop trying to fight it. Let it in. Let the wind be the blood in your veins. The breath in your lungs. It is your birthright. You've paid the blood price for this power, and now you must use it. Embrace it or it will destroy you. It is the only way.*"

Val tried. She tried to control the storm, bend it to her will.

It was too strong, roaring and swirling like a living thing. She was an insect trying to turn a flood.

"I can't," she groaned.

"*Do not fight it. You must accept it. Let it in. The wind is your ally, not your servant.*"

She tried again, tried letting down her barriers, opening herself to let the wind in.

It took her breath away, literally yanking the air out of her lungs. She couldn't breathe. Couldn't do anything. The blackness at the edges of her vision expanded, the tiny thread of consciousness slipping away from her.

"*Accept it. Accept it or it will kill you.*"

Accepting was hard. Val had been fighting her entire life. Fighting against the other children. Against her parents. Against the orderlies at the institutions. She was a fighter, it was who she was.

Mister E whispered in her ear. "*You cannot do everything alone. Let the wind be your ally.*"

The blackness at the edge of her vision covered everything. The thread of consciousness was slipping ... slipping ... slipping ... and then it was gone.

Val let go.

Air rushed back into her lungs. Her eyes flew open. She drew the sweetest breath she had ever taken.

She was no longer being buffeted by the wind. Now she floated in a pocket of calm, a self-contained eye in the storm.

Around her, the tornado whirled and roared and growled. Jack was flung about like a toy, his light spinning in the murk.

But for Val, all was calm.

She could feel every inch of the tornado, from its base upon the bridge support pillar, all the way up into the clouds. She was the storm, and the storm was her. She turned her attention to Jack. He was shouting and cursing, struggling with all his might. But his words were ripped away by the wind before they even left his mouth. Even with the Scepter of Sutro, he was an infant kicking against a giant.

Val tore him apart.

In the space of a single breath, she shredded his wings. The wind slammed him from several directions, pulling feathers out in a flurry of white. Jack screamed, and Val seized the breath carrying that scream. She refused to let him draw another one. He gasped, his face growing red, tendons bulging in his neck as he tried to fill his empty lungs.

Val watched his face go from red to purple. That beautiful face. A face that would sink a thousand ships. A face that men and women would die for. It blackened and bulged, and finally slackened as he lost consciousness. His body went limp.

As the scepter fell from his grasp, Val exhaled a breath she didn't even know she'd been holding. She had done it. She'd defeated an angel.

Val allowed the tornado to dissipate, gently setting Jack down on top of the tower.

"*Kill him.*" Mister E's grin was bigger than his face. "*He's prey. We've earned this kill.*"

Val looked down at Jack's body. He looked so innocent in repose, like a sleeping baby. As if he could never harm anyone.

"No. I've plucked his feathers and humiliated him. He's helpless. I won't kill him in cold blood. I think I'll leave him up here. Maybe this will teach him a lesson."

"*His kind do not learn. He will come after you again. He'll come for revenge.*"

Val shrugged.

"Let him come. I beat him once, I can beat him again. He doesn't scare me anymore."

"*What about retribution? What about your friend Ruby?*"

A wave of emotion threatened to drag Val under at Ruby's name. An image of her friend's body flashed up, lying in her own fluids in the lot behind the Alley Cat, intestines uncoiling in dull grey ropes.

But the emotion threatening to overwhelm her wasn't anger this time. It was sorrow.

"Killing him isn't going to bring Ruby back. Does he deserve to die? Probably. Am I going to be the one who kills him?" She gazed down at Jack for a long moment, the wind rising around her, responding to her agitation. It would be so easy to slit his throat. Or stab him through the heart. "No. I've got enough blood on my hands."

As she turned away, a gust of wind swept the top of the tower like a giant hand, pushing Jack's unconscious body off the surface in one clean motion. Val whirled, rushing to the edge of the platform.

She watched the pale shape of his body tumble down, getting smaller and smaller, until the dark waters of the bay finally swallowed him.

She kept her eyes focused on the spot, but Jack did not resurface.

"Shit."

"*I think your heart is less forgiving than you believe it to be.*" Mister E circled her ankles, rubbing his back against her shins.

Val sighed and scrubbed her hands over her face.

"I'm trying to be a better person. I guess I'm not there yet."

"*You are a predator. Embrace it.*" The cat extended his claws in front of him, arching his back and stretching as he dragged them across the metal. They left bright gouges in the steel.

"I'm a person. I decide what I am, not you," Val snapped.

"*Keep telling yourself that. You cannot deny your nature.*" Mister E laughed and leapt lightly onto her shoulder. *"What of the scepter? What will you do with the Scepter of Sutro?"*

Val lifted the golden rod, examining it closely for the first time. It was beautiful, flaring into a fist-sized knob at one end, meticulously engraved in the art nouveau style. A grand scepter for the end of the nineteenth century.

She thought about the things she could do with it. All the wrongs she could right. If she could force people to do the right thing, she could create a better society. A better world.

"No," she murmured. "That's what Jack would do. It's too powerful. No one should have that much power."

She set the scepter down upon the platform. It gleamed up at her, golden and beautiful. It was a work of art. A talisman of a bygone era. An era of San Francisco's history when anything was possible.

With a cry, she brought her heel down upon the center of the rod, snapping it in half. She stomped on it again and again, breaking it back down into the pieces from which it came. On the last stomp, she couldn't get it to break.

"Oh, well. Five pieces will have to do."

She summoned the wind and lifted the broken pieces of the Scepter of Sutro gently, like a mother lifting a child. Then she scattered them far across the bay. One by one, she flung them into the murky water, where no one would ever find them again.

"Foolish child," Mister E hissed. *"We could have ruled this city."*

Val laughed.

"That sounds like the shittiest job ever. I can barely handle my own life; why in the world would I want to control the lives of millions of other people?"

"Your lack of imagination is appalling. Your life is small." Mister E turned his back on her, sulking.

"Yes, it is. It's just the size I want it to be."

Val summoned the wind and let it carry her into the night. Back to her city.

47

The Alley Cat was even louder than usual. Every table was full, and the noise of conversation was so overwhelming you could barely hear the music coming through the speakers. It was like one of the busiest Saturday nights Val had ever seen.

Except it wasn't a Saturday night. It was a Tuesday. And the people were here to mourn, and to remember. They were here to celebrate a life.

They were here for Ruby.

"Hey, bartender. Who do I have to bribe to get some service around here?"

Val gritted her teeth and turned on the voice, brandishing a bottle. She'd been running for hours, pouring drinks nonstop. Most of the people had been polite and patient. But if this joker thought...

She stopped when she saw who it was, her golden eyes shining.

"Alain, I was hoping you'd make it."

The shifter grinned at her. "Wouldn't miss it for the world."

She poured him a shot of whiskey and slid it across the bar. Then she poured one for herself.

"To Ruby," she said, raising her glass.

"To Ruby." He downed the shot and leaned across the bar, shouting over the din. "This is quite the party."

"A celebration of life."

"She definitely lived a life worth celebrating," Alain agreed.

Val looked over the crowd. There were hundreds of people in the club. Men and women. Young punks and retirees. People from all walks of life.

"I had no idea Ruby had so many friends. I never really knew her outside the club."

Alain smiled a sad smile.

"Everybody loved her. She always had time for you, day or night. She was a great listener."

"Well, I hope she's listening now." Val poured them another round of shots and raised her glass again. "Godspeed, Ruby."

Alain cleared his throat. "I wanted to say thank you."

"For what?"

"For getting the bastard who killed her."

Val felt Mister E's satisfied smile on her shoulder. The bloodthirsty little shit.

"He deserved it."

"Still, I would've never been able to get him on my own. A seraphim? With the Scepter of Sutro?" He whistled. "You're something else, Val Keri. You're really something else."

Val rolled her eyes. "That's what my therapist always said."

Alain nodded at the saran wrap on her shoulder. "Fresh ink?"

Val looked down at the twilight sky on her shoulder, the new green star sparkling like a sequin against the purple and blue hues.

"It's a memorial. For Ruby."

Alain nodded. "That's fitting. She certainly loved art."

What she didn't tell him was that the new ink was just a piece of a larger memento mori that stretched halfway across her chest. Over her heart. There were pieces there for everyone who had ever died because of her: Katrina. Her mother. Silvio and Amber. Now Ruby. There were others too, too many of them. She carried the guilt graven into her flesh.

Val had to turn away to help another customer, then another after that. By the time she looked back toward Alain, he was gone. Just another face in the crowd. One of the many there for Ruby.

Another face caught her eye through the crowd. A young woman with haunted eyes. The receptionist from Royal Construction.

Hillary Linscomb looked uncomfortable surrounded by so many people. Jumpy. Like she was trying to hide in plain sight.

The young vampire caught Val watching her and froze, her eyes widening. She looked scared and indecisive, like she wanted to both run away and ask for help. Val opened her mouth to call out to her, but the crowd shifted, blocking Hillary from her view.

By the time the crowd shifted again, the young woman was gone.

"Another stray for your collection?" Mister E yawned.

Val brushed off his sarcasm. "Maybe. Everyone needs a hobby, right?"

She scanned the crowd but couldn't find the young vampire. Her stomach tightened. She hoped the young woman was all right. A nagging voice told her that if Hillary was here to ask for her help, that would also put Val even more firmly onto Ms. Pearl's bad side. As if the vampire didn't have reason enough to hate her already after their battle over the Scepter.

"You did offer to help," Mister E reminded her.

"True. Maybe one of these days I'll learn to keep my big mouth shut."

"Somehow, I doubt that."

Val chuckled mirthlessly. "Yeah, me too."

She sighed and ducked back into the kitchen to grab a clean rack of glasses, where she found Lisa and Junior with their mouths full of cheese fries. They both froze when they saw her.

"Really guys? I'm busting my ass out there and you two are in here eating cheese fries?"

"Sorry, Val," Junior mumbled, avoiding her eyes.

Lisa shrugged, wiping cheese from her chin with a pink nail.

"We were hungry. We've been running nonstop for hours. Who would've thought Ruby had so many friends?"

Val shook her head. "Just don't let Tommy catch you eating. We'll never hear the end of it."

She dropped the empty rack by the dishwasher and grabbed a clean one.

"I've got that Val." Lisa started across the room.

"No, you eat your fries. Everyone's here for Ruby tonight. If they want a drink, they'll just have to wait. They can get it on my time."

Lisa looked embarrassed. "Thanks, Val. I'll be out in a minute."

Val nodded and carried the clean glasses back out front. She ran her eyes over the crowd again, amazed. Maybe half the people in there were shifters from Ruby's community. It wasn't obvious, but the signs were there if you knew to look for them. A pair of extra sharp incisors here. An extra thick mane of hair there.

But that only accounted for half the people. She had no idea where the other half came from.

It made her sad to see them all. Ruby's life had touched hundreds of people. She was beloved in the city, and Val had been completely unaware of it. All she'd seen was the needy, attention seeking woman that Ruby became when she worked at the Alley Cat. Was that all an act? Was Ruby playing a role because that's what she thought the customers wanted? Had Val actually known her at all?

She thought about Junior and Lisa in the kitchen. Malina sitting up in the DJ's station, bobbing her headphoned head. Tommy doing lines in his office. And Gina on the stage, strutting up and down with her striped stockings and top hat.

What did she know about any of them?

Aside from who they were when they were in the Alley Cat, almost nothing. Which, if Ruby was any indication, meant she didn't know them at all. She'd make an effort to change that. Get to know some of the people around her. Before it was too late.

Tommy Walker hurried down the stairs, waving to her as Vasilevski and his crew occupied their corner table. Val amended her earlier thought. There were still some people she didn't want to get to know.

She delivered their shots of vodka, and Vasilevski slid a fifty onto her tray. She eyed it suspiciously.

"What's that for?"

"For services rendered," Vasilevski said.

Val frowned. "What services are we talking about?"

"Word on the street is, someone brought justice to the man who murdered our *solnyshka*. A woman with golden eyes. You have our gratitude." He raised his glass. "To Ruby. May her sunshine rest in peace."

The gangsters all downed their vodka.

"May she rest in peace," Val echoed. She was caught off guard by the gesture, and she blinked back sudden tears. Ruby really did have friends everywhere.

Still, she eyed Vasilevski skeptically.

"You aren't mad at me?"

"For what?"

"For that scene in the plaza. We weren't exactly on the same side there."

He waved away her concern.

"This is not time for business. Tonight is personal. Business and personal operate on different clocks. You want to talk business, come see me in my office." There was a dangerous glint in his eye. A warning, maybe. Let it go.

Val swallowed and forced a smile.

"Right. Well, let me know if you boys need anything else."

As she slid back behind the bar, a familiar voice spoke behind her.

"I haven't had to take you in for questioning in almost a week. Starting to miss you around the station."

She turned to face Detective Chen.

"That's funny. I don't miss you."

Chen put a hand over his heart. "Ouch. You really know how to hurt a guy, Keri."

"It's the first thing they teach us. You can't work in a strip club unless you're a heartbreaker."

"Ha." He eyed her across the bar. "Rumor has it that Ruby's murder has been avenged. You wouldn't know anything about that, would you?"

Val gave him her most innocent smile. "I hear the rumors, same as you detective."

"So is it true? Did someone"--he made air quotes with his fingers-- "handle my case for me?"

"Again, Detective, I only know what I hear. But I don't think we have to worry about Ruby's murderer being loose on the streets anymore."

Chen glared at her. "Do me a favor. Pass a message on for me. You tell this mysterious person that vigilante justice is not justice. You can't just take the law into your own hands."

"With all due respect, some things are bigger than the law, Detective. Sometimes the city needs someone who can operate independently."

"People like that are no better than the ones who break the law in the first place," Chen growled. "Whoever this vigilante is, tell them I'm gunning for them."

Val stared back at him, her golden eyes hard. "Thanks for the advice, Detective. I'll be sure to pass on your message. Now, if you'll excuse me, I've got work to do."

As she turned back to the kitchen, another voice interrupted her.

"Valora Keri?"

She turned to the stranger, an angular, dark-skinned woman in a long black coat.

"Who wants to know?"

The woman held out a manila envelope and Val took it. "This is an official notice from The Council of New York. Judgment will be rendered at the time and place of our choosing. You have now been served."

Val stared at Paula's graceful, looping cursive on the front of the envelope. A cold ball of dread clenched in her stomach. The council wanted her to answer for her crimes. For the murder of Amber and Silvio. They wouldn't rest until she did.

And the worst part was, they were right. She did have a lot to answer for.

She'd tried to live a good life since New York. Tried to fight for what was right. Tried to balance the scales.

But could the scales ever be truly balanced? She had so much blood on her hands, so many stains on her soul. Her mother. Katrina. Amber and Silvio.

And no matter how hard she tried, she kept adding more. Edward. Jack.

No matter how hard she scrubbed, maybe some things could never be erased.

"*You are a warrior.*" Mister E appeared on the shelf behind the bar, lounging among the liquor bottles. "*An avenging angel. Killing is part of your nature.*"

"That's not an excuse," Val muttered. "You don't get to just walk away from your crimes. Maybe the council is right to come after me. Maybe I do need to be judged."

"*Yours is a higher calling. Only the gods may judge you.*"

Val laughed bitterly.

"Try telling that to the council. Or Detective Chen."

"*Their opinions mean nothing to me.*"

"That's great for you. For me, things aren't so simple."

Someone at the far end of the bar flagged her down with an empty glass. Val sighed and poured another beer.

Hours later, she steered the Ural through the silent streets of the sleeping city. The big motorcycle rumbled beneath her, the sound oddly muffled in the fog. Her leather jacket was warm against the chill.

A flicker of movement caught her eye as she crossed the Van Ness bridge. A shadow, there and gone so fast she wasn't sure she hadn't imagined it.

Maybe it was nothing. Or maybe it was something murderous.

Either way, Val would be here to face it.

This was her city and, as she'd told Chen, there were things out there bigger than the law. The police couldn't handle murderous seraphim, or vampires, or the dozens of other things that lived in the shadows. The police couldn't protect the people.

Stopping them was up to her. It may not be the role she wanted, but it was the one she had. She had to work to balance the scales somehow.

The Council of New York might have other ideas, but the council wasn't here now. Val was. She might not be perfect, but she was trying. She would do her best to be the line between the innocent people and the things that went bump in the night. She would be San Francisco's protector, for better or for worse.

She lifted her chin and cranked the throttle. The Ural roared. Icy wind stiffened the skin on her cheeks.

Above her shoulder, a smile gleamed without a cat.

Valora Keri's golden eyes shone in the darkness.

Thank you for reading Dead Wrong, the first book in The Keri Chronicles! Before you go, I have a small favor to ask.

Reviews are vitally important for book publishing, especially when launching a new series.

If you could take a minute to leave a review on Amazon or Goodreads, it would really help a lot. It doesn't have to be large: Even just a few words can make a world of difference.

Thank you so much.

Yours,
A.C. Arquin

COMING IN AUGUST 2022

PALE MIDNIGHT: THE KERI CHRONICLES BOOK TWO

PRE-ORDER NOW!

ABOUT THE AUTHOR

A.C. Arquin lives in his own worlds. At least, that's what his teachers always told him when they caught him reading a book in class instead of paying attention to the lesson.

Now all grown up, he still prefers realms of imagination to reality. The only difference is that nowadays, he dutifully writes down his adventures and shares them with the world.

When not writing, he is also a very busy audiobook narrator, under the name J.S. Arquin.

He is hard at work on the next book in the Keri Chronicles.

Get a FREE KERI CHRONICLES PREQUEL STORY as well, as all the latest news and deals, by joining his Reader's Group at www.arquinworlds.com/

ALSO BY A.C. ARQUIN

The Itch (A Gaslamp Fantasy Thriller)

The Crimson Dust Cycle (A Dystopian Space Adventure. Published as J.S. Arquin)

Ascent (Book 1)

Slide (Book 2)

Peak (Book 3)

Twist (A Crimson Dust Prequel)

The Crimson Dust Cycle Box Set

Printed in Great Britain
by Amazon

21298824R00154